The Adults in the Room

The Deep State

Second Edition

A novel by

By Jeffrey D Mechling

This novel would not have been possible without the research and editing talents of Kathleen Ryder, to whom I owe everything.

AND

Marie Groves, whose friendship has guided me through good times and bad.

AND

Don E. Gibbin

The Good as Gone Group LLC
Middleburg, Virginia and Los Angeles, California

FOR KATHLEEN

CHAPTER 1

Tim Hall was a former spy for the Central Intelligence Agency. As a matter of fact, his official title was "Case Officer" and he spent much of his career in Central America. In 1981, Tim participated in the training of a paramilitary group known as the Contras and participated in the fighting of the Nicaragua civil war. Although this was a very controversial time in the United States, Tim was proud of his contribution and had no problem telling his friends at The Blue Goose about his exploits. The problem was that no one believed that Tim had ever been out of the City of Baltimore Maryland, much less a spy and Tim really had no way to prove that he did what he claimed. Unlike the local Police Departments, The Central Intelligence Agency did not issue "Retired Spy Identifications. As a matter of fact, the Agency was more than happy if their former employees did not brag about their exploits. The only thing Tim could prove related to his United States government employment was the two years spent working as a clerk for the Social Security Administration. He had been assigned to work there after he had recovered from the accident. The accident that took the life of his wife Pam and about four years of his memories.

Tim had woken up at the University of Maryland Shock Trauma Center with little idea how he had arrived there. A world class hospital, the University of Maryland Shock Trauma Center was known to save the lives of those who would or should have died if they had not been treated within what was known as the Golden Hour. The general concept of the so-called Golden Hour was in cases of severe trauma, such as internal bleeding, required surgical intervention within 10 minutes of the accident. Other issues such as shock may also occur if the person was not treated appropriately. Patients whom did not receive treatment with such injuries within this time frame often died sometime days or even weeks later but if treatment could be administered within the Golden Hour, the survival improved exponentially. This was however not without controversy since some in the medical community felt that the complications that a survivor would be forced to live with may not outweigh the benefit of death, but such subjects were not openly discussed.

After Tim recovered from his traumatic injuries, he was transferred to Johns Hopkins Hospital department of neurology under the care of Doctor Felix Gray. It was Dr. Gray who told Tim that his wife Pam had died in the accident and explained to Tim that he was suffering from "Retrograde amnesia". Tim's recall was limited to the fight that he and Pam were having that day. It was an uncommon condition, but it did indeed occur. Tim did remember his wife Pam but his memories of her mostly existed in the 1990s and the years beginning in 2000 but it was 2012 when things became fuzzy. Pam was also a Case Officer with the CIA, but they rarely saw one another because of an Agency rule about married couples working in the same locations. It just was not allowed and is even still discouraged today. This was a big reason that one spouse of a CIA marriage would often resign so they could remain together. The majority of the spouses taking that option were the women and that fact bothered Pam to no end. That part Tim remembered well.

It had taken Tim a full year to recover before he could even begin to consider returning to work and the transfer to the SSA made sense, since that agency was located in Baltimore and was close to the hospital where Tim still needed occasional treatment. Besides, there was nothing for him to go back to in Northern Virginia, where Tim and Pam had owned a house. A second cousin from Tim's mother's side, Tim's only living relative, appeared and handled the sale of his house and found Tim a condo in Baltimore. Tim was not even sure what he and Pam had been doing in Maryland the day of the accident, but none of this made any difference now. Pam was gone, and now Tim only had incomplete memories of her.

Before the accident, Tim, like many, had considered amnesia to be a condition that only happened on daytime soap operas and old movies. Tim watched a lot of old movies on TCM while recovering from his accident, and one film in particular called *Random Harvest* had a strong impact on him. In the movie, a man played by Ronald Coleman suffered amnesia due to an injury during World War I. His faithful girlfriend (played by Greer Garson) followed and supported him through the entire film. "If only," Tim had sighed after seeing the film for the first time.

He did not remember much of anything from the year 2015 going back to 2013. Tim's doctors told him that he was lucky that he was only missing a two- to three-year gap. Many who suffered from retrograde amnesia had much longer periods of memory loss. Occasionally, Tim would remember something, but would have to ask if it had actually happened or if it was from a dream. He read newspapers and magazines to try and catch up on all that he had missed, although he occasionally needed to remind himself that he was physically present during those years. To make matters worse, Tim had no one to fall back on to help with his memories. If anyone had been close to either Tim or Pam before the accident, they were not making themselves known. The CIA, or "the Agency" as Tim called it, was certainly living up to its reputation as a secretive organization. The Agency seemed to be happy that Tim had no lasting memories of the previous three years. Tim did not even know if the second cousin who showed up to sell his house in Virginia was really his mother's relation or just someone the Agency had hired —but he was happy at the time that anyone was willing to help him, so he'd decided not to question it.

Tim did feel that it was odd that no one from the Agency stopped by and explained his retirement or Pam's death benefits which all Federal Employee received. He tried to speak with the Human Resource Officer at the Social Security Administration but each time she tried to access Tim's information, a red screen would appear with the words Access Denied in black and white letters. Although she assured Tim that she would get to the bottom of "his issue", she seemed to "change her tune" the next and last time they met. She informed Tim that since he was hired under the old Federal Retirement System that he was only eligible for 10,000 dollars a month plus free medical. She reminded Tim that few federal employees received over

100 thousand dollars a year and if she were him then she would not complain. This response appeared to Tim to be something that the woman had been told to say and his years of experience in interrogation techniques told him that something or someone had scared her. He decided to let the subject drop since he now had more money than he could possibly spend but why put the fear of god in this lady? This simply told Tim that somebody was hiding something. As the HR lady walked Tim to the door, she mentioned that perhaps he could obtain more information from his Congressmen or US Senator. Tim thanked her but had to keep from laughing out loud. Both the Maryland and Virginia Congressional delegations were in the pocket of the CIA.

CHAPTER 2

"I'm telling you; Ed Walker is alive today because he was able to grow a new kidney."

The argument the two men were having was becoming a little too loud at the other end of the bar. The disagreement was over stem cell research, a subject Tim Hall knew little about but was very interested in.

"Randy, I agree that one day science will do wonders with stem cells, but right now it's all experimental."

"Experimental!" Randy shot back; his voice raised two octaves. "They are curing cancer right now, today even, and I'll tell you something else—"

"You two shut the fuck up or you're both out of here!" ordered Mary Ann, the bartender and owner of the Blue Goose Bar and Grill, where Tim had spent most of his time since his retirement.

Mary Ann Layback was a 40-year-old ex-biker chick (her own description) who wore black t-shirts and tight jeans with a motorcycle chain belt. She had long brown hair with a reddish tint, which she pulled back in a ponytail most of the time. Although Tim found Mary Ann attractive, he'd never dated anyone like her before and thought she was also a little scary. Tim wondered if he was even capable of handling a woman like Mary Ann. Recently, he had been having a hard time "getting it up" when watching internet porn, and he was becoming concerned. The thought of the humiliation of not getting hard for Mary Ann was simply unthinkable.

"I'm out of here, anyhow," remarked the man who Tim had met but couldn't remember the name of, which was something he noticed was happening more and more lately.

As the man paid his tab and got up to leave, he said to Mary Ann, "Buy Ben Casey here another drink on me." He was laughing as he walked out.

"Who the fuck is Ben Casey?" asked Mary Ann as she made Randy another rum and coke.

"He was a doctor on a show of the same name back in the '60s, played by an actor named Vince Edwards," answered Tim, not looking up from his iPhone.

"Wow, Tim, you are just a fountain of useless knowledge," Mary Ann laughed as she opened a bottle of Budweiser and placed it next to the one Tim had not finished.

This indicated that the beer was on the house. Mary Ann was always giving Tim free drinks, and Tim felt that she had a different and perhaps closer relationship with him than with the other regulars who frequented the Goose, as the bar was known. Perhaps they were kindred spirits, although at other times Mary Ann could be as cold to Tim as she was to the other regulars.

"You're not that fucking smart, college guy,"

Mary Ann had said to him once in front of the others, and everyone had laughed, which made Tim feel lower than whale shit. But for the most part, he felt that Mary Ann liked him more than the other regulars at the bar.

Snapping out of his reverie about Mary Ann, Tim noticed that Randy had slid down the bar to the seat next to him. "So, how goes it, Secret Agent Man?" he asked.

That was a nickname Tim had picked up from the other barflies at the Goose based on his general knowledge of a number of subjects in a number of areas and his claim that he was once an agent for the CIA. Tim was one of the few regulars who had finished college. As a matter of fact, Tim had a Ph.D. in Chemistry, but no one knew it. Actually, Tim himself did not feel that he was particularly bright—he felt that most of the regulars at the Goose were just slow. But they were his friends, and Tim was happy he had some now.

"Well, Randy, I am looking into getting some dental implants because my dentist says I'm going to lose a lot of my teeth from some kind of gum disease." Tim always found it best to keep things simple with his friends at the Goose.

"Dental implants? Those things are going to cost you an arm and a leg!" Randy exclaimed.

Randy was correct. The initial estimate from Tim's dentist had been over thirty thousand dollars.

"For that kind of money, Tim, you could get an entire new body with stem cells!" Randy was becoming more animated. "Even new teeth—but the trouble with the teeth grown with stem cells is that they don't know how to make them stop growing." He laughed loudly. "You'd look like some kind of monster, Tim."

Mary Ann slammed an empty beer bottle on the bar to get Randy's attention. "What did I say about keeping it down, Randy?"

"Yeah, yeah, I know," Randy mumbled, making a retreat out the front door. Tim watched Randy disappear around the corner.

"I think you scared off my friend, Mary Ann."

"I'm the only bar left that will serve your friend, so he'd better be fucking afraid."

Mary Ann bent over to change beer kegs, and Tim took the opportunity to look at her butt. He really did want to ask Mary Ann out on a date, but he just felt that he was now too old for her. Tim was finding that he hated getting old. Besides his lingering injuries from the accident, Tim could feel age creeping up on him. His eyesight was going, his hair was thinning, and he tired more easily. Getting old just sucked. Tim picked up his iPhone and Googled stem cells.

Tim's brand new fear was Dementia or early onset Dementia. His mother had died from it after all so Tim felt that he was a very strong candidate for the disease. He wondered if embryonic stem cells could regenerate dead brain cells. He thought back to his studies in chemistry at UC Berkley and such a thing did seem theoretically possible, but he studied chemistry over thirty years ago and a lot had changed.

Ironically Tim was recruited by the CIA because

of his PHD in Chemistry yet they never really used him for it. Instead they teamed him up with a woman named Rebecca Scott and sent them to the jungles of Central America to train the Contras on military tactics which they had only recently learned themselves. Typical CIA Tim thought and wondered what Rebecca was now doing. Was she working at Langley? These were the types of things Tim could not remember yet he remembers that he had a relationship with Rebecca while separated from Pam who was working in the Asian continent at the time. Tim had only slept with three women at that point in his life and Rebecca was number three. This made Tim wonder if women placed numbers on things such as how many different men they slept with as men did with women. Probably not or not as much Tim speculated.

Mary Ann came from around the bar and sat next to Tim, peering over Tim's shoulder at the screen. "Stem cells, Tim? What are you planning on using stem cells for?" she asked.

Tim shrugged. "My understanding is that stem cells have been used for a variety of different purposes. And it does make sense, Mary Ann."

"But why do you need stem cells, Tim?"

Tim sensed that Mary Ann was actually interested, not just being nice. "Has anyone ever told you about my memory issues?" he asked.

"You mean that big dark secret that you carry around, Tim? The one where you have gaps in your memory? You know back when you were a spy?" Mary Ann was now laughing at him.

Most of the regulars at the Goose knew about Tim's amnesia issues and it had also got around that he was an agent for the CIA which no one, including Mary Ann believed. Sometimes, the regulars would ask Tim something about the year 2014 just to watch Tim struggle to remember. Unbeknownst to Tim, though, Mary Ann had been looking out for him to keep that from happening for a while.

"Yeah, well, I suffered a memory loss," Tim explained. "It's actually a kind of amnesia, where I have these very annoying gaps in my memory between the years 2012 and 2015. I was wondering if stem cell therapy might help. It won't hurt to look."

Tim suddenly noticed that he and Mary Ann were alone, and he saw that she was staring directly at him but what she did next was a total surprise.

Tim was drinking his beer using his left hand and held the iPhone in his right hand. Mary Ann grabbed Tim's right wrist and twisted it hard into Tim's back, but Tim made a counter move and shoved his left elbow towards her solar plexus but missed it. Tim's move however broke Mary Ann's hold on his right wrist. Tim turned to face Mary Ann with both of his arms now turned in to a 90-degree angles from his elbows. Mary Ann however was now in a boxing stance and threw a right hook aimed at Tim's jaw, but Tim was able to block her punch with his left arm. She followed with a left hook that Tim blocked with his right arm. This continued for another 45 seconds as Mary Ann continued to throw punches and Tim was successfully blocking them, but he could also tell that she was slowing down on purpose which was a good thing because Tim was now breathing hard. All of a sudden it occurred to Tim that this was not a fight but a test. Mary Ann wanted to see what basic fighting skills Tim possessed. If she had been able to twist Tim's arm and have him in pain, with his face on the bar top, then she would have known that he was a fake. Mary Ann allowed Tim to grab both of her wrists and use his weight to push her against the wall where he kissed her.

"OK, the first kiss is free, but you are going to have to work for a second one. Okay, Tim?" she said with a grin. "So, when are you going to ask me out on a date?"

The bell attached to the door suddenly jingled indicating that somebody had come into the bar. Mary Ann quickly moved from Tim to her place behind the bar. The regular payed no attention to Tim as he ordered a boiler maker.

"And what about you Timmy? Ready for another?"

Tim shook his head indicating that yes, he did desire another round but was just beginning to finally catch his breath. He watched Mary Ann speak with her customer but wondered. Women do not naturally fight like Mary Ann just did unless they are trained to. Even bad ass biker chicks do not fight that well. No Mary Ann Layback was no biker chick but then what was she or more importantly, who was she?

CHAPTER 3

Tim's big date with Mary Ann was set for two weeks from Sunday because she needed to find someone to run the Blue Goose in her absence. Meanwhile, Tim's coffee table in the living room of his condominium was becoming covered with glossy brochures, the results of his inquiries into stem cell treatments. *Take a Medical Vacation in Beautiful Santo Domingo and Return Home a Changed Person.* This particular brochure featured beautiful 40-something men and women who were trim and fit. The women in that picture wore a two-piece bathing suit. Some of the advertisements were rather simple, as in *"Bring Us Your Double Chin and Leave it Here!"* Others were more mysterious, such as *"We aren't the fountain of youth, but we are the next best thing!"*

Yet, every glossy brochure was somewhat vague on what was actually done, and price lists were nowhere to be found. One thing that was apparent was the fact that no one accepted any kind of insurance, period. Not in the Dominican Republic, not in Thailand, and certainly not in the United States, where only certain procedures involving stem cells had been approved by the FDA. Even in those cases sanctioned by the FDA, most insurance would not cover stem cell treatments. Yet, the internet contained lists of diseases and conditions that had been successfully treated by stem cells —everything from cancer to mental illness. And there were lots of testimonials from actual patients, but Tim had seen this kind of advertising before and was generally suspicious of it. "It seems that you can get people to say anything these days on the internet, but how do you know if anyone is telling the truth?" Tim thought to himself. "There is just no accountability."

After ten days of searching online, Tim was beginning to feel like an expert in stem cell treatments. He had joined two internet chat rooms where he posted questions that were met with quite a number of different responses. Many replies were actually warnings not to fall into the trap of "endless hope met with constant disappointment," as one chat room member put it. "Your new life will be one of new bankruptcies" was another negative response. There were a number of stories of someone who had a chronic or fatal condition and a stem cell clinic would offer hope for just a little more money, but the money never seemed to be enough and the cure never came. On the other hand, there were almost an equal number of stories where a patient with no hope was given a new life thanks to treatments using stem cells. The clinics were another story. Some appeared to be very legitimate, while others were just money-grubbers.

But there was one clinic that caught Tim's attention: the Clinton-Bush Stem Cell Research Centre.

The Clinton-Bush Stem Cell Research Centre (or the CBSCRC) was typical in the sense that they used the name of former occupants of the White House. The name by itself always seemed to lend a certain air of legitimacy, which was something every center desperately looked to establish, and the CBSCRC had two names! But what really struck Tim the most was the absence of any mention of money, be it called treatment fees or accommodation expenses. Instead, they simply said, "We would like to meet you to see what we can accomplish together."

There was nothing else. Tim clicked on the new patient form, which appeared to be seeking certain types of people instead of medical conditions. Tim's curiosity got the better of him, and he filled out the form and pressed the "Submit" button. An automatic response showed up in Tim's email inbox that simply said, "Thank you for your interest, we will be in touch."

Later that evening, Tim posted about this in the stem cell chat and asked if anyone else had ever had contact with the CBSCRC. Tim received one reply: "The CBSCRC rejected me out of hand. Within 5 minutes of submitting my application, I got an answer that said, 'We are very sorry, but CBSCRC is not accepting applicants with your particular qualifications. This in no way reflects poorly on you. You simply do not fit our profile. Best Regards, Nurse Jennifer, Director, CBSCRC.'"

Tim replied to the post with the hope that the poster would expound a little more, but that didn't happen. This made him wonder what separated the CBSCRC from everybody else. Perhaps it was important for the CBSCRC to maintain standards; maybe this was proof that they were not in this business just for the money. At least, that was what Tim was hoping. In any event, Tim needed to find out what was going on in his brain.

Before the accident, Tim had always prided himself on being clear-headed. For instance, he always knew what to do. He never overreacted, and most of all, he never panicked. Now, he seemed to do all three on a regular basis. This in itself was annoying, but when Tim read that these were also symptoms of dementia, he became afraid.

What would happen to him, if he had a mental illness? What could he do? He was a widower with no children. He had no siblings or any family or friends to speak of. Tim was hoping that he would make a connection with Mary Ann, but certainly not for the purpose of a caregiver. Would he take all of his money and just hand it over to some nursing home with the hope that he would be taken care of for the remainder of his life?

Tim sat down and took a deep breath. He needed to get control of his emotions. After all, there could be a hundred different things wrong with him. Had he even taken his medication for the day? Tim took at least fifteen different pills every day, most prescribed by his neurologist Dr. Gray. Fifteen pills a day was a lot of pills. God, did he need that many? All of these fears only convinced Tim that he should consider at least looking at the CBSCRC. Maybe they really could help him.

One of the pills Dr. Gray had prescribed for Tim was a blue one named Xanax. This one did have a calming effect on Tim, and he soon began to feel a little better after he took another. Tim thought about his teeth and how his dentist had told him that he may soon be a candidate for dentures. That was just fucking wonderful. I'm old and will soon be toothless, but I'm going on a date with a woman in her late 30s, he thought to himself. Maybe even younger. Maybe he should just call it off—but Mary Ann had basically asked him out, so what did he have to lose? Maybe she was just into older guys. Tim hoped so, because that's what she was getting.

He closed his eyes and fell asleep.

CHAPTER 4

The night of Tim's big date with Mary Ann had arrived, and he waited anxiously at the corner by his condo.

"Over here, handsome!" Mary Ann yelled as she walked from the opposite direction.

Mary Ann was wearing her usual tight jeans and black t-shirt, but with a white linen jacket over it and no motorcycle chain belt. Her hair was down instead of tied back in the usual ponytail, and it looked like she had applied a little more mascara for the occasion.

Taking Tim's arm, Mary Ann walked him to the street and hailed a cab. Talk about taking charge, Tim thought to himself. At least it relieved him of some of the evening's stress.

Mary Ann gave the cabbie an address and immediately moved closer to Tim until their shoulders touched. "I thought we would go down to Fell's Point for dinner. I know a great little Italian place. Did you know that I'm half Italian?"

Tim had never heard Mary Ann say so much at one time and was a little taken aback by it. However, it was making the date much easier. Tim had been on lots of dates where he'd had a difficult time getting the woman to say two words, so Mary Ann's newfound verbosity was a welcome change.

"Italian? With a last name like Layback?" Tim challenged playfully.

"Well, I'm Italian on my mother's side. I have no clue where Layback came from, but I sure got a lot of shit about it as a kid. But I took care of that." Mary Ann seemed to go a little dark as she said the last sentence.

How did she take care of it? Tim wondered.

He decided that he needed to change the subject. "Well, I love Italian food. Who doesn't?" he responded cheerfully, hoping that Mary Ann would continue the conversation instead of shutting up.

His wish was granted. "I'm also a great Italian cook," she murmured. "Maybe I could cook for you sometime."

The food at the Blue Goose was awful. Tim could only hope that this was not the food she was considering cooking for him.

As they approached Fells Point, Mary Ann changed subjects. "I just love this neighborhood. It reminds me so much of Amsterdam. Have you ever been to Amsterdam?"

Mary Ann's question gave Tim a very strange feeling. No, he had never been to Amsterdam—but he knew exactly what Mary Ann was talking about. Row houses by water. How the hell did he know that?

"No, I've never been there...or, at least, I don't think I have," Tim replied, which made Mary Ann laugh.

"You either have or you haven't, Tim. You're a funny guy."

Tim was not sure if Mary Ann thought he was a funny guy in the "ha-ha" sense or the strange sense, but they had arrived at their destination, so he didn't bother to ask.

"Pay the man, Tim, and don't forget to tip him," she said as she exited the cab.

The 'maître d' appeared to know Mary Ann and welcomed her with a hug. She did not bother to introduce Tim. The maître d led Tim and Mary Ann to a corner table, where Mary Ann ordered a vodka martini. Tim ordered the same.

"So, how is the stem cell research going?" Mary Ann asked.

Tim was a little taken aback by the question. He recalled that Mary Ann was with him when he'd decided to Google stem cells, but he hadn't spoken about it to her or anyone since then.

Still, he knew Mary Ann was perceptive. "Well, I was really just looking into dental implants at first. I got kind of sidetracked into stem cells, but I don't think stem cells can grow new teeth."

Mary Ann reached across the table and placed her hand on Tim's lower jaw. "Let's see them, then. Yep, you have extensive bridge work on both your uppers and lowers. I'd give them about a year."

"A year for what?" Since Mary Ann still had her hand on Tim's lower jaw, his response sounded a bit like Duffy Duck.

"A year before you lose them. Not all at once—just a few at a time." Mary Ann removed her hand from Tim's jaw and started reading the menu.

Tim's dentist had told him the same thing, but how the hell had Mary Ann known that? "So, are you a dentist as well as a restaurateur?" Tim asked, trying to sound sophisticated.

"I used to own a dental lab, and I've seen lots of bridges. Do you like calamari?"

"Love it. But you think my teeth will start falling out?" Tim was beginning to panic.

"Well, they will start hurting first, and you will go to the dentist, and she or he will tell you that there is nothing more to do and will start pulling the few real teeth you have left." Mary Ann was still reading the menu, and her response sounded almost absent-minded.

She closed the menu and looked at Tim. "But that's not going to happen tonight, so relax. I am going to have the eggplant parmesan. Have you decided on anything?"

Tim ended up ordering a steak. May as well while he could still eat one, he figured. Mary Ann laughed at his choice and joked about finding an Outback Steakhouse the next time they went out for dinner, although the steak at the Italian place was delicious and Tim thought it was one of the best he had ever tasted. Italians do excellent steaks, Mary Ann informed him, then started talking about gangsters in Chicago during Prohibition and steakhouses.

Tim was beginning to think that this was the best date he had ever been on. Mary Ann was different here from when she was behind her bar, tossing one-liners back and forth with the regulars. Here, she spoke freely and expounded on all kinds of subjects, although Tim also found that she was a good listener. She surprised him by how well she recalled all of the little comments he'd made about life while sitting at her bar. Tim figured that she, like most people, really did not care what he thought about anything—but Mary Ann certainly impressed him.

They had consumed two martinis each as well as one bottle of red wine, and any inhibitions Tim may have had at the beginning of the evening had gone out the window.

"So where is Mrs. Hall?" Mary Ann asked playfully.

"Dead and gone, I'm afraid," Tim responded, not really meaning to sound so cold.

Tim's response created a kind of pregnant pause at the table where neither of them could think of what to say next. Finally, it was Mary Ann who broke the silence. "Tim, I am so sorry. I had no idea at all. I just thought you were divorced like everyone else—"

Tim cut Mary Ann off by taking her hand in his. "It was an accident, and I wish I could tell you more about Pam—that was my wife's name—but after the accident, I just don't remember much about anything. I mean, we had a good marriage, we both worked, too busy to have kids, the usual story...but, the thing is, I mean, the thing is that I don't remember if I loved her or not."

This statement almost brought Tim to tears, which was the last thing he wanted, but what he said was true. He just didn't know if he'd loved Pam or not.

Somewhere in all of this, Mary Ann had paid the check, and they were both now walking down Thames Street arm in arm.

"Mary Ann, I am so sorry. I feel like I have sabotaged our entire evening. I just was not expecting that question, and—"

Mary Ann placed her hand on Tim's cheek.

"Tim, you can shut up now," she said, and they started to kiss.

Their kissing continued during the cab ride back to Washington Hill. Both Tim and Mary Ann's hands were all over one another. Tim was surprised by how assertive Mary Ann was, but should he be? He'd never been on a date with anyone like Mary Ann before.

As they headed upstairs to Tim's condo, Tim's mind began to race with questions like, did he make his bed that morning? And did he have coffee? But the kissing suddenly stopped when they reached Tim's door.

Mary Ann turned and faced Tim. "This is as far as I go on a first date, but..." Mary Ann stopped speaking and gave Tim a long kiss, pushing her tongue deep into his mouth. "...I wanted you to know that I had a simply fabulous time."

Mary Ann kissed him again and started for the elevator. Tim called after her, "Can I at least walk you home?"

"No, I have an Uber coming," Mary Ann responded. The elevator door opened, and Mary Ann stepped in.

"Well, can I walk you to the..."

The elevator door closed, and Mary Ann was gone. Tim opened the door to his condo, entered, and headed to the window. He saw a black car pull up to the front of his building, perhaps a Mercedes, and Mary Ann got into the front seat. Tim thought that riding in the front seat of an Uber was a little strange, but this was Mary Ann, after all, so he decided to let it go.

Tim sat on his couch and considered the evening. The date had certainly gone much better than he'd expected. He was sorry that he didn't get to close the deal but getting a woman into bed was no longer the big thing that it used to be for him.

Tim's iPhone sounded the text message alert. Tim picked it up and saw that he'd received two texts from Mary Ann. The first read, "I had a wonderful, wonderful evening. Let's do it again" followed by two red hearts. The second message said, "And if you mention anything about our date to anyone at the Goose, I will kill you."

CHAPTER 5

Tim was slightly surprised that post-date Mary Ann was actually a little colder to him when she was bartending at the Goose. A few times, she was even downright mean.

"I think he looks like a porcupine," she'd said, referring to Tim's new haircut.

"At least you are not a weirdo like Tim," was another comment Mary Ann made while she was attempting to help the young busboy ask a girl out. Sure, it was sweet for Mary Ann to help the kid, but why do it at Tim's expense?

On the other hand, Mary Ann would purposely pinch him or grab a piece of Tim's anatomy when she felt that no one was looking. So, Tim figured he could tolerate Mary Ann's put-downs for the time being.

Tim was also close to giving up on stem cell treatments. After all, he wasn't suffering from any of the major conditions stem cells could treat, and all he really wanted in the first place was dental implants to replace his failing teeth. This probably would have ended it, if not for the persistent emails from the CB-SCRC. Tim had been sent a questionnaire, the type one might fill out when applying for a job at a large corporation. Tim was familiar with these types of tests and knew it was a process of asking the same question several different ways. The purpose was to determine the applicant's characteristics, like if the applicant was a team player who got along with others. But why would the CBSCRC even care about anything like that?

Soon afterwards, Tim began to get emails from the CBSCRC. "Please contact us at the following number" one email read in the subject line. Another said, "We can help you live longer," and still another read, "We will save your life!"

This was the one that got Tim's attention. "What do these guys know about my life?" Tim thought to himself.

Each email included a phone number that Tim should call. Tim finally decided to do this, if only to find out what the CBSCRC really wanted.

The person who answered the phone sounded like a receptionist. After Tim identified himself, he was put on hold for what seemed like an eternity. He was close to hanging up when a man with a southern accent picked up. "Mr. Hall? This is Dr. Richard Justice speaking. How are you today, sir?"

Tim was somewhat taken back by Dr. Justice's familiarity. "Ah, fine, doctor. And you?" he managed.

"I am fine, sir. It's always a fine day here in lovely Santo Domingo, and I am very much hoping that you will be joining us soon."

Tim was once again taken aback by the doctor's enthusiasm. "Well, sir..." Tim could hear the nervousness in his own voice. "Well, that's just it. I mean, I'm not sure why I'm coming down. I mean, I only really wanted some dental implants."

Dr. Justice cut Tim off. "Dental implants, Mr. Hall? I am offering you another 80 years of life, and you're talking about dental implants?"

Dr. Justice went on to explain the advanced algorithm that had been used to cull Tim from the thousands of applicants who'd applied to the CBSCRC program. The use of the term "advanced algorithm" impressed Tim, since he was a big believer in computer science. Humans had natural biases, after all, and although some computer programmers included their biases in their programing, Tim trusted computers a lot more.

After getting off the phone, he began to research stem cells again. Tim was still researching and making notes when the buzzer in his condo sounded. He glanced at his watch to see that it was 11:30 at night. Usually, any ringing at this time of night would just be some homeless person wandering the streets. He stood and made his way to the intercom, then pushed a button and said, "May I help you?

"Hey, let me the hell up. I'm freezing my butt off", came the unmistakable voice of his maybe-girlfriend, Mary Ann Layback.

Tim looked around to see if there was anything lying about that Mary Ann could use to make fun of him, but the three knocks on his door came quicker than he expected.

Tim opened the door, and there she was. Black jeans, black sweater, black leather jacket, and a black watch cap on her head. She carried two bottles of wine.

"For what do I owe the pleasure—" Tim started to ask.

He didn't get the rest of his sentence out before Mary Ann had placed the two wine bottles on the table and began to kiss him. Mary Ann soon had her hat, jacket, and sweater off and began to pull off Tim's sweatshirt as well.

"Do you have a place where you want to do this, or shall we just do it right here on your carpet?" Mary Ann looked at the floor as she said this.

Tim motioned to the bedroom.

Tim had a large double bed with no head or foot boards. Once they reached the bedroom, Mary Ann playfully pushed Tim onto the bed and began to remove her jeans. Tim was not sure if he should help remove any of Mary Ann's clothing, since she appeared to be performing a somewhat modified striptease. Mary Ann's pants were now off, revealing that she was wearing a tiny black thong. She reached behind her back and undid her bra, which she threw at Tim.

Mary Ann then pulled Tim's sweatpants off, got down to her knees, and began to go down on him. Tim just about lost it at that point, but he held off until Mary Ann got on top of him and managed to turn around, so her ass was facing his chest. She began to move her hips up and down and around. She raised up and took Tim's penis in her hand and placed it close to her ass, but then reinserted it in her vagina. When she began to repeat the move, Tim could no longer hold on and found himself ejaculating all over the place.

Mary Ann was now lying on top of Tim, who was sweating. Mary Ann blew on Tim's forehead to cool him off. No woman had done that to him for years, Tim thought to himself.

Mary Ann got off and went into Tim's bathroom, coming back with a warm washcloth that she used to clean Tim's genitals. After that, she laid back down next to Tim, who turned and kissed her.

"Hey, Mary Ann," Tim said as he placed his hand on her cheek.

"Hey, Tim," Mary Ann answered softly.

The two fell asleep in each other's arms.

Tim and Mary Ann both woke up at 7 a.m. and made love again. This time, it was in a more traditional way, with Tim on top. Tim seemed to orgasm at about the same time as Mary Ann. He usually couldn't tell if a woman did or did not orgasm, but he no longer worried about it.

He was in the kitchen making scrambled eggs when Mary Ann asked if she could check her email. He told her sure, not wondering why Mary Ann didn't just check her email on her phone.

Mary Ann was now standing in the doorway of the kitchen. She was wearing one of Tim's suit shirts, which just about covered her privates. "So, are you going to go to this stem cell place?" she wondered. "They sound like they really want you to come down there."

Tim had forgotten that he had left his email open with all of the information about stem cells and the CBSCRC.

"Is this something you will be making fun of me for doing in front of everyone at the Goose?" he wondered. He really wanted to address the subject of Mary Ann acting mean towards him.

"Hey, I'm sorry I hurt your feelings," Mary Ann said defensively, "but a couple of the guys already suspected that we went out, and I just can't have those clowns know we're lovers. You won't be able to come in there anymore because they'll all accuse me of giving you preferential treatment, and I just don't need to hear some 'your boyfriend this, your boyfriend that' kind of thing."

Tim felt that Mary Ann was making way too big of a deal about the entire subject and could also see how upset the conversation was making her. He placed three strips of bacon next to her eggs and put the plate on the table, then kissed Mary Ann on her forehead.

"Is that what we are now," Tim asked, "lovers?"

Mary Ann kissed him back, on the lips this time. "Well, I guess—but it all depends on how good your eggs are."

Tim and Mary Ann sat and ate in silence after that until she returned to the subject of stem cells. "You didn't answer my question about if you're going to this place in the Dominican Republic."

"I don't know, Mary Ann. I mean, it sounds interesting, and I sure don't have anything better to do." Tim took a long pause, then added, "I used to have a life, and it was not as a clerk for the Social Security Administration—but I can't really tell you about any of that."

"Because you were some kind of top-secret spy?" Mary Ann remarked somewhat sarcastically

Tim wished again that he had never told anyone that he had worked for the CIA. The only reason he had mentioned it in the first place was to settle an argument someone was having at the Blue Goose. Tim simply mentioned that he had worked at the CIA and everyone in the bar that night stopped talking and stared at him.

"Hey look, James Bond is in the room" someone said with a laugh and he had not been able to live down his statement since. This was an old, former Polish neighborhood of West Baltimore and everyone was thought to be a "bull shit artist". Why would any CIA type spies live there they wondered, and the patrons of the Blue Goose had a point? Even Tim was not sure why he was living there.

"Well yes, that is part of it" Tim confessed to Mary Ann "But since the accident, there are some very large gaps in my memory, and no one will fill them in for me."

"OK, cool down, cowboy." Mary Ann reached over to hold Tim's hand.

"I'm sorry, Mary Ann, but I just seem to live from one day to the next, and it's becoming exhausting." Tim took Mary Ann's other hand in his own. "You are the best thing that's happened to me in years, but it's not fair for me to make any of this your problem."

"So, what are you going to do, Tim?"

Getting lost in the deep brown of Mary Ann's eyes, Tim leaned over to kiss her again. "I don't know, but I'll keep you in the loop."

They both laughed at that and started to make love once again. Tim fell back to sleep afterwards, but he woke as Mary Ann was getting dressed to leave.

"I've got to go and open up the Goose. I'm already late," Mary Ann explained. She kissed Tim on his forehead.

"Maybe see you later?" Tim asked.

"Maybe. You'll just have to wait and find out," Mary Ann replied. With that, she turned to the door and was gone.

After Mary Ann had left, Tim got up and walked to his computer. He opened his emails with the CBSCRC and started a new one.

"Hi, I am interested in receiving treatments with stem cells," he wrote. "I am available any time. Please email the details so I can make travel arrangements. Regards, Timothy Hall."

Tim sent the email and went back to bed, thinking about his night with Mary Ann.

CHAPTER 6

For the next two weeks, Tim was busy making plans for his trip to the Dominican Republic and saw little of Mary Ann. He did go to the Goose, but Mary Ann was doing her usual "you're just another customer" routine.

Tim was getting better at not paying attention to her. Tim was becoming so good at not paying attention to Mary Ann, in fact, that he was also missing the loving looks she would occasionally send his way. Mary Ann even sent him a text asking if he still liked her, which Tim responded to with three red hearts.

But Tim's mind was on his trip.

The night before Tim's flight, Mary Ann came over with a pizza. She made Tim give her his contact information at the CBSCRC, then helped him pack and spent the night with him. In the morning, Mary Ann made sure he was in a cab headed to BWI, kissed him goodbye, and watched him drive away.

Tim watched as they turned the corner and suddenly wondered if he was making the right decision. Maybe he should just try to get Mary Ann out of that bar so that they could live out their lives together—but he wondered if Mary Ann would ever consider giving up her independence to be with him. Perhaps Tim should just see this stem cell treatment through and decide about Mary Ann when he returned. Sure, that made sense...or he hoped it did, at least.

Tim's flight to Santo Domingo from Miami was uneventful (as all of Tim's airplane flights had been), and two large and smiling Dominican men met him as he exited through customs. One held a sign that read, "Mr. Timothy Hall, Baltimore, MD."

"Are you Mr. Hall?" the man with the sign asked.

Tim just nodded.

"From Baltimore, Maryland?"

Tim mumbled, "Yes," and began to look around the small but very busy airport.

"Welcome, sir. How was your flight? May we take your luggage?"

Before Tim could answer, the man took Tim's bag, saying, "Please, sir, this way."

Tim followed the man with his bag and noticed the other man falling into step directly behind him.

There was something going on out in front of the airport, perhaps a protest of some kind. There were police and maybe soldiers all around, but Tim's escorts paid this little mind and continued to walk through the crowd.

They stopped at a black SUV that was waiting in the parking lot. There was a third man in the driver's seat. The man with Tim's bag sat next to the driver, while the big man sat next to Tim.

"I have been to Baltimore. It's a beautiful city," the man said to Tim.

Tim ignored the comment and continued to observe the protest. Two soldiers were dragging a screaming woman from the airport parking lot. "What's going on here?" he asked.

"They are just having a fight," the big man answered with a smile.

Tim decided to drop the matter.

The SUV traveled almost a quarter of a mile through lush flowers and exotic trees before it reached the main entrance to the CBSCRC, which looked more like a resort than a hospital or clinic. The car took one loop around the circular driveway and stopped at the front.

At that point, another smiling man stepped forward and opened Tim's door. "Mr. Tim?" he asked.

Tim looked up and replied sleepily, "Yeah, my name is Tim..."

The man cut him off. "Mr. Tim, my name is Amin, and I will be your guide as you embark on your new journey."

At first, Tim had thought that Amin was another Dominican man, yet he was somewhat smaller, and his accent did not sound as French. More Middle Eastern or Pakistani? Tim wondered how he would even know what nationality someone was, anyway.

"Come," Amin said. "The doctor would like to see you right away."

Before Tim could say another word, he was led to an elevator, taken one flight up, and escorted into the waiting room of Dr. Richard Justice. Amin led Tim to a chair and disappeared through a door.

The same door opened a minute later, and an attractive nurse with shoulder length red hair appeared. "Tim? I'm Jennifer, Dr. Justice's nurse. If you will come with me, we can take some blood."

Tim followed Nurse Jennifer down a short hallway and into a room with a large chair with straps on either side of the arms. Nurse Jennifer smiled. "This is my chair of torture. Please take a seat."

Somehow, Tim found her request a little sexy and did not think twice about sitting in a chair that included restraints.

Nurse Jennifer looked at both of Tim's arms before deciding on the left one, then looped a Velcro strap around it. Next, she picked up the largest needle Tim had ever seen in his life, softly saying, "If you're afraid of needles, I suggest you look the other way."

Tim closed his eyes, but he still felt Nurse Jennifer stick needles in his arm several times in different places. Every so often, Nurse Jennifer would reassure Tim that she was almost finished, yet the blood-taking seemed to last forever.

Finally, after twenty minutes or so, Nurse Jennifer cheerfully remarked, “All done.”

Tim glanced over at his arm and counted seven bandages. “What the fuck?” he said, but Nurse Jennifer had already left the room.

Amin was now standing in the doorway, saying, “Dr. Justice would like to see you now.”

Amin led Tim into a large office with a window overlooking the water. Tim had no clue what water he was looking at, since he hadn’t bothered to look at any maps, but he assumed it had to be some part of the Atlantic.

There was a knock on the door, and a stout man in his 50s entered the room and extended his hand. “Richard Justice at your service, Mr. Hall.”

The doctor sat behind his desk and opened a file, which Tim imagined to be his own. They sat in silence, minutes passing before the doctor spoke again.

“Mr. Hall, you are 70 years old?”

“I’m in my late 50s.”

Doctor Justice didn’t seem to hear Tim. “And I would say that you have probably five more years to live. Would you agree with that, Mr. Hall?”

Tim was shocked to hear such a prognosis. “How the hell can you make that prediction? I’ve only been here an hour.”

Dr. Justice held up his hand for Tim to stop. “Calm down, Tim,” he said, taking a more personal tone. “I have in front of me your medical records for the last

10 years. Without going into great detail, that is how it looks to me. I assure you; I have been doing this for a very long time."

The doctor pulled a paper out of Tim's file and began to read. "For example, your most recent blood work, the blood you provided to your dental implant clinic, shows me a number of markers that indicate that you will have a stroke before you are 70. Your body is really not programmed to live much beyond 80 years. That's a fact...but perhaps we can change it."

Tim sat back, astounded. How the hell had these people gotten his medical records? Wasn't that illegal? But he was in the Dominican Republic now, where American laws did not apply, he remembered.

"Mr. Hall, we feel that we have discovered a process using stem cells that will completely rejuvenate your cell structure. At a certain age, we no longer produce new cells, which is why we age. However, if the human body could continue to grow new cells, well, sir, we could become immortal."

Tim had been looking down at the floor, but now looked up to see Dr. Justice standing by the window, staring out to the ocean. "You were chosen out of thousands, Mr. Hall, because your body is at the correct stage to begin such a treatment," he continued. "So, it is we who need your help. Will you help us?"

Tim got up and joined the doctor at the window. "Now look, doctor, I came down here with my life savings of $20,000. After deducting my airfare, $17,500 is what I have left. The price of immortality would be somewhat higher than that, would you not agree?"

Dr. Justice turned and placed his hand on Tim's shoulder. "Tim, I am a doctor and scientist. I am not seeking to make a fortune."

The doctor returned to his desk and sat down. "However, every bit of funding helps our research, so your $17,500 donation is greatly appreciated."

Amin, Tim's guide, suddenly appeared at the door. "Amin will make sure that your donation is successfully transferred from your bank in Baltimore, Mr. Hall," the doctor added. "At that point, we can begin your treatment."

Dr. Justice turned and slipped through the door.

Amin turned to Tim. "Mr. Tim, would you follow me to my office?"

Tim stared at the door the doctor had left by, then followed Amin downstairs.

Later, Tim laid back on his bed in the oceanfront room the CBSCRC had given him and logged into his bank account from his smartphone. Gone was his $17,500 left in savings, and only $575 remained in his checking account. They certainly didn't waste any time, did they?

Tim did have a lot more money in other accounts, but he certainly was not going to let anyone at the CBSCRC know about it. Tim also thought that it was strange that he observed no other patients on the premises.

There was a TV in his room and a phone, chairs, table, and a small desk like any hotel room would have, plus a balcony looking out to the ocean. Tim also had access to the beach, but little else. Anytime Tim attempted to wander around the facility, he was stopped by one of the friendly Dominican men, who directed Tim back to his room. It had been two days since his meeting with Dr. Justice, and Tim was beginning to become suspicious. Was this all just some elaborate scam to get a hold of his lousy $17,000?

A soft knock sounded on his door all of a sudden, and Amin entered Tim's room. "Mr. Tim? We are ready to begin your procedure."

"At four fucking o'clock in the afternoon? What kind of place is this?" Tim demanded.

Amin simply ignored Tim's outburst and held out his hand.

Tim put his shoes on and began to follow Amin down the hallway. Amin used an ID badge to open another door, which led to another hallway. Tim now noticed that an additional Dominican man was behind them. This was all becoming a little strange to Tim, and it began to occur to him that maybe he should reconsider the entire procedure. Tim turned to make a retreat but felt the strong hands of the man behind him placed on both of his shoulders.

Amin turned to Tim. "Mr. Tim, you have come too far," he said gently.

Amin opened a door for Tim to see a brightly

lit room that was crammed with a variety of medical equipment. There were also six doctors or nurses waiting inside of it, all gloved, gowned, and wearing surgical masks. With the Dominican still holding Tim, a woman who Tim thought was Nurse Jennifer stepped to his right and administered an injection, saying, "Tim, this will help you relax."

Tim felt his entire body go limp, although he was still very awake.

"Amin prepare the patient," said a voice that Tim recognized as Dr. Justice's. Tim tried to speak but found himself paralyzed to the point where he could only make unintelligible sounds.

Amin and the other Dominican man took Tim into a side room and began to undress him. Tim was soon in a hospital grown and laid out on an operating table. Tim was completely freaking out now, yet there was absolutely nothing he could do.

Dr. Justice stood over Tim and spoke. "Tim, I apologize for proceeding in such a manner, but we have our reasons, which I will explain later. Now, we are going to be performing several kinds of injections that may feel uncomfortable. Some of these injection sites will be in and around your eye sockets, and we need you to be completely still, which is why we needed to use certain sedative medications. For the remainder of the procedure, we think it is best that you are unconscious."

Dr. Justice turn and nodded to someone. "Now, Tim, if you just start counting backwards... 10, 9, 8—"

Tim made it to 7.

He woke up on his back, staring at a white ceiling fan. He slowly started testing each of his limbs for movement. He did have a tremendous headache, a type of headache that he had never experienced before.

"Mr. Tim, Mr. Tim, are you back with us?" a voice next to Tim called out.

"Yes, yes, I'm back. You're the man in charge, right?"

Tim knew right away that he was making no sense. Coming out of anesthesia was always a strange occurrence, but in this case, getting back to reality was important. Tim tried harder.

"My name is Tim Hall, correct? And I am in, am I, am in..." Tim paused for a moment. "I am in a place where the laws do not apply," he finally decided to say.

That statement even made the stoic Amin laugh out loud. "Yes, Mr. Tim, you are in a land where American law does not apply, but you must hurry. You have a plane to catch back to your home in Baltimore that you will not want to miss."

"Plane? Baltimore?" Tim exclaimed. "What about seeing the doctor? What about aftercare?"

Amin laughed once again. "You have received the treatment that Dr. Justice prescribed. The doctor may indeed want to follow up with your progress, but there is no—how do you call it?—aftercare."

Tim had never been to any medical facility

where he did not have to sign a stack of forms in order to be released. He was getting the feeling he was getting the bum rush out of the CBSCRC—but why?

"Amin, don't you think I should speak with Dr. Justice or at least Nurse Jennifer before I leave?"

Tim could tell that Amin was becoming impatient. "Mr. Tim, both doctor and nurse have examined you thoroughly, and they have given you permission to leave. Your passport is only valid for seven days, and you have now been here for six, so it is imperative you leave today."

By this time, Tim was dressed, and his bag was packed (although he didn't have a clue how any of that was done). Before he could ask any more questions, he was seated in the SUV with Amin heading back to the airport, then aboard flight United 2259 to Dallas-Ft. Worth International Airport. Tim was not pleased with the small 50-plus seat jet or the connection he needed to make at DFW, but he soon fell asleep.

He was awakened by the flight attendant welcoming everyone to the greater Dallas-Fort Worth area. All of the passengers deplaned directly onto the tarmac and were required to take a bus to the main terminal.

On arrival, Tim was disappointed to discover that he, along with the rest of the passengers, would need to be screened through the TSA once again. When Tim arrived at the checkpoint, he encountered the longest line he had ever witnessed. In addition, there did not seem to be any order to the screening process. Apparently, a group of travelers had attempted to bring some sort of *energizer beverage* on board that was forbidden by the current FAA rules. Somehow, this act by itself had shut down the entire DFW TSA, and the line through screening was becoming longer and longer.

Tim's line was slowly merging with another line, which was leading to the one TSA gate in operation. To Tim's right was a young blond man with an even younger blonde woman. The man wore sunglasses and looked like he was going on a skiing vacation. When he spoke to his girlfriend, Tim noticed some kind of accent, maybe English or Australian.

As the line moved another inch, Tim inadvertently kicked the younger man's bag (everyone's bag was on the airport floor at this point). The blond man shot Tim a look and remarked, "You got a problem with my bag, mate?"

Feeling angry or perhaps just frustrated, Tim replied, "I ain't your fucking mate, you asshole."

As Tim was turning back, he saw the blond man's fist coming straight at him through the corner of his right eye. Tim instinctively raised his right hand and caught the man's fist, beginning to squeeze.

The blond man cried out in pain and fell to his knees. "Let go, let go!" were the only words he could get out. The blond man's girlfriend also screamed, yelling at Tim to leave him alone.

Tim released his grip and took a step back, not totally understanding what had just occurred. An airport cop approached and asked Tim and the blond man if there were any problems, but the blond man just shook his head and told the cop that everything was okay. At that point, the TSA line finally began moving, and Tim passed right through.

Tim's flight was scheduled to leave, and he found himself sprinting to the gate just as the door was closing. As he sat in his seat and fastened his seat belt, he noticed that he was not nearly as winded as he would have expected. Tim wondered what that fight had been all about and how he'd been able to bring a younger man to his knees simply by squeezing his hand. Something was going on...but what?

Tim arrived at BWI expecting Mary Ann to meet him, but then remembered that he hadn't told her when he was coming back. Tim was supposed to call her from the Dominican Republic, but he hadn't had time. Hell, he had not had much of a chance to do anything, since he'd slept on both of the return flights.

He wandered through the airport until he found himself at the ground transportation section, then in the back of a taxi. "I need to go 5456 Lovettsville Road," Tim told the driver.

"Lovettsville Road? Where the heck is Lovettsville Road?" the driver responded.

Tim thought the same thing. Where the hell was Lovettsville Road?

"I mean North Washington Street in the city," he quickly corrected.

"That address I know," the driver laughed. "But Lovettsville Road is a new one to me."

It was a new one to Tim as well.

It was early Sunday morning, and the Goose would not be open until sometime that afternoon. Tim considered going to Mary Ann's apartment above the Goose but decided that probably was not a very good idea. Showing up at a woman's home uninvited had never worked out well for him—something about the invasion of their space. Tim couldn't remember the exact reason, but he'd decided long ago never to show up uninvited again.

Tim made his way to his condo, opened the door, and threw his bag on the floor. He went to bed and began to dream. In his dream, he found himself on a road with trees on either side that was close to a river. There was also a house, a large brick house that overlooked the river. A woman was coming out of it.

Tim woke up and saw that the time was 4 p.m. Maybe the Goose would be open now. He could not remember the last time he'd eaten.

Before he could get dressed, though, Tim turned on the TV in his living room and fell right back to sleep. This time, Tim dreamed of being in a car with other people that he did not know. They were driving in a city, and they were escaping from someone. Tim woke again and saw that it was now 7 p.m. Why all these dreams, he wondered. Tim usually had the same dreams over and over, but these dreams were new and extremely vivid.

Tim decided to take a shower. He undressed and stood in front of the full-sized mirror in his bathroom to examine his body. Tim removed several band aids, which revealed numerous needle marks. What the hell had those maniacs done to him at the CBSCRC?

After the shower, Tim dressed in a sweatshirt and pants and laid down on his couch. This was the last thing he remembered.

CHAPTER 7

Tim opened his eyes to see another white ceiling fan, just like the one in the Dominican Republic. "What the hell?" he said out loud.

He attempted to get up, only to find that both his arms and legs were restrained to the bed. A hospital bed.

"Hey!" Tim yelled, not knowing who he was yelling to.

"Shut the fuck up," said a voice to Tim's right.

Tim looked over to see a man with a food tray in another bed. The man was eating what appeared to be breakfast while watching TV.

"Where the fuck am I? How the hell did I get—" M

The man in the bed next to Tim cut him off. "You're in the Johns Hopkins Psych Ward, pal," he answered, not bothering to look at Tim. "But I don't have a clue how you got here. I just know that they brought you in last night and woke me the fuck up."

Tim was beginning to calm down somewhat. At least he was someplace safe, but how and why was he in a hospital room?

Tim decided to take a nicer tone with his new

roommate. "So, they brought me in here and I woke you up? I am very sorry, but can you tell me anything else?" Tim was trying his best to stay calm, but he could feel his heart racing.

"You kept asking if there was a plan B and calling out for some chick named Pam." The man was now looking directly at Tim. "Look, pal, if you got women problems, then let me give you a piece of advice. They ain't worth it."

Two nurses entered the room (or, at least, that was what Tim figured they were). The female nurse spoke first. "Good morning, Mr. Hall. How are you feeling today?"

"I'd be a lot better if I knew how I got here," Tim said, but he noticed that the female nurse was writing down his vitals on a clipboard instead of paying attention to him.

Tim again attempted to be nice. "So, is there any way I can be untied?"

"Perhaps," the nurse replied, "provided you can behave yourself. Dr. Ryan will be here in a moment, and we will have to see how she feels about that."

Tim could tell that he was being treated like a preschooler and decided that he should cooperate.

A woman in her fifties entered the room and had a conversation with the female nurse. She next walked to Tim's bedside, while the female nurse drew the privacy curtain. Meanwhile, the male nurse stood silently at the head of the bed with his arms crossed. Must be here in case I start any trouble, Tim thought, which he found somewhat amusing. Tim had never imagined he could be considered dangerous.

"Mr. Hall? My name is Dr. Ryan. Do you have any idea why you are here?"

"Not a clue," Tim responded.

"Well, you were brought here by the Baltimore police, who found you running up and down Washington Street at 11 p.m. last night. They report that you appeared to be having a psychotic episode. Do you know what a psychotic episode is, Mr. Hall?"

"I have a pretty good idea. It's the official name for acting crazy." Tim was trying not to sound too much like a wise ass, but he was finding it difficult given the situation. If nothing else, Tim had always considered himself sane.

"Yes, Mr. Hall, that would be an appropriate description," the doctor agreed. "Have you recently taken any drugs, legal or illegal?"

"Not that I am aware of." Tim had decided to try and keep his answers short.

"Have you been out of the country recently?"

That question stopped Tim cold. Yes, he had, but did he want to go into all that when he didn't know exactly what had happened himself? Yes: he decided he'd need to be straight with the doctor if he ever expected to get out of the psych ward.

"Dr. Ryan, I recently traveled to the Dominican

Republic to take part in a study involving stem cells, but now I believe there never was a study and I was simply robbed of $18,000. I returned yesterday, I mean Sunday morning, and just have not felt very well since then."

Tim studied the doctor's face and saw what he interpreted as a look of understanding. "Well, that certainly may explain a lot. For example, your blood work from last night was all over the place, but this morning, your blood levels seem about normal. Actually, for a man of your age, I would say you are in excellent health."

Tim did not remember any blood work from this morning, but he did not remember last night, either. Tim noticed that the doctor seemed be taking a more friendly attitude toward him now.

The doctor turned to the male nurse. "Toby? I think we can take the restraints off of Mr. Hall now."

Nurse Toby stepped forward and undid Tim's wrists and feet. Meanwhile, the doctor made more notes on Tim's chart and handed the clipboard back to the female nurse.

"Mr. Hall, I would like to keep you in the hospital for another day for observation, but I feel that your episode was related to your experience in the Dominican Republic, and I would of course advise you never to try something like that again."

The doctor was now smiling, which Tim saw as a good sign. She continued. "The Baltimore police did charge you with disorderly conduct, but I will write you a statement saying that your behavior was caused by a reaction to medication. That should allow them to drop the charges. Later today, we will move you out of the Psychiatric Ward to a regular room. In the meantime, you must be hungry."

Dr. Ryan finished writing notes on Tim's chart and asked him if he had any questions. Tim thanked her and said that he did not. The doctor and the two nurses left the room, and Tim began to relax.

His roommate spoke up. "You're lucky, pal. I know some people who never leave this place. But I got to let you know something."

"And what would that be, my friend?" Tim replied, feeling confident.

"You say you got back to Baltimore Sunday morning? Well, today is Wednesday."

CHAPTER 8

Tim was relieved as an attendant rolled him out of the Psychiatric Ward to one of the regular medical units, but he was still extremely worried about the missing two days. At least now he had a medical explanation for the blackout, but where in the hell had he been? He certainly hadn't been running up and down Washington Street for that length of time—although this was Baltimore, where acting strange would not attract much attention.

Tim was taken to a room with two beds, but fortunately the other one was empty. He was able to get up from the gurney to the bed without any help from the attendant and was in the process of making himself comfortable when a nurse arrived with several papers attached to her clipboard.

"Mr. Hall, I have your discharge papers here."

"Discharge papers? Dr. Ryan told me this morning that she wanted to keep me another day."

Tim was slightly surprised at this news, but he really did not want to spend another night in the hospital, so he decided not to make too strong of an argument.

The nurse laughed. "You guys come in here all of the time and we tell you to stay, but before we know it, there's a phone call from upstairs telling us to let you out."

Tim was confused. What did the nurse mean by "you guys" and "a phone call from upstairs"?

The nurse continued. "Now, when the local cops are admitted, we can't get rid of them—but you Feds, well, I guess it's a different world."

"I think you may have me mixed up with somebody else. I'm retired from the government, and I am not cop—Fed or otherwise," Tim explained.

"Yeah, sure, and I'm a Secret Service Agent," the nurse responded as she handed Tim her clipboard and a stack of papers to sign.

Tim was still convinced the nurse had somehow made a mistake, but he decided that he wanted to get out of Johns Hopkins before anything else happened.

"Here are your clothes, Mr. Hall." The nurse handed Tim a plastic bag that contained a pair of his blue jeans, a pullover shirt and sweater, shoes, and a jacket. There was another bag that contained Tim's wallet and house keys. The last thing Tim remembered doing was falling asleep in his living room, but it appeared that he had purposely gotten dressed and gone out. But where did he go?

Tim had finished dressing when there was a knock on his hospital room door. He looked up to see a smiling Mary Ann.

Mary Ann walked directly to Tim and began to hug him tightly. "Where have you been? I've been looking all over town for you!" she exclaimed.

"I don't know, Mary Ann, but I'm hoping you can tell me," Tim answered.

Tim and Mary Ann navigated their way out of the massive hospital center and found a coffee shop around the corner on Madison Street. Tim sat and gazed out at the traffic while Mary Ann brought two coffees to the table.

"So, tell me something that I don't know?" Tim said, trying to be funny, but he was very worried that he was beginning to lose his mind. Wasn't this the first symptom of dementia?

"Well," Mary Ann began, "you woke me up at 1 a.m. on Monday morning. You were banging on my door, and I almost called the cops because I didn't know it was you."

"But you did not," Tim said.

"No, but I wanted to. But you said that you had to tell me something important, so I let you in, and..."

"And what?" Tim was becoming slightly impatient.

"You picked me up, carried me to my bed, and said that you were in love with me. And then, well, then we had sex." Mary Ann grabbed Tim's hand. "And it was the best I have ever had. I just didn't think a guy your age could have so much energy. You don't remember any of this?" she added.

Her face was beginning to register a look of disappointment, so Tim lied and told her that he did remember. Mary Ann began to smile again and continued. "So, we stayed in bed all day Monday, and I didn't even bother to open up the Goose. I went down and put a note on the door—and remember, we could hear the regulars down on the street banging on the door, and you said, 'Fuck em if they can't take a joke?'"

Tim shook his head yes, and suddenly he did remember. He remembered waking up at midnight in his condo, getting dressed, and walking to the Goose. He knew that the Goose closed early on Sunday night, so he'd gone up the stairs to Mary Ann's apartment.

"You told me to go away when I knocked on your door, right?"

"I told you to go the fuck home," Mary Ann responded.

"And I said who cares what anybody thinks."

"Yes, you did." Mary Ann was now laughing, which made Tim feel good.

Tim began to recall their lovemaking and how long he had lasted, but what was really amazing was the short amount of time it took him to be ready to go again. It had been a very long time since Tim was able to get it up twice in one night, but it seemed that the love fest had gone on the entire next day.

Tim's memory was coming back a little bit at a time. He remembered that they'd ordered a pizza for dinner on Monday night, watched something on HBO, and had more sex. He recalled Mary Ann telling him on

Tuesday that she had to open the Goose, and Tim told her that he was going home and would be back later on. Tim then recalled walking downstairs and around the corner, where there was a black Mercedes SUV and Amin from the Dominican Republic. Was that a dream, or did that really happen?

"Earth to Tim, Earth to Tim," Mary Ann said as she shook Tim's hand. "Where did you go, honey?"

"Oh, I'm just thinking," Tim answered absently. He was still thinking about the black SUV.

"What I want to know is how the hell you ended up at Johns Hopkins." Mary Ann was now sounding concerned.

"That, I don't know," Tim answered. "I really wish that I did. The cops picked me up on Washington Street and said I was acting crazy."

"Yeah, that's how I found out where you were. The Irish cop, Danny B., came by to ask if I knew you. I told him that you were one of my regulars, and he told me the rest. I was very disappointed that you didn't call me, but I figured you just fell asleep."

"Mary Ann, I have no idea what happened in the Dominican Republic, but I should not have gone. I was ripped off."

"Well, they did something to you, Tim, because you seem like a new man."

Tim leaned over and kissed Mary Ann, and they both go up to leave. It was close to 4 p.m., and Mary Ann had to go and bartend at the Goose. They agreed to meet at Tim's condo later that night.

Tim watched Mary Ann walk up to Washington Street and wondered why it had taken her so long to ask about his trip to the Dominican Republic, but he decided to let it go. After all, a lot had happened since he'd returned.

CHAPTER 9

Tim decided to get a sandwich on his way back to his condo. A good sub shop was close by, and he ate there often. CNN was on the sub shop's TV, and although the sound was turned down very low, Tim could hear a panel of talking heads discussing the President's job performance, it was not a particularly positive review. Tim had an opinion on just about everything but was surprisingly neutral about the current President—and, for that matter, about all of the Presidents going back to the first President Bush. Tim simply felt that the President was for the most part a figurehead and that it didn't matter who held the position. The fact that everyone in the press seemed to hate this particular President was a mystery to Tim. He knew the man was a racist, but he recalled hearing a recording of one very progressive President making an extremely racist remark as well.

Tim suddenly realized what he was thinking. How the hell did he hear a recording of a former President making a comment about African Americans and Jews? Was this another one of his dreams? What was going on? Tim thought about seeing his neurologist to get an opinion, but the prospect of more MRIs and CAT scans scared him. Maybe he should speak to Mary Ann about what was happening...but did he want to scare her off as well? Why would she want a senile boyfriend?

Tim's sandwich was now ready, and the talking heads on CNN had apparently finished talking. The station had gone to commercials, so Tim paid for his sandwich and Diet Coke and headed out the door for North Charles Street and his condo. As Tim walked, he noticed a car, no, an SUV, out of the corner of his left eye. Tim had begun to notice how much his vision had improved lately, and he could see that a black SUV was slowly tailing him as he walked up to Charles Street. Was somebody following him? Why?

Tim decided to find out, so he stopped, turned, and faced the street. The black Mercedes SUV pulled up right in front of him. Tim had to bend down slightly in order to see in the vehicle, and he spotted two men. He could not make out the driver, but the man in the passenger seat had graying hair and a light brown complexion. Maybe from India or Pakistan, Tim thought to himself.

"May I help you?" Tim was somewhat surprised by how direct he was becoming. It felt like he was pretending to be a different person, yet his new behavior also seemed natural.

The man in the passenger seat smiled and said, "Yes, I certainly hope that you can. We are looking for North Charles Street." The man had a slight accent, perhaps from the UK. One might call it posh. Yes, Tim thought. He had a posh British accent.

"That's interesting," Tim replied. "I'm headed that way myself."

Tim immediately felt stupid. Why the hell did he

just tell two strangers where he was going?

Then again, maybe he was just being paranoid.

“Well then,” the man in the SUV replied, “perhaps we can give you a lift?”

Paranoid or not, there was no way Tim was going to get into that car. “Thank you, but my mother told me to never accept a ride with strangers.” Tim was now laughing, although he was still on guard. “But if you take a right turn at the light and then go down two blocks, you’ll see North Charles.”

Tim pointed while walking, hoping to put some distance between himself and the black SUV. The man in the passenger seat gave Tim a friendly wave and drove on.

Tim knew that he had seen the man before. He was just too familiar. Tim thought once again that he was acting paranoid, which might also be a sign of some medical condition. He decided to call his neurologist after all.

Tim made the call to his neurologist as soon as he got home. At first, the doctor’s receptionist told Tim that the doctor would not be able to see him for more than six weeks, but when Tim told her that he was having new symptoms, she relented and a made an appointment for Friday in two weeks. Thirty minutes later, the neurologist’s nurse called Tim back and told him that they had arranged for a number of tests, including a CAT scan and an MRI with contrast plus some blood work to be done before the examination. They also made appointments for Tim to be tested on his cognitive ability and IQ. All of that could be done the week before the appointment.

Tim sat down and began to make notes about the coming appointment in his day planner when he heard a heavy-sounding knock on his door. There were three knocks, to be precise—and then nothing.

When Tim looked through the peep hole, he didn't see anything. He slowly opened his front door and cautiously looked each way, but he still saw nothing.

However, at his feet was a thick, padded envelope. Tim bent down, picked it up, and returned to his couch. He placed the package on his coffee table.

All that was written on the large envelope was Tim's full name, Timothy Robert Hall. He didn't usually use the Robert, since that was the same name as a low-end men's clothing store that existed in the 1960s. Tim remembered that some kids used to call him "cheap suit" at school.

Tim had been remembering little things about several subjects all day long but had been unable to connect them with anything. And now he had a mystery package on his coffee table. Tim took stock of the entire week. First, he'd traveled to the Dominican Republic, where something he couldn't explain had been done to him. Next, he came home, went out with his girlfriend, and took her to bed for a day and a half, not to mention that he'd almost broken a guy's hand at the Dallas-Fort Worth airport. But what was really beginning to worry Tim was that his personality appeared to be changing. He found himself thinking and saying things that he ordinarily would never say.

Perhaps his memory was returning. The doctors had said that it might, after all—but Tim also knew that a personality change could be an early sign of dementia, which just plain scared him.

Tim looked back down at the package. There were no stamps or postage of any kind on it, no return address. Tim's address was also not present on it, which told him that it had been hand-delivered. There was only a white label with his full name printed on it.

When Tim picked up the letter opener and carefully opened the top, a book with plastic binding fell out of the envelope onto the coffee table. The book was similar to an employee manual and was certainly not very fancy. The paper could have come from any copy machine.

Tim opened the book to the first page and saw the title "Who Am I?" That is a very good question, Tim thought to himself, but he was fully aware that he was a former employee of the CIA. He was just a little unclear about what his job had been for the last 5 years or so before the accident. Tim had tried to tell some regulars at the Goose that he was a CIA Case Officer but only Mary Ann believed him. Once you retired from the Agency, you were pretty much dead to them. Sometimes, you got the feeling that they would prefer you to actually be dead. Nothing annoyed Agency management more than retired officers shooting off their mouths to civilians at cocktail parties...or worse, write a book. The best the Agency could do was to issue what was known as the Stump Speech, which said, *we can neither confirm nor deny (fill in the blank and your name here).*

Most people had general misconceptions about the Agency. Generally speaking, CIA employees were usually either analysts or technicians. The ones known as the case officers were actually what people would consider to be spies. Both analysts and technicians could be case officers. These employees worked at CIA Headquarters at Langley and at most US Embassies around the world. Often, the analysts and case officers would be responsible for different tasks—but the one aspect they all held in common was lying. They all lied so often that you never really knew when a case officer or analyst was telling you the truth. Therefore, you just had to accept the fact that you were being lied to most (if not all) of the time.

The other CIA employees you would likely encounter were known as contractors. These men and women performed much of the dirty or unpleasant kinds of work that the CIA was known for. For example, if anyone had a gun, it was probably a contractor, especially since contractors were responsible for Agency security. The case officers tended to feel that they were above that kind of work (although they planned and supervised all of it), but the case officers would be lost without the support of the contractors.

The fourth type of CIA employees were known as assets. These were the people who supplied the CIA with valuable information. Although the assets were not considered paid employees of the Agency, many were actually paid very well for the information they provided. Other assets believed that they had a moral obligation, and a few others were simply blackmailed by the Agency. Most of the assets reported to a case officer, who would be known to the assets as their handler. The assets perhaps had the most dangerous jobs of anyone, since if they were caught, the result was usually a very unpleasant death.

It was also not lost on Tim that someone had gone out of their way to erase his past after his accident. Tim accepted that he was suffering from retrograde amnesia, which was the name his condition was given, but the fact that no one came forward and tried to explain anything about his past life before the accident just did not make any sense. Did he not have any friends or coworkers from the Agency? Why didn't anyone take him to his old house or the town where he lived just to see if any memory would return? He remembered that his doctors had suggested this course of treatment, yet no one ever followed up on it. Tim did not even know where his late wife Pam was buried or where her ashes were scattered. He'd been told by the doctors and nurses in the hospital that Pam had died in the car accident, but that was all. No police officers ever visited Tim in the hospital to take or follow up with a report. Wasn't that the common practice? Tim's mysterious second cousin showed up one day to take care of his home, and she did present him with a check for $478,000, which was apparently the sale price of his house and car. He was given a do-nothing job at the Social Security Administration, where he tried to look himself up in the system until the words "Denied Access" appeared in big red letters. "Classified," it also said.

Tim tried going directly to human resources after that, but all they would tell him was that he'd been transferred from another agency, and its name was redacted. Tim asked if his wife had life insurance. All Federal employees had life insurance provided to them with double indemnity for accidental death, yet no one had any information about that. The manager of the human resources department sympathized with Tim and suggested that he contact his Congressman, which he considered doing until he thought about what he was going to say. *"Hi there, I was some kind of spy, but I'm not sure for who or where."* It sounded crazy because it was.

He finally had to face the fact that someone no longer wanted him around and had decided that Tim needed to retire. The message "Just stay in Baltimore and collect your pension" was loud and clear. Tim's retirement annuity was almost 90K per year, plus he had money in the bank from the sale of his home. And now that he had a girlfriend, so what was there not to like about life?

Well, for one thing, why the trip down to the Dominican Republic? Tim had been lured there, but for what purpose? Now, those two men had appeared in front of the sub shop, and this book was delivered. Tim wondered if the two men were in Baltimore to kill him. Maybe the people who had worked so hard to erase Tim's former life had decided to retire him for good.

CHAPTER 10

Tim had finished all of the tests and scans prescribed by his neurologist. He'd even had a sleep study and an EEG performed. After the accident, Tim hated seeing doctors and especially hated waiting for test results, yet now he did not really seem to mind at all. Tim needed to understand his physical condition before he could think about any future with Mary Ann, after all. He also needed to know if there were any side effects from the stem cell treatments he'd received, or at least thought he'd received, in the Dominican Republic. Although he felt great, Mary Ann was concerned about what doctors may have done.

"God, Tim," Mary Ann had said the other night. "You're lucky they didn't take a kidney or something." She'd even made him lie down on his stomach so she could look for scars.

That happened two weeks ago, and Tim had not seen much of Mary Ann since then. Tim wondered why Mary Ann seemed to disappear every two weeks or so. Perhaps she was seeing someone else. Their sex life was good for the most part, but Mary Ann sometimes behaved as if her mind was on something else entirely. He had been hoping that she would come with him to the neurologist, but apparently, she'd made other plans.

Tim got a cab ride over to the doctor's office.

The driver let Tim off at the Medical Office building, and Tim began his journey through the maze of floors looking for room 876, Drs. Clarkson, Gray, and Harris, Neurology. Tim once again felt sad that Mary Ann was not with him. She hadn't even bothered to call or text him that morning, which was something they had started to do every day. On the other hand, the smiling Indian man in the Mercedes SUV and his driver had not been seen for at least two weeks, and there were no more books delivered or imaginary attempts on his life. Tim chalked both Mary Ann and the man from India up to his paranoia.

When he found the right room, Tim was led directly into Dr. Gray's office and told to sit on the examination table. Dr. Gray soon came in with a stack of results under his arm and got directly to the point. "Mr. Hall, I can find absolutely nothing wrong with you, at least neurology related," he explained. "I have studied your scans, and my partners have studied your scans, and none of us could find anything medically wrong with you."

Tim was happy with the good news. He really was convinced that he was suffering from the early symptoms of dementia, yet he sensed that something else was troubling the doctor by the look on his face.

The doctor opened to another page of Tim's report and started to speak. "What is unusual, Mr. Hall, is that we did not detect any shrinkage in the size of your brain. As we age, most of us experience an amount of brain shrinkage, which is normal—but your brain appears to be the brain of someone 35 to 40 years old. In addition, the results of your cognitive tests also indicate the brain of a younger man, not someone who is 58. Your other scans have all come back clear as well as your EEG. You show no sign of seizure or strokes. There are no structural issues such as growths or lesions. Your blood flow through your brain appears excellent. Your blood pressure is exactly normal. We do not see any dead or damaged areas which would indicate dementia. Your vision is 20/20. Your reflexes are above average, and you have an IQ of 128."

The doctor made his way over to Tim and shone a light in one eye, then the other. He next ran a few simplistic neurological tests on Tim. Tim seemed to pass all of them.

"Dr. Gray," Tim began, "Are there any radical treatments for retrograde amnesia?"

"Radical or experimental treatments?" the doctor repeated. "There's a whole list of them."

"What about stem cell treatments, doctor?"

"Using embryonic stem cells to treat anything these days would be considered radical, Mr. Hall, and the FDA will only allow for a small amount of any treatment using stem cells. That said, I am not aware of any study where stem cells were used to treat amnesia. The treatment plan I developed for you was designed to help restore your memory. Have you continued to take the medicine I prescribed?"

Dr. Gray had prescribed several medications for Tim to take every day. One was a compound medication that needed to be filled at a special pharmacy, which Tim found to be a royal pain in the ass.

"Yes, religiously," Tim replied. "But what kind of treatment plan?"

"Well, nothing particularly radical, I assure you. I recommended that you should visit as many places as you can that you were formerly familiar with in the hope that this might stimulate your memory, but I have no follow-up notes to indicate whether any of this was done."

Dr. Gray began to look through his notes for the results of Tim's therapy, but Tim knew he wouldn't find anything. He wondered if anyone had actually prevented treatment to restore his memory.

After a thorough search of Tim's medical folder, Dr. Gray continued speaking. "Well, Mr. Hall, it appears that the treatment plan was never implemented."

Tim wondered why the doctor just did not just ask him about this instead of looking for notes, but he guessed that the man didn't trust Tim's memory, either.

"Dr. Gray, who did you give your treatment plan to?" he wondered.

The doctor was still going through Tim's folder, so he answered without looking up. "It was given to the two men from your agency."

"Agency!" Tim exclaimed, beginning to laugh. "Doc, I'm retired. I have no agency."

The doctor seemed truly surprised at Tim's assertion. "I assure you, these two men had proper identification."

"Oh, I'm sure that they were who they claimed to be," Tim agreed sarcastically.

The doctor turned and walked over to his desk, inviting Tim to sit down. "Mr. Hall, I have no knowledge of the world which you and others inhabit. I just know that it exists. Over the years, I have had several patients who were employed by the CIA, FBI, NSA, Defense Intelligence. And because our job here is to treat injuries to the brain, the people who you work for have a vested interest in your condition."

Tim found himself agreeing with the doctor. After all, you certainly didn't want your spies running around the hospital giving away sensitive information without realizing it.

"So, are you telling me that you provided my medical records to my former employer, the Central Intelligence Agency?"

Tim's doctor looked perplexed. "I cannot really answer that, Mr. Hall, because I don't know—but it does appear as if that particular agency is interested in following your recovery."

"And you just gave them all of my information?" Tim was becoming indignant.

"Well, Mr. Hall, they have been paying your medical bills."

Tim was shocked, but he'd never really thought about who had paid for all of the treatment he'd received over the years. He'd just assumed it was his insurance.

"Mr. Hall?" The doctor was speaking again. "Have you had any treatments performed outside of this office?"

At that point, Tim decided to confess everything about the trip to the Dominican Republic and the supposed stem cell treatment he'd received there. The doctor just shook his head and made some notes as Tim was describing what he could recall. Finally, the doctor put down his pen.

"Mr. Hall, I would really like to repeat all of the tests we have performed in three months and see where we stand."

"Where we stand, doctor?"

"Yes, Mr. Hall. As of right now, you seem to be fine, but now that you tell me that you may have had some treatments with stem cells, I would like to revisit your scans in three months."

This made sense, so Tim decided to ask about something else that was bothering him. "Dr. Gray, will I ever get my memory back?"

"It is unlikely that your memory will ever be fully restored," the doctor answered, "but it is possible that enough of your past will return to allow you to live a normal life."

Tim nodded to indicate that he understood the doctor, then turned to leave. The doctor called after him. "Remember, I would like to retest you in three months."

Tim turned back to the doctor. "Dr. Gray, I would not repeat our conversation today with anyone," he cautioned. "If someone asks, just tell them my appointment was a routine checkup."

Tim left the doctor's office and didn't bother to make the follow-up appointment.

CHAPTER 11

Leaving the doctor's office, Tim began to walk the long hallway to the elevators. The doctor's office was in an older building on the Johns Hopkins campus, and the hallways were maze-like.

Tim had reached one end of the hallway and was trying to decide whether to go right or left when a voice behind him spoke.

"It doesn't matter if you turn right or left. Either direction will lead you to the same place."

Tim turned around to see the smiling man who looked to be from India with another man. The other man was much taller and larger than the first. Tim wondered why he had not heard either of them approach from behind.

Before Tim could think of anything to say, the first man spoke again. "Tim, my name is Sebastian Oak, and this is Toby Wheeler. I do believe you have already met Mr. Wheeler."

Yes, Tim had met Toby Wheeler. He was the same Nurse Toby who'd stood guard over Tim while he was in the psychiatric ward next door. This Sebastian guy also seemed familiar as well.

Tim's fight or flight response was beginning to kick in. Seeing an exit to his right, he thought about making a dash for it—but Sebastian spoke again.

"Now, calm down, Tim. We really mean you no harm, but we do need to speak with one another."

Sebastian gave Toby a silent look that apparently told him to go away, since he turned around and walked in the opposite direction. "Toby can be slightly intimidating, so it would probably be better if he takes a break so the two of us can talk," the man explained.

Sebastian reached into his suit jacket pocket and produced a large billfold that contained his identification, which read the United States of America, Central Intelligence Agency and the name Sebastian P. Oak. Below it was Sebastian's picture. Tim studied the picture, then looked at Sebastian, then down again at the picture. Sebastian was the same person as Amin from the CBSCRC in the Dominican Republic, but Tim was convinced that he had also met him before.

Tim and Sebastian rode down together in the elevator without saying a word. They entered a coffee shop, where they both ordered black coffee. They found an empty table and sat.

Tim spoke first. "So, Sebastian—or should I call you Amin? What is this all about?"

"You don't remember me at all, do you?" Sebastian replied.

Tim studied Sebastian's face. Yes, he did know Sebastian Oak...but, for now, Tim decided to lie. "Other than the guy who lifted $18,000 from me in the Dominican Republic, no, I can't say that I do."

This made Sebastian laugh. "That is the one thing I really miss about you, Tim: your sarcasm. No matter where we were or what we did, you always kept things amusing. Here, let me show you a picture."

Sebastian produced an old Polaroid picture of a young Tim Hall sporting long hair with another younger man, also with long hair. The two were seated at a cabana in what looked like someplace south of the US border.

"That is, you and me in the mid-seventies in El Salvador. We were just two students on a road trip."

"Except we weren't students, and we weren't on any road trip," Tim surmised.

"Unfortunately, not, my friend. But we accomplished our mission."

Tim stared out the window. He did vaguely recall traveling on the Pan American Highway, but when and why was just a blank.

"So, Sebastian, you and I have been friends?" he asked.

"I like to think that we were very close friends, Tim," the other man agreed.

"Then why don't you and I cut the shit? If you know me, then tell me why I've been hanging out here in fucking Baltimore for the last four years," Tim demanded. "Can you do that for me, Sebastian?"

A couple from another table looked over at Tim's outburst while Sebastian held up his hand, trying to get

Tim to lower his voice. "Maybe we should take a walk outside," Sebastian suggested. He ordered two more cups of coffee and followed Tim out the door.

Sebastian and Tim walked down Washington Street towards the harbor and then over to Patterson Park without speaking. Tim had just about had enough of people keeping secrets from him. If they knew who he was and what he'd done before his accident, why didn't they just tell him?

As the two men walked, Tim did not feel that he was in any immediate danger—with "immediate" being the keyword. He was bigger than Sebastian, but he also figured that Toby was somewhere close by. Toby did worry Tim. Toby was a big guy, like NFL linebacker big. Tim figured Toby to be at least six feet four and 285 lbs. This made Tim and his six-foot, 175 lb. frame feel small in comparison. Toby had not yet spoken a word to Tim, but he got the distinct feeling that the big guy did not like him. Tim figured that Sebastian was most likely unarmed since CIA officers didn't carry weapons, as a rule—but Toby, who was probably a contractor, would likely be armed.

Sebastian finally broke the silence. "Tim, ask me anything. What do you want to know?"

"Well, first, who am I?" Tim knew this was a dumb question since he was pretty sure that he was the same person as it said on his driver's license, but he had to ask.

"Your name is Tim Hall, and up until four years and five months ago, you were an officer with the CIA,"

Sebastian replied.

"How did I end up here in Baltimore?" was Tim's next question.

"That is a long and somewhat complicated story," Sebastian replied.

"I got time," Tim said as they sat at opposite ends of a park bench.

Sebastian took a deep breath and started speaking. "You, me, and your wife Pam were on a mission to China. We were employees of a software company located in Silicon Valley. That was our cover. Our real purpose was to sell intellectual property and information to the Chinese government. Our target was a Chinese national named Lilly Lin. Our objective was to turn Lilly Lin and make her an asset using any means necessary to do so. Our information on Ms. Lin was that members of her family were part of the 1966 Cultural Revolution and had been able to maintain a high standing in the Communist Party of China. Therefore, if Ms. Lin could be placed in a highly embarrassing, perhaps sexual situation, that would give us the necessary leverage to make her an asset."

"Wow, you guys sure know how to have fun," Tim remarked sarcastically.

"I suppose that's true, since it was your plan," Sebastian answered.

He continued. "Apparently, Ms. Lin was known to play around with other women, which was something that your wife Pam had no trouble participating in."

Tim felt like saying, “Hey, that’s my wife you’re talking about, pal,” but he let Sebastian keep going.

“So, you and Pam and Lilly had planned a dinner when all of that was supposed to happen—but then, as you say, things went south.”

“How did things so south?” Tim wondered.

“You tell me, Tim.” Sebastian gave him a hard stare. “Your wife shot Lilly Lin, and you and she came racing out of the house. I’m behind the wheel, but you push me aside and drive. We drive, but you crash the car. You are unconscious. I have to get you out and to the contact’s house, and I still don’t know how I managed to do all of that because now we have a murdered Chinese national and the Chinese police are looking for an American. I was able to get you to Hong Kong and on a diplomatic flight out. You ended up in Dover, Delaware and were transported to Baltimore Shock Trauma.”

At this point, Tim was overloaded with information, but he believed Sebastian. As Sebastian was retelling the China story, Tim was having flashbacks of him driving a car on some winding road and losing control. It seemed to make sense, but Tim now felt remorseful. What kind of person would devise such a plan to entrap a woman so she could do his bidding? Well, apparently, he was that kind of person.

Tim looked up and saw that Sebastian was glancing at his watch. It was getting late and would be dark soon. Tim thought that they should leave the park before it got dark since it was not the safest place to be.

But he had one more question to ask—and he wasn't looking forward to hearing the answer. "Sebastian, what happened to Pam? How did she die?"

Sebastian looked at Tim, then out to the street. He seemed to be stalling for time.

"Well, the thing is, Tim...the thing is that your wife Pam is still alive."

If Tim had been subject to fainting spells, now would be the time to have one. The China story had been hard enough to hear, and God only knew what details Sebastian had omitted...but to end it with Pam actually being alive, well, that was just too much.

It was now dark out, so Tim and Sebastian began to walk back over to Washington Street. Tim was still digesting the news of Pam when Sebastian spoke again.

"Tim, the China operation was extremely messy in so many ways. When we all made it back home, well...let's just say that management was not very pleased, not to mention that the Chinese's Embassy in DC was on the phone to the State Department. Take my word for it—it was a mess. The Chinese knew that there was a man-and-woman team involved, so keeping you and Pam apart just made sense, plus the fact that you two were apparently close to a divorce."

"If you say so, Sebastian." Tim knew that he had to take Sebastian's word for everything, but he was beginning to regain some of his sarcasm. "Did she ever come to visit me here in Baltimore?" he asked.

"We both did, although Pam did not tell the hospital staff that she was Mrs. Hall. When you finally woke up, you remembered nothing."

It was true that Tim recalled very little of those days. Sebastian continued, "At first, we just hoped that your memory would return...but after six months, it appeared that would not happen. The doctors told us that you were most likely suffering from retrograde amnesia and that your full memory would probably never recover."

Sebastian and Tim continued to walk until they reached the edge of the Johns Hopkins campus. Sebastian turned and faced Tim.

"Look, we did not exactly desert you up here, Tim. Pam and I made sure that you had proper medical care and a place to live. And when you were ready, we found you a job."

"Yes, as an auditor for the Social Security Administration. Thanks for that," Tim deadpanned.

"It was that or as an inspector in charge of monitoring the air quality in the Baltimore Harbor Tunnel," Sebastian answered.

Tim couldn't help laughing at that. "Okay, Sebastian," he agreed, "I understand—but the plain and simple truth was that you and Pam were going to leave me up here forever. Except now, you're here. Why is that? What do you want from me?"

"We need you, Tim. We need you to come back to help us."

Tim was at a loss for words and just stood on the

corner, staring at Sebastian. "Come back? Come back to what?"

Sebastian placed his hand on Tim's shoulder. "The country needs you to come back and help us."

At this point, the black Mercedes SUV drove up and started waiting at the curb. Tim could see that Toby was behind the wheel.

Sebastian waved at Toby, then turned back to address Tim. "I'm not one to use hyperbole, but the fate of the nation depends on you and your help, Tim."

Toby beeped the horn of the Mercedes to remind them that he was waiting.

"You better go, Sebastian. I don't think your friend likes me very much."

As Sebastian walked toward the SUV, he grinned. "Toby does not like you because you're dating his girlfriend, Mary Ann. Isn't that her name?"

Sebastian entered the SUV and was gone.

CHAPTER 12

As soon as Tim got back to his condo, he sent Mary Ann a text message that said, "Met your boyfriend Toby this afternoon. He's a real babe." Maybe that was a little below the belt, but Tim wanted to get her attention.

He did. Mary Ann began to send him a string of text messages. "HE IS NOT MY BOYFRIEND" was the first. Two minutes later, another text said, "At least not anymore." Tim shook his head and smiled. He had figured that Mary Ann must have an ex hanging around somewhere but considering all of the new information Tim now had to process, the last thing on his mind was Mary Ann's previous love life. The one thing that did concern Tim was the fact that if Mary Ann knew Toby, she was most likely aware of Sebastian and was probably involved with this entire plot of "Let's get Tim back in the CIA."

Tim quit reading Mary Ann's texts after a while. Mary Ann had told him that she would be over after work, so he supposed he would find out all about it then. In the meantime, he needed a drink.

At exactly 11:45 p.m., Mary Ann slammed open Tim's front door, which had the effect of waking him up. Despite all of the excitement Tim had experienced earlier in the day, the second vodka tonic had put him right to sleep.

"Where is he?" was the first thing out of Mary Ann's mouth.

"Mary Ann, I said I met Toby. I didn't say I brought him home."

Mary Ann still looked around the condo anyhow. After she seemed convinced that Toby was not hiding anywhere, she asked Tim what he was drinking. Tim offered to make her a vodka tonic, but Mary Ann made one herself.

She seemed to relax somewhat and turned to look at Tim. "Does this mean that we're breaking up?"

Mary Ann appeared to be truly concerned that this was Tim's intention. "Why, because you have an ex-boyfriend?" he wondered. "Well, you may want to break up with me when I tell you that my wife is still alive."

"Yeah, I knew that," Mary Ann agreed casually.

"You knew that my wife Pam was still alive and did not bother to mention that to me?" Tim demanded, floored. "How long did you know?"

"I knew she was alive when we went on our first date."

Tim felt like he was having an "I Love Lucy" moment, and he was Ricky Ricardo. Meanwhile, Mary Ann continued to sip her vodka tonic, appearing to be totally oblivious to his shock and anger.

Tim collected himself. He realized that he would

get nowhere yelling at Mary Ann, so he decided to be nice.

"So, Mary Ann, when I was baring my soul to you about my wife, me not being sure that I loved her and all, you knew that she was alive?"

Mary Ann nodded.

"So, can you tell me why you did not mention that Pam was alive?"

"Because Sebastian told me not to tell you."

At this point, Mary Ann started to cry. Tim was beginning to think that Mary Ann had to be the best actress of all time. He knew that she was lying to him now and had been lying to him during their entire relationship, yet she was managing to break his heart.

Tim sat down next to Mary Ann and placed his arm around her, kissing her on the cheek. "Why don't you start at the beginning?" he suggested.

The beginning was this: Toby Wheeler and Mary Ann Layback were both licensed private detectives in the state of Nevada, primarily working in Las Vegas. Their bread and butter was chasing down bail jumpers, and apparently, they were very good at it. They also did background checking, which included something called "honey trapping." Honey trapping was a method that determined the fidelity of prospective husbands. Essentially, this involved Mary Ann attempting to pick up the men while they were sitting at a bar while Toby would record the entire event on his iPhone. Often, they were hired to do this by a relative of the brideto-be, and Mary Ann would always want to know how much they wanted the guy "caught," since she was convinced, she could pick up any guy, be he young or old.

These kinds of jobs should have provided Toby and Mary Ann with a very good living, except for Toby's gambling problem. Toby was convinced that there was not a game or table in Vegas that he could not beat. Toby thought he was a major player, whereas most dealers considered him a major sucker. Of course, no one except Mary Ann ever told Toby this.

Since Toby was always in debt to several bookies at a time, both Mary Ann and Toby supplemented their income in other ways. Mary Ann would bartend, and Toby would work security. Life just went on from one day to another for the two of them until the day Toby got a call from Big Doug Smith, Bail Bondsman.

Big Doug Smith was one of the bigger bail bond outfits in Las Vegas. Big Doug himself was no longer around, having died of a sudden coronary some years back, but his picture was the first thing you saw as you walked into the company's office. Many said that Doug had a striking resemblance to Satan, or at least what they imagined Satan to look like. He'd sported a goatee that was pointed at the bottom plus both of his eyebrows were pointed—but it was Doug's wide smile that completed the look of the Fallen Angel himself. Under Big Doug Smith's picture was a gold-plated placard with the words "You Can Trust Big Doug" on it.

Big Doug Smith Bail Bondsman was now run by Doug's daughter, Grace Smith. A small, attractive woman who was nothing whatsoever like her father,

Grace was married to an accountant who worked at one of the casinos. She had two children, a boy and a girl. Grace was president of the women's group at the First Methodist Church and otherwise lived a quiet life. However, she ran her late father's business with an iron fist. She'd kept the Smith name for business purposes, and her husband also went by the name Smith, so no one knew what his real name was.

Grace stayed in an office behind the large plexiglass enclosure and rarely made an appearance out front. Three large men with shaved heads manned each of the three windows where the business of bailing men and women out of jail took place.

Grace used Toby and Mary Ann because Grace loved Mary Ann and wished that she could be more like her instead of the suburban mom she had become. Ironically and unbeknownst to Grace, Mary Ann wished she had Grace's life.

Grace dialed Toby and Mary Ann's number, hoping to get Mary Ann. She got Toby instead. "Hello, Toby," she murmured, "Grace Smith here. Is Mary Ann around?"

"She's bartending," Toby answered. He was a man of very few words.

"Oh dear," Grace said. "When will she be back?"

"Late, I guess." Most business owners would know if they were speaking with one of their top customers, but Toby was one of a kind.

"Oh dear," Grace said once again.

At this point, Grace knew that she had no choice but to summon Toby for a routine but important errand, but she decided to call Mary Ann just to be sure that she was aware that she was sending Toby out on a job.

"Toby," Grace began, "I need you to come over to the store. I need you to run out to Barstow and bring back a client who decided to leave town without letting us know."

"Got it, Mrs. S. Is there anything else?"

"Yes Toby. You will need to take fifty thousand dollars with you. That money goes to the Barstow Sheriff's Office to cover the client's bail for whatever crime he committed up there."

It was important to Grace to get the bail jumper back to Las Vegas, even if it meant she would be shelling out fifty thousand dollars. She would be out one hundred thousand if he failed to return from California. The money would all even out in the end.

With Toby now on his way, Grace dialed the number to Mary Ann's cell phone. It was important that Mary Ann be made aware of what was going on. Toby was good at one thing: being a tough guy. He'd never lost a bail jumper, and very few ever jumped bail again once they spent an afternoon with Toby—but in other matters, Toby was as dumb as a bag of rocks.

Mary Ann's phone went to voicemail. Grace began to speak. "Hello, Mary Ann? Grace Smith here. I just wanted to let you know that I've hired you and

Toby to bring back a client from Barstow, and I've given Toby fifty thousand dollars so the client can be released into his custody. I hope everything is good with you and do hope to see you soon. Bye-bye."

"Oh dear," Grace Smith said as she hung up the phone.

Mary Ann would have received Grace's phone call if she had been allowed to use her cell phone behind the bar, but that was against casino rules. Personal cell phones could only be used during designated breaks. The casino wanted you to be attending to the customers, not speaking with your boyfriend. Boyfriends, Mary Ann thought to herself. Probably time for a new one. Because of Toby's gambling losses, both Mary Ann and Toby were maxed out on their credit cards. They'd gotten cash advances to keep Toby's bookies at bay. If not for the fifty thousand in credit card debt, Mary Ann would be, well, anywhere but the evening shift at casino bar #2, also known as the Cowboy Bar because of the Western motif. This included Mary Ann's cowgirl uniform, which she was required to wear at all times while on the job. Well, at least she was behind the bar and not on the floor pushing drinks to drunk gamblers. Those girls had to wear short pants with their cowboy shirts and hats. Although the tips were better working on the floor, Mary Ann liked it fine where she was, plus there were men who she could flirt with at the bar. Out on the floor, you were not supposed to distract the customers from gambling—at least not too much. Just smile and laugh at their dumb jokes, then move on to the next one.

Mary Ann was making a sweep from one end of

the bar to the other to check if anyone needed a refill when she saw the well-dressed man with the light brown skin. He had been in the night before, and Mary Ann had had a very pleasant conversation with him then. He had a slight English accent that certainly made him sound sophisticated. He also paid his check using an Amex Black Card, which meant he was rich. Mary Ann also thought that the man had a very cool name: Sebastian Oak. Mary Ann had never met someone with a name like that.

As Mary Ann approached Sebastian, he gave her what she thought was a perfect smile and spoke before she could. "Well, good evening, Mary Ann. It's so nice to see you once again."

"Wow," Mary Ann thought to herself. "What a gentleman."

"Tonight, I think I will start with a Dewar on the rocks."

"Now, Mr. Oak, I'm supposed to greet you first," Mary Ann playfully said as she slid a beverage napkin in front of Sebastian. Whipping around, she grabbed the call brand scotch and gave Sebastian an extra half pour of liquor. She quickly garnished the drink and had it in front of him within 45 seconds.

Sebastian took a sip and said, "Yes, that's exactly what I needed."

"Have a hard day, Mr. Oak?" Mary Ann asked as she pretended to clean something below the bar top.

"Oh, just the usual stuff," he replied. "I'm just

waiting to see if someone accepts a deal, and then I can head back east."

"Where are you from, Mr. Oak?" Mary Ann figured that she might as well start digging for information on Sebastian, since you never knew what you might learn.

"Originally, I am from London, but right now I live outside of Washington, D.C."

London and Washington, D.C. sounded positively exotic to Mary Ann compared to Las Vegas. Mary Ann never could understand the attraction of this fucking town. To her, Las Vegas seemed to be nothing but drunks, drunks losing money, and loveless sex. Sure, there were people who lived here and liked living here, but she never thought the town was sophisticated like New York or D.C. As a matter of fact, she thought Vegas was pretty much a redneck town, and she wanted out of it. The maxed-out credit cards were all in Toby's name, and there was nothing holding her here. All Mary Ann needed was an offer to leave. She looked back at Sebastian and thought to herself that a girl could dream.

On any other night, Toby Wheeler would have taken the fifty thousand dollars from Big Doug Smith, driven up to Barstow, and picked up the bail jumper for return to the Clark County Detention Center. However, earlier that day, Toby had caught wind of a poker game. There were some would-be high rollers in town looking for a local game. One high roller had lost his shirt the night before and was looking to win his money back before he headed back east. This was the kind of game that Toby always missed out on, mostly because players needed to bring twenty-five grand to get in, and

Toby couldn't remember the last time he'd anything close to that kind of cash. Toby knew it was wrong and knew that Mary Ann would not approve even if he did win, but why the fuck did she even have to know? He could get in the game, double his money, get up to Barstow, and be back before anyone knew anything.

It was 10 p.m. before Mary Ann could take her first break of the night. She was a firm believer in the "no news is good news" view when it came to her boyfriend Toby, so her heart skipped two beats when she saw two messages from Grace Smith and one from Toby. Mary Ann listened to the first message from Grace, then the second.

"Mary Ann? Grace Smith here. Earlier today, I gave Toby a job which entailed driving to Barstow to take custody of the bail jumper we have up there? Well, I've talked to the sheriff, and he has not seen Toby as of yet or my fifty thousand dollars, so I've sent Larry and Barry out to look for him. Hope to see you soon. Bye-bye."

Mary Ann could almost hear Grace say "Oh dear" at the other end of the phone call. The third message was from Toby.

"Babe, I'm out back."

That was code that meant Toby was at their special meeting place, the place where they'd agreed to meet when it was time to skip town.

Mary Ann walked directly out of work and got in her car. There was no point in asking to leave early. She was able to grab her cash tips, at least. She drove fast and reached the rest area on Interstate 15. Toby's red pickup was there with Toby in the front seat. Mary Ann jumped in.

"Toby, you asshole, what the fuck have you done now?"

"Shhhh," came a sound from the rear. Mary Ann turned around to see Larry of the Larry and Barry twins holding a 9mm pistol to the back of Toby's head. She then saw that Toby's hands were cuffed to the steering wheel and a piece of duct tape covered his mouth. Sitting next to Larry was Grace Smith.

"Well, hello, Mary Ann. I was hoping that you would make it out here." Grace seemed truly glad to see Mary Ann despite the circumstances.

"You know, there was a little voice inside of me that said, now, Grace, it's not wise to let Toby have this kind of money without Mary Ann. And as usual, that little voice was right."

"Look, Grace, we can work something out here, can't we?"

"Oh dear," Grace said. "I'm afraid things have already been worked out." She sounded truly sorry.

Another car pulled into the rest area and parked next to Toby's truck. Two men got out. Mary Ann could see that one of them was the other twin, Barry, but she didn't recognize the second man.

Grace and Larry both got out of the truck and spoke with the mystery man. The man gave Grace a briefcase, which Grace opened. She then closed the case and walked back to the truck.

Grace opened the passenger side door. "Mary Ann? I am sure going to miss you, and I hope one day you'll come back for a visit...but if you do, leave Toby at home."

Grace smiled and walked back to her car. Larry opened the door for Grace, and she gave Mary Ann a little wave. Larry, Barry, and Grace then drove away.

The door of the truck opened once again. Mary Ann was truly surprised to see Sebastian Oak standing there. "Mr. Oak?" was all she could say.

"You may call me Sebastian. Mary Ann, you and your boyfriend will be working for me now, at least until you pay me back the one hundred thousand dollars you owe."

Toby, who still had the tape across his mouth, seemed to disagree with the deal, judging from the sounds he was making—at least until Sebastian offered to bring back Larry and Barry.

For her part, Mary Ann had been more than happy to begin working for Sebastian Oak. "And that's how we ended up here in Baltimore," she finished. She was smiling now, having told Tim the whole story.

Tim had only bought about half of Mary Ann's tale, but he totally believed that Sebastian had played both Toby and Mary Ann much more than they would ever comprehend.

He was tired, so he decided to get up and head to the bedroom.

Mary Ann was still seated in the big chair. "Are you coming?" he asked, turning back.

"I thought you would never ask," Mary Ann replied as she followed Tim to the bedroom.

CHAPTER 13

Tim was dreaming that someone was working on the street in front of his house. Bang, bang, bang was the noise. Why could they not stop the banging?

As Tim opened his eyes, though, he realized that the noise he was hearing was not roadwork, but someone pounding on his front door.

Tim pulled himself out of bed and started towards the door. He glanced at Mary Ann, who was sleeping in the opposite direction with her head at the foot of the bed. How the hell did she get in that position? Tim wondered to himself.

When Tim was five feet from the door, he yelled, "Okay, okay, okay!" His head was pounding along with the pounding on the door.

Tim opened the door to see Sebastian and Toby. Not unexpected, but not welcome, either. Tim turned without a word and headed to the kitchen.

Sebastian followed Tim, and Toby followed Sebastian. Tim started to make coffee. "Good morning, Tim," Sebastian said.

"What can I do for you, Sebastian?" Tim asked without bothering to turn around.

"It's actually what I believe that I can do for you,

Tim," the other man replied smoothly. "What would you say if I told you that I could help you get your memories back?"

"At this point, I'm not sure if I want them back," Tim muttered in response.

"You were always the joker, sir," Sebastian laughed.

Tim poured cups of coffee for himself and Mary Ann and headed back to the bedroom. Sebastian yelled after him, "Tim, get dressed! We need to take a ride. Your wife Pam is expecting us by 1 p.m."

The mention of Pam and the prospect of actually seeing her created a strong feeling of anxiety in Tim's stomach. God, did he want to see her again after all of these years?

Tim entered his bedroom to see that Mary Ann was already awake and dressed. He handed her a cup of coffee and kissed her good morning.

"Sebastian and your boyfriend are here, and they want to take me on a ride to see my wife."

"Yes, I heard that," Mary Ann replied. "I think you should go."

Tim was a little surprised that his girlfriend thought that he should get reacquainted with his wife...but Mary Ann was not the usual girlfriend.

"Well, unless they just intend to kill me," Tim deadpanned.

Mary Ann snorted. "Why do you think they

would do something like that?" she asked as she began to brush her hair. Tim noticed for the first time that Mary Ann had brought a hairbrush to his condo along with other little personal items. Women had a tendency to start moving in after you sleep with them a few times, Tim thought to himself.

"Besides," Mary Ann continued, "if they had intended to kill you, they would have done it yesterday."

Tim figured that Mary Ann was right and started to think about what he should wear to the reunion. He settled on a pair of khakis, a white shirt, and a blue sports jacket. He next jumped into the shower and considered whether to shave or not. He decided not to, since he'd shaved the day before.

When Tim returned to the bedroom, he saw that Mary Ann had joined Sebastian and Toby in his living room. He could hear the three of them talking, and he began to consider again how much he could really trust Mary Ann. She was obviously a plant by Sebastian for the purpose of keeping an eye on him and god only knew what else. Was she really not with Toby anymore? Tim had listened to her story the night before and figured that some of it was true, but the rest was probably BS, like the part about Big Doug Bail Bondsman. That said, Tim knew that he was already a part of whatever plan Sebastian was hatching, and he had to figure that Toby and Mary Ann had no clue what that plan was. Toby and Mary Ann were not typical Agency contractors. Real contractors worked for big companies that were known for other things, such as building airplanes and tanks. Real contractors were also usually ex-military, Army Rangers or Navy Seals, not dipshit private investigators from Las Vegas. No, Toby and Mary Ann were expendable pieces in Sebastian's plan. They just didn't know it yet.

Tim entered his living and saw Sebastian, Toby, and Mary Ann all sitting at his dining room table. Mary Ann said, "Looking sharp, dude," Sebastian smiled, and Toby just stared, his face showing no expression.

Tim realized that he had not yet heard Toby speak and wondered what he sounded like. He did not have to wait long. "We better get a move on if we're going to make it to Virginia by one," Toby told Sebastian with a Boston accent.

How unexpected, Tim thought to himself. "Hey, Tub, are you a Southie?" Tim asked, referring to the South Boston neighborhood.

"He doesn't like being called Tub," Mary Ann warned Tim.

"Aw, we're just fooling around," Tim replied, knowing he'd hit a nerve. "Aren't we, Tub—I mean Toby?"

Toby just continued to stare at Tim. A true psychopath, Tim figured. He would have to be careful from now on. The only person standing between him and a very violent reaction from Toby was Sebastian.

As Tim, Sebastian, and Toby got up to leave, Mary Ann walked over to Tim and gave him a kiss. "Be safe, honey," she whispered in his ear.

"What are your plans?" Tim asked, not knowing what else to say.

"Oh, I'll be at the Goose as usual," Mary Ann said with a smile. "But I'll see you tonight."

Toby was first out the door without a word to Mary Ann, followed by Tim and Sebastian. On the street, Toby opened the back door to the Mercedes SUV.

"The two of us will sit in the back," Sebastian told Tim, getting in first. Tim followed, and Toby slammed the door just a tad too hard.

"He'll be okay as soon as we get out of the city," Sebastian said to reassure Tim.

Toby walked around to the driver's side, got in, started the SUV, and headed south.

As Toby approached Interstate 695, Sebastian told him that he and Tim would need some privacy. In response, Toby reached into his jacket and produced his iPhone and a set of earbuds. He placed the earbuds in his ears and began to listen to music. Tim could hear that Toby was listening to the band Guns N' Roses. Loudly.

Sebastian turned and smiled at Tim. "That's a little method I worked out. Sometimes, there are things that Toby doesn't need to hear."

"And Mary Ann?" Tim replied. "Do you have a little method worked out for her as well?"

Sebastian just laughed. "Yes. They are quite the pair, are they not? Did Mary Ann tell you how I found them?"

"She gave me some song and dance story of you

rigging a poker game or something," Tim answered, wondering if Sebastian was going to start trashing Toby and Mary Ann.

Sebastian laughed again. "Oh, I wish it was that interesting. The truth is that I found them in Las Vegas, and they did owe some money. I paid that off on the condition that they would work for me for at least one year. I installed Mary Ann at your bar, and yes, it was to keep an eye on you. I did not anticipate that you two would become emotionally involved with each other."

"What can I say, Sebastian? It must be my charm."

Toby had exited on Interstate 70, and Tim wondered if they were still headed for Virginia.

"Well, I certainly did not tell her to become involved with you in a sexual manner. If anything, it just complicates matters. Mary Ann does have a bad habit of not doing what she's told."

Tim sensed that Sebastian was telling him the truth. It certainly would complicate things if your hired muscle had a broken heart. The last thing anyone needed in an operation was a distraction. That's how mistakes were made.

Tim was also bothered by Sebastian's remark about Mary Ann not following orders. It indicated to Tim that Sebastian may be considering ending his relationship with Mary Ann in a negative way.

Sebastian continued to speak. "If you would try hard not to mention Mary Ann around Toby, that would help a lot. He still has feelings for her, and I'm not sure I could control him if he gets angry."

Toby was now approaching Frederick, Maryland and the junction of I70 and I270. He exited onto US Route 340, and Tim saw a sign for US Route 15 and Virginia. Tim now knew where he was and where the three of them were going.

Leaving Maryland, US Route 15 began to follow a gentle hill, which led to an old iron-frame bridge that crossed the Potomac River into the Commonwealth of Virginia. Once across the bridge, Toby made a sharp right turn onto another road. Tim looked at the signpost to see the name Lovettsville Road and recalled giving that address to the taxi driver at BWI.

Toby traveled another half mile and made a sudden left onto a gravel road that took what seemed to be a 90-degree angle. There was a clearing at the top of the hill which revealed a large brick home with a circular driveway, a black Mercedes S Class parked out front and an older Land Rover parked in a garage. The Land Rover was the classic type that you might see on the old TV show *Daktari*.

As Tim got out of the SUV, he noticed that the house had a commanding view of the Potomac River. "I used to live here," he said out loud.

"Yes, you did. Welcome home, darling," a woman's voice said from behind him. Tim turned around and saw that the woman was his wife, Pamela.

Pamela, or Pam, as she was generally known, was in her early fifties, but could certainly pass for a woman in her forties. She was 5'6" and had shoulder-length blonde hair. She wore makeup and was dressed smartly, perhaps like a high-end real estate agent.

She gave Tim a hug, but not the type of hug a wife might give a long-lost husband, Tim thought. More like the hug one would give a friend that they hadn't seen for a while—which was pretty much the case, Tim realized.

"Please come in. We have a lot to catch up on," Pam said.

As Tim and Sebastian walked past her, Tim heard Pam call out to Toby. "Toby, dear? Can I get you anything?"

"No thanks, Mrs. H," was Toby's reply. He seemed perfectly okay to stay outside.

Toby dear, Tim repeated to himself. Nothing like getting personal with the help. But Pam was that kind of person—just nice to everyone.

The house was immaculately furnished with various antiques, mostly from Asia. China, Thailand, and maybe India. Tim recognized most of the furnishings, but there were some new items, like a life-sized Buddha standing at the end of the hallway. "Where did he come from?" Tim asked.

"Oh, I bought him home last year. I actually bought him at an antique store here in Virginia." Pam pointed in a southerly direction, which was her way of expressing 'here in Virginia.' "You know, I'm a practicing Buddhist now," Pam added.

That did not surprise Tim in the least. He remembered that Pam was always New Age, and becoming a Buddhist was just a natural progression for her. But he highly doubted that she'd give up material possessions, which was part of the Buddhist teachings.

The tour of the downstairs ended in the kitchen. "Let go upstairs now," Pam said, leading the way to a back stairway.

Once they reached the second floor, she turned left and walked toward the master bedroom. It was a magnificent room that took up the entire front of the house and offered a stunning view of the Potomac River and Lovettsville Road. There was a canopy bed that was at least three feet high and required steps. Tim had a faint memory of falling out of this bed at one time or another. There were also walk-in closets on each side of the room and a master bath. Pam opened the closet on the right side and turned on a light. The closet was full of men's clothing. Tim's clothes.

"These are yours, honey," Pam said as she walked through. Next, Pam opened another door, which led to a smaller bedroom. The room was furnished with a large single bed in an oak frame. There was a matching chest of drawers across from the bed and next to a door that led to the master bath. There was also a small table and two chairs next to the window. Tim walked over and looked out. Straight ahead were woods, but when Tim looked to his left, he saw that he also had a view of the river.

"I thought Tim would start out in here," Pam mentioned casually as she walked out the door so she could show off the other two rooms on the second floor.

"So, this is my room," Tim said to himself. It was so WASP-y for the husband to have a separate bedroom from the wife. Tim turned and followed Pam and Sebastian as Pam showed off the other two bedrooms and bath on the second floor. Next, the three descended down the main staircase, where Pam opened a door which led to the basement.

"Wait until you see this, Tim," Pam said with a bit of excitement in her voice. Probably some new dungeon Pam built while I was gone, Tim thought, almost believing it to be true.

Pam flipped the light switch at the bottom of the stairs. A bank of florescent lights came on that revealed a finished basement. In the middle was a large worktable with a granite top. That was a sink with hot and cold-water taps sunk into the table and a gas line used for a Bunsen burner. The table appeared to come from a science laboratory. There were several cabinets lining the walls. Pam opened each one of these to reveal a number of instruments, glass test tubes, plus boxes and tubes of chemical compounds. There was also another cabinet filled with chemistry and biology books.

"I think you will find everything you'll need right here, Tim, although we can get you anything that we don't have. Now, you have to see this."

Pam walked to what looked like a stone wall. She removed one stone in the wall, which revealed a lock. She took a key from around her neck and placed it in the lock. A door that appeared to be part of the wall opened to another large room.

They descended down about ten steps as the lights came on. Tim saw what appeared to be a very sophisticated safe room. The room looked to be at least three hundred square feet with a nine-foot-high ceiling.

Pam walked over to a bank of TV screens and turned on a switch. They could now see each room in the entire house as well as outside. There was also a screen showing CNN, where a talking head was calling the President an idiot. Tim could not remember a point in his lifetime where newscasters had ever called the President of the United States an idiot, even if he really was one.

On another screen, he could see Toby leaning against the SUV, smoking a cigarette. There was also a microphone. "Can I speak to Toby?" Tim asked.

"Sure," Pam replied as she pressed a button next to Toby's screen.

"Toby?" Tim said. "This is the Surgeon General speaking. I have determined that smoking is very bad for your health."

Toby did not move except to raise his hand and give the finger.

Pam laughed. "Leave poor Toby alone. He knows all about the surveillance system—he helped me design it. Toby was a top private investigator in Las Vegas."

"Yes, so I understand," Tim deadpanned.

Sebastian shot Tim a look as if to say to lay off Toby.

As Pam, Tim, and Sebastian left the safe room, they passed what Tim recognized as a gun safe. "So, what's in here, honey?" Tim asked sarcastically.

Pam walked in front of Tim and keyed in a combination. She was at an angle where Tim was unable to see, but it sounded like a four-digit code. The door opened to reveal four M16 type rifles and two 12-gauge shotguns. Below that were six 9 mm pistols and two revolvers of some caliber.

"Well, we are certainly prepared to rob the Bank of Lovettsville," Tim joked, but neither Pam nor Sebastian laughed. Pam closed the safe and started back upstairs.

"For security purposes only," Pam said, referring to the gun safe.

Yes, Tim thought. The Agency was not about guns. Guns were for the cowboys at the FBI and ATF. The Agency only resorted to firearms when absolutely necessary. Tim always laughed at that rule, since "absolutely necessary" seemed to occur much more often than anyone at Langley would like to admit.

With the tour of the Lovettsville house now concluded, Pam, Tim, and Sebastian retired to the library. Pam made drinks for the three of them, then sat in a chair in front of Tim and Sebastian. "What do you think of the setup, Tim?"

"It's great, assuming you'll be hosting some

chemistry students," Tim deadpanned, "but I don't get what it has to do with me."

Pam shot Sebastian a look which seemed to ask what the fuck was going on, but Sebastian just held up his hand. "Tim," he started, "will you recite the periodic table and its symbols for Pam?"

Tim's first reaction was to say that he had no idea what the periodic table was, but, almost automatically, he began to recite.

"Well, you start with, I mean do you want it listed by element and symbols alphabetically?"

"Yes, that would be fine," Sebastian agreed.

"Okay, well, actinium is Ac, silver is Ag, aluminum is Ai, americium is Am, argon is Ar..." Tim's recitation made it to potassium before Sebastian held up his hand for Tim to stop.

"That's quite the parlor trick, Sebastian, but does he remember what it all means?" Pam was looking directly at Sebastian.

"Eh, I'm in the room too, Pam," Tim remarked with a wave.

"Of course, you are, honey," Pam replied, but Tim detected a somewhat patronizing tone in her voice.

"It's all still in there someplace, Pam," Sebastian said as he looked at Tim's head. "We determined that in Santa Domingo."

"Okay, but can he remember enough to use it?" Pam said, still acting as if Tim was not in the room.

However, Tim no longer cared about the etiquette of conversation. He was more concerned about how Sebastian was able to get him recite the periodic table. It had come to him automatically, as if it had been programed into his brain: a table of the chemical elements arranged in order of atomic number, usually in rows, so that the elements with similar atomic structure appear in vertical columns. Tim could also see a picture of the table in his mind.

Tim had not noticed Pam walk over to one of the bookshelves, where she removed two books. He looked up as she was walking back toward him.

"Here you go, Einstein. See if you can remember anything in here." Pam handed Tim the books. "I've made chili and beans if anyone is hungry," she added as she headed back to the kitchen.

Tim looked at the two books. One was a college-level textbook named *Advanced Chemistry*. The other was called *The Practical Applications of Chemical Formulas* by Dr. Timothy Hall.

CHAPTER 14

Tim opened *The Practical Application of Chemical Formulas* and went straight for the copyright page. 1974, University of California Press. This was the book Tim had written during his doctoral work at Berkeley. He hadn't really forgotten this, but since he had no use for that information, he'd just put it out of his mind. Now, though, it was all coming back. He'd studied chemistry at UC Berkeley for, god, six years and had started working on his Ph.D. when he was recruited by the Agency. The book was the last thing he had finished before he traveled east to spy school, where he met Pam.

Spy school was the first time Tim had ever been east of the Mississippi River, and that was just a short trip to visit Northwestern University in Chicago. Tim was born and bred in Fort Bragg, California, the only child of two schoolteachers who Tim recalled paid very little attention to him. His parents made sure that he was clothed and fed but did little else. Tim could not even recall having one conversation with either of his parents of any significance.

Tim's parents did put aside a sum of money for his higher education. Tim's college fund, as it was known. He'd picked Berkeley because it was close to home and the only life he had ever known.

After earning his undergraduate degree, Tim decided to become a teacher like his parents and return to the Fort Bragg area. This plan changed when both of Tim's parents died within six months of each other, effectively leaving him an orphan at the age of 22. Tim buried one and then the other parent, then sold the small house where he was raised. He took the proceeds from his parents' estate and returned to Berkeley. He got an apartment and moved in with his college girlfriend, a woman named Sarah.

With his girlfriend's encouragement, Tim decided to enter the graduate program in chemistry in order to obtain his Ph.D. From there, Tim thought he would eventually become a college-level chemistry professor. This particular plan seemed to work out very well. Tim was popular with the professors in the Chemistry Department and was even able to publish a textbook with their support. Tim also got along with Sarah very well and thought seriously about asking her to marry him. The two of them could then become teachers, just like his parents. The irony of this was not lost on Tim, yet he determined that it was the life he wanted.

All of that would change the day Tim was visited by two men in dark suits.

Tim had already been recruited by a number of large corporations such as Dow Chemicals and DuPont, but he had little interest in that kind of work. Teaching, on the other hand, seemed to offer a sort of relaxed, easygoing lifestyle. And if he could become a tenured professor at one of the many colleges and universities in the state of California, then he and Sarah would have it made for life.

Tim expected that these two men in the dark suits were just two more recruiters from some major chemical corporation. Therefore, he was quite surprised when they told him that they represented the United States government and that his talents were needed to help save the world from total destruction.

In 1975, the Vietnam War may have ended, but the Cold War was still going strong. Men and women were not only needed to work in laboratories, but also to analyze what was happening on the other side. The men were rather vague in describing exactly what they needed from Tim, but they continued to stress nuclear deterrence. They concluded their sales pitch by telling Tim that men like him were the future and that the safety of the world would be in his hands. Tim asked where he would be working, and they replied that, after training, he would initially be working in the Washington, D.C. area—but after that, anywhere in the world. The thought of "anywhere in the world" was what convinced Tim there and then to sign up.

That decision did not sit too well with Tim's girlfriend Sarah. She was a holdover from the Berkeley of the mid-sixties and the protests that went with it. The thought of Tim even considering working for the government was more than she could stand, and she moved out of the apartment at the end of that week. Tim left for spy school the following month.

How green the state of Virginia was, Tim thought to himself as his unmarked bus took a special exit off of Interstate 64. Tim was used to the tall redwoods and yellow fields of Northern California and had never seen such dense green foliage. He had done some research about the area and discovered that he was not far from the first permanent English settlement at Jamestown. He thought about what a strange wilderness this all must have been back then.

The bus stopped at a guard's gate, where two Army MPs boarded. The MPs stopped at each passenger and examined their IDs. Tim noticed that the MPs had pictures of each person on the bus on a clipboard.

After the MPs were apparently satisfied that everyone was who they said they were, the bus continued down a tree-lined road, which opened to a clearing. Spy school looked pretty much like any small college campus, with a large expanse of grass, buildings with classrooms, and dorms. There was also a dining hall and a gymnasium. The bus pulled in front of the gymnasium, and the man who was acting as a kind of proctor announced, "All right, kids, this is home."

Everyone made a single file line and entered the gymnasium. There were ten rows of ten folding chairs, but everyone ended up sitting where they liked. Pam was sitting directly in front of Tim. Her hair was much longer in those days, almost reaching the small of her back. She wore what smelled like patchouli oil as a fragrance, which seemed to go well with her turquoise jewelry. Pam turned, smiled, and asked if Tim had an extra pencil. He did have one and gladly gave it to her. Tim had already fallen in love with her.

Speaker after speaker spoke about what would

be expected of everyone, including what offenses a student could be dismissed for. One speaker, a woman, told the class that fraternization between the men and women of the class was prohibited. She also mentioned that there were more women in this particular class than ever before. The government had made an effort to recruit more women into the FBI and CIA and had even gone so far as to set up phony schools for airline flight attendants in order to give the agencies opportunities for vetting. Pam had told Tim that this was how she had been hired, although Tim was never really sure if that story was true or just another Agency myth. There were quite a few Agency myths.

Although he saw Pam from time to time during school, there was never a good opportunity to get to know her. Eventually, however, Pam and Tim did have some classes together, and they always sat next to one another. Tim was never athletically inclined and initially had trouble with the various obstacle courses. Pam was a natural athlete and had not had trouble passing any, and she took the time to work with Tim. During one such session, while Tim was doing push-ups, they began to kiss each other right in the middle of the football field—but that was as far as it went. Before either of them knew it, they graduated and were given different assignments. They promised to stay in touch but were unable to keep the vow. Tim had no idea where Pam had gone or what assignment she'd been given. Tim was assigned as an Analyst based at CIA Headquarters in Langley, Virginia. It was not until almost two years later that Tim was finally able to ask Pam on a date, when they happened to meet by chance at the Langley cafeteria. They were married a month later.

As Toby crossed the Baltimore County and city line, Tim thought again about the Agency recruiter telling him that he could be assigned anywhere in the world. He wondered if that included downtown Baltimore. Baltimore was a city that was always on the cusp of revitalization, yet never seemed to quite get there. This was still apparent from the number of vacant storefronts Tim could see as they traveled down Lombard Street.

Sebastian told Toby to drop him off at his hotel and then take Tim back to his condo. This would be the first time Tim and Toby would be alone together, and Tim wondered if Sebastian was doing that on purpose.

Sebastian turned to Tim as Toby entered the driveway of the hotel. "Take a look at the textbooks tonight, Tim. In the morning, I'll tell you what our mission is about." With that, he exited the SUV and headed into his hotel.

Before Toby started to drive again, he turned to face Tim. "Would you like to see a very funny video?" he asked.

"Sure, Toby," Tim said, almost happy that Toby seemed to be acting friendly toward him.

Toby handed Tim his iPhone. "Just press the start button," he said as he began to drive the few blocks back to the condominium.

In the video was a woman with dark hair in a kitchen, washing dishes in a sink. Suddenly, a man wearing a ski mask that covered his entire face appeared. The man entered from behind and grabbed the woman by her neck, placing her in a chokehold. He next forced the woman onto the floor, where he produced a coil of rope. He bound the woman's hands and feet, then hog-tied those together. The masked man then produced a roll of duct-tape. He shoved something into the woman's mouth and began to wrap the duct-tape several times around the woman's head. He next pulled down the women's top to expose her breasts. The masked man then left the frame, leaving the woman to roll around on the floor.

"Gosh, Toby, do you get your rocks off watching bound and gagged women rolling on the floor?" Tim asked with a fair amount of sarcasm.

"I'm always interested in women who are willing to be humiliated," Toby replied. "For example, look at the woman in the next video."

The next video featured what looked to be the same woman, but this time she was already bound and gagged, naked while sitting on a couch.

"Take a closer at look who it is," Toby said, and Tim placed his finger on the pause key for a closer look.

It was Mary Ann Layback, and so was the woman featured in the first video.

Tim handed the iPhone back to Toby. "So, Toby, is there a reason you're sharing this with me?" he asked.

Tim knew that this was just Toby's method of trying to psych him out. This was actually one of the first things Tim was taught in spy school. Recording subjects in compromising sexual situations used to be one of the most effective ways for agents to control their assets. Frankly, it was just plain old-fashioned blackmail, except that the sexually compromising situations were no longer as effective as they had been, especially in regard to homosexuality. Now that many men and women had "come out of the closet", recording a man receiving a blow job in a restroom no longer had the impact that it once did. Even catching men dressing up in women's clothing no longer had the same damning effect. This was not to say that pictures of subjects in sexual situations no longer had any value. For example, a man or even a woman with an underage person would be career-ending, if not a criminal prosecution. But people just having sex was no longer the big deal that it once had been.

"So, what's your point, Toby?" Tim repeated. "What should I garner from your bondage videos?"

"I think you really need to know the kind of person you are letting share your bed, Tim."

Toby actually sounded sincere, as if he was concerned about Tim's wellbeing. "Mary Ann is a compulsive liar," he added. "Sometimes, she doesn't even know when she is telling you the truth. It took me a year to understand that, which is why we are no longer together, although I'm still in love with her."

That was certainly a mouthful, Tim thought. Was Toby really trying to tell Tim that he was still in love with Mary Ann despite the fact that she was a known liar? Over the years, Tim had become pretty good at evaluating people, or "subjects," as the Agency called them. The word "subjects" kept everything impersonal, and Tim often looked at Mary Ann as a subject as opposed to his lover. He knew that Mary Ann might be dangerous and was most likely capable of cutting his throat while sleeping, although he felt that the chances of that happening were slim. Tim had met a number of men and even a couple of women who were programed to kill with little remorse, but Tim felt that the lack of remorse was something that typically had to be trained. *It's not personal, it's just part of my job. I may not like doing it, but there is a reason it needs to be done* was the mantra that was taught in the classroom. On the other hand, sociopaths and psychopaths (Tim really did not distinguish between the two) were basically just plain selfish people who were working solely for their own gain. In Tim's opinion, Mary Ann was a somewhat complex and confused person, whereas Toby was just a run-of-the-mill psychopath. Toby was attempting to manipulate Tim to his side by pretending that he and Tim had some mutual affection for Mary Ann. Toby was certainly up to something, but Tim could not figure it out—at least not at this point.

As the SUV pulled in front of Tim's condo, he collected the two textbooks from Pam's library, then looked at Toby. "Well, I do appreciate you sharing the video. It has certainly opened my eyes to a couple of things," he said.

Tim was referring to deciding that Toby definitely possessed a number of psychopathic tendencies.

Toby made a fist and offered Tim a fist bump. "Anytime, my man," he replied as their knuckles touched. "We will see you in the morning."

Tim got out and watched Toby drive away. He quickly reviewed his day and thought about how each new day seemed to reveal more than the day before. He turned and walked toward the entrance of his condo, still thinking.

CHAPTER 15

"Well, I didn't think it was a big deal," Mary Ann said in response to Tim's inquiry about the bondage video.

Tim had expected that this was what she would say and basically agreed with her, but he didn't understand how a woman would submit to that level of humiliation.

When Tim put that question to Mary Ann, though, her response was, "Yes, Tim. And us gals all love getting down on all fours and letting you ram us from behind. That's so empowering."

The conversation was becoming uncomfortable, so Tim decided to make a drink and offered to make one for Mary Ann as well.

"I assume Toby showed this to you?" Mary Ann asked as Tim handed her a vodka tonic. "Did he mention that he played the part of the masked man? For that matter, he also directed it."

"He's a very talented man," Tim said with a smile, attempting to lighten the mood. "Look," he added, "I'm sorry I even mentioned this to you. It doesn't bother me at all that you performed in a kinky sex video, but I thought you needed to know that your ex showed it to me."

"So, you're not breaking up with me?" Mary Ann wondered.

Tim sat down and gave her a kiss. "Of course not. I think this is the third time you've asked me if I was planning on breaking up with you. Why is that?"

"Because all of my boyfriends have been like Toby," she explained. "You're the first guy who's had any class."

"Well, I wouldn't go that far, but thanks. Let's drop the subject," Tim said. He was not comfortable about receiving compliments, plus Mary Ann was probably lying.

But she had more to say about the video. "Well, it was Toby's idea, and it really did pay very well, plus I didn't have to fuck anyone on camera. We might have done some more videos, but then Sebastian came along."

Mary Ann began to retell the story about how she and Toby met Sebastian, but Tim's mind started to wander. He really was not surprised about the video, since Tim knew that Mary Ann was the kind of woman who would be up for just about anything sexual. No, the question was why Toby decided to show the video to him in the first place. But Tim also had a lot of other things on his mind, chemistry being the main one.

It had been a long day, so he took Mary Ann in his arms and fell right to sleep.

Morning came sooner than Tim would have preferred, but he was out of bed, dressed, and drinking his second cup of coffee by the time Mary Ann got up at 9 a.m. She saw Tim sitting at the dining room table reading one of the two textbooks he'd brought home from Pam's house. "Interesting book?" she asked, kissing the top of his head.

"Not really, but this guy Tim Hall is a fucking genius," Tim joked.

Tim really was impressed with his book. It wasn't that he had forgotten that he studied chemistry in college—it was just something that he had not thought much about in the last 35 years. Now, he regretted that he had not continued his career as a chemist. The Agency had originally hired Tim as a Technician II Chemist GS 9, but he'd ended up being asked if he minded taking a position in the Forensic Psychology group. Tim had minored in Psychology at Berkeley and, although the laboratory was his first love, he was also interested in the science of the mind.

He'd figured that anything he did not know could be learned on the job, and he was correct. He spent the next year visiting a number of secret Agency camps known to the public as "Black Sites," where he learned enhanced interrogation techniques. This was a term that had become a euphemism for torture, but Tim never thought that any of the interviews he conducted were torture, unless one considered boredom a form of it. Most of the time, he would ask a question to a detainee, and the detainee would then tell him a lie. Tim had had the advantage of knowing when someone was lying, since he usually knew the truth. But in the current situation, he had no clue why Sebastian and Pam had brought him back from retirement.

"Would you like some scrambled eggs?" Mary Ann called from the kitchen.

"Yes, I would," Tim replied as he stared at her backside.

Mary Ann was really a piece of work, he thought to himself. She had been lying to him since the moment they met. He thought back to their first date and about how Mary Ann had told him that she once owned a dental lab. Could that possibly be true, or was it just part of a running story Mary Ann was making up as she went along? Most lies Tim had encountered through his enhanced interrogations where attempts to cover up something, usually some kind of plot or conspiracy—but most of these liars could be tripped up by pointing out the contradictions in the stories they were telling. However, in Mary Ann's case, her entire life seemed to be a contradiction. Nevertheless, Tim felt that they had made a strong connection. He also felt that Mary Ann needed to be protected. Tim sensed that Mary Ann had most likely stumbled into a very dangerous situation with no clue of the possible consequences. Tim knew that he was also in danger, but he was aware that neither Pam nor Sebastian would go away empty-handed, so he would have to stay around long enough to figure out their plan.

The buzzer buzzed in Tim's condo, and he looked up to the clock. 10 a.m.; it must be Sebastian and Toby time. Tim went into his bedroom and came back with an overnight bag. "I may be gone for a couple of days, Mary Ann, so hold the fort," he murmured.

Mary Ann was surprised at this news. “A couple of days? What’s going on?”

Tim noticed that Mary Ann actually seemed disappointed that he might spend a night without her. “I don’t know yet, but don’t worry. Everything will be okay.”

There was a knock at the door, and Tim opened the door to meet Sebastian and Toby. Tim beamed at them. “Good morning, guys. Are we ready to hit the road?”

Sebastian looked surprised to see Tim ready to go. “By all means,” Sebastian replied as he nodded to Mary Ann, who was standing behind Tim.

Tim turned and kissed Mary Ann goodbye. “Don’t worry,” he repeated. “I’ll see you in a couple of days.”

As Toby drove them out of the city, Sebastian motioned to him that it was time to put in his earbuds. When Sebastian could hear Guns N’ Roses come out of the earphones, he turned to Tim. “So, do you remember any of your chemistry, Tim?”

“Actually, I remember quite a lot more than I thought I would, but you know I wasn’t a chemist with the Agency. I was an operations guy like you.”

Sebastian once again seemed pleased that Tim now recalled his time as a spy. “Yes, an operations guy. I always enjoyed your terminology, Tim. So, here’s the question: what do you remember about making poisons?”

Poisons? Tim wondered. These two are taking me out of retirement for poisons.

"Well, Sebastian, I certainly know enough to be able to concoct something to put our friend Toby to sleep, but I don't think I know enough yet to cure cancer."

Sebastian gave Tim a funny look, but then he got the joke. "Besides," Tim continued, "you have enough real chemists at Langley and Quantico to develop anything you need...so why are you asking me?"

Sebastian thought for a second, then answered, "Suppose you had a mission that only a handful of people were aware of, and you needed something created. Something that could not be traced back to Langley. Who would you turn to?"

Though it was long and somewhat rhetorical, Sebastian's question told Tim what he wanted to know. Pam, Sebastian, and whoever else was involved wanted to keep the operation tight and bringing in a bunch of chemists from Langley was not the way to accomplish that.

"Okay, I get it, Sebastian. You and Pam want me to develop some sort of poison...but why?"

Sebastian responded without hesitation. "There is a current world leader who is creating havoc, and our analysis is that if this person continues unchecked, it could affect the world as we have come to know it."

Sebastian had certainly said a mouthful, but who were they going after? After all, there was trouble in

Central and South America, but Russia was once again becoming a pain in the ass, and China had also become a major concern.

"So, who's the target and why?" Tim asked. May as well be blunt.

"Aw, that will all be revealed in time," Sebastian said, obviously enjoying his role as the mastermind. "But first, let's talk about poisons. Would it be possible to administer a poison to an individual over a period of time that would eventually kill him or her?"

Tim thought about Sebastian's question. Sure, there were poisons that could be administered over time, like arsenic—but the problem with that was that they'd have to be administered every day, which might be difficult to do without the cooperation of the subject.

"We would need a sort of timed-release poison," Tim volunteered, "but I would have to think about how we could do that."

Tim was beginning to wonder how all of his spycraft suddenly seemed to be coming back to him. Could the stem cells really be responsible for his recovered memory?

The SUV had crossed the Potomac, and they were now back in Virginia. Toby took the sharp left turn onto Pam's driveway, and the SUV made the slow climb up the hill.

When they parked, Pam came out of the house to meet them. "Did you make any progress, Tim?" she asked. "Can you help us?"

"I guess it all depends on exactly what you want me to do, Pam," Tim replied. "Let's go in and talk about it."

Pam shot Sebastian another one of her looks, but Sebastian just shrugged. The three of them entered the house while Toby took his usual place outside guarding the SUV.

It was just after one in the afternoon, and Pam, being the perfect hostess, had prepared a light lunch consisting of ham and cheese and tuna sandwiches. After some polite conversation about the drive, the three got down to business. "So, Tim, what has Sebastian told you about our mission?" Pam asked.

"He has indicated—or should I say, insinuated—that you two would like me to develop some kind of poison in order to eliminate some head of state. At least, that's the impression I've received."

Pam glared at Sebastian. "Sebastian, is it possible for you to be direct for once in your fucking life?"

Sebastian appeared to be somewhat stunned by Pam's reprimand. Tim felt a little guilty for making him sound too obtuse. Still, Pam was correct. Sebastian just seemed incapable of telling someone exactly what he wanted without playing some kind of game.

Pam looked back at Tim. "I'm sorry, Tim. Yes, we need you to come up with a poison that will gradually kill someone, and we also need to develop a method to administer the poison to the individual without their knowledge. What thoughts do you have?"

Tim was looking out the window and thinking about how beautiful everything was. It was springtime, and the trees along the river were beginning to bloom. Tim thought how strange it was that the conversation they were having was about murdering another human being, but he redirected his thinking back to poisons.

"Well, I feel that in order to accomplish a slow death for the subject, we would need to employ two poisons. Perhaps a combination of arsenic and thallium delivered via a common device like a tool, maybe even a knife or a fork."

Pam raised her eyebrows. "A knife or a fork? How would that work?"

"We could place two very small needles in a piece of silverware." Tim got up and walked into Pam's dining room, coming back with a very nice silver fork.

"Be careful, that's my best silver," Pam said, half-joking.

Tim held the fork in his right hand and then his left hand, remembering that he used his right hand for the knife. "See, if we could place the needles on the bottom of the fork, then you may have two or three injection sites." Tim showed Sebastian and Pam his fingers and where the possible injections sites would be located.

"Will you be able to make some thallium and arsenic?" Sebastian asked Tim.

"It all depends on what Pam has in her chemistry set downstairs, but thallium was used up until 1978, so it's not a secret," Tim replied. "The arsenic should not be a problem at all."

"I actually have some thallium already made," Pam said as calmly, as she would tell someone that she'd baked an apple pie.

"Somehow, you are having thallium on hand doesn't surprise me in the least," Tim said as he closely examined one of the tuna sandwiches she'd made for lunch.

"I think the main issue will be obtaining the silverware," Sebastian added.

"We should be able to get anything we need," Pam replied, "but, in the meantime, Tim can use the fork he's already picked out."

"And ruin a piece of your best silver?" Tim commented sarcastically.

"Well, anything for the cause," Pam replied.

Tim got up with his fork and half-eaten sandwich and headed for the basement. "I'm going down to the lab to start working on this." Tim looked down at his bag. "Is it okay if I spend the night?"

"Sure," Pam replied with a smile. "After all, it is your house too, sort of."

"Okay." Tim looked at Sebastian. "You and Toby can take the night off, Sebastian, but I will be returning to Baltimore in the morning."

Tim turned and headed for the basement as Sebastian and Pam watched.

"I believe your memory restoration project in Santa Domingo worked a little too well, don't you think?" Pam remarked to Sebastian when Tim was out of earshot.

"Yes, Pamela, you may be correct. You just may be."

CHAPTER 16

It took Tim almost three hours to set himself up to begin constructing the deadly fork. Actually, the more he thought about it, the more he determined that a fork may not be able to carry as much poison as would be needed, so he decided that he would have to include a knife and possibly a spoon. The amount of thallium needed to be a fatal dose was a little tricky to gauge, but the good news (or, at least, the good news to Tim) was that thallium could be absorbed through the skin, which meant that perhaps Tim could cover the knife and spoon with enough poison to accomplish the mission. Pam had brought down her package of thallium, which was way more than he would need. Tim also considered using the arsenic as a kind of decoy. If the victim thought that he or she had been poisoned with arsenic, then perhaps the doctors would not check for thallium poisoning—at least, not until it was already too late. Tim also thought about using ricin, which would be almost guaranteed to work, but would also perhaps work too quickly, defeating the whole purpose of the assignment.

Tim was also able to find a number of hypodermic needles of various sizes. He labored to work these downs to the point where they were almost microscopic. If he could place these on the fork and spread poison around the pins, it just might work.

Using a large magnifying glass, Tim cut down two of the hypodermic needles until they were each less than a millimeter in diameter. Next, he drilled two extremely small holes for the needles and glued both into the fork. The general idea would be to fill the two needles with the poison, then cap them with a little bit of wax. Additional poison or poisons could be spread around the needles. The needles would barely break the skin, and the poison in them would provide enough moisture to activate the additional poison spread on the fork. This was all rather primitive, of course, but it would most likely do the job.

In order to test this, Tim took some Xylocaine and painted it on and around the needles. He then picked up the fork with his left hand as if he were eating and felt the two pins pierce his skin. Tim's fingers began to feel numb, indicating that the trick had indeed worked. Happy with his progress, Tim decided to call it a night.

As Tim began to walk up the stairs, the basement door opened, and a large African American male began to descend. Tim stepped back down to the basement in order to allow the man to pass. "Hi there. My name is Tim. I'm doing some work here," he offered.

"Yes sir, I am aware of who you are and what your purpose is," the man replied, sounding neither friendly nor unfriendly. "My name is Darrel Murphy. I am responsible for security."

Tim looked at Darrel a little more closely and realized that he had a striking resemblance to one of the Dominican men who picked Tim up at the airport. Tim considered asking Darrel about this for a second, but he was afraid he would be accused of racial profiling. "Yeah, we all look alike" was the response Tim feared, so he decided to let it drop and ask Pam about it later.

"Well, nice meeting you, Darrel," Tim said.

Darrel was opening the gun safe. "You too, Mr. Hall. I'm sure we will see each other around."

Tim had a feeling they would.

As Tim came upstairs, he noticed that the time on the clock was 8 p.m. Pam was sitting in the library reading a book, but got to her feet when she saw Tim. "I have dinner ready, but would you like a drink first?" she offered.

"Yes, a drink would be great, dear," Tim answered. He'd placed a little too much emphasis on the last word, but Pam ignored it and made Tim his vodka tonic.

At that point the basement door opened, and Darrel came out. "Good evening, Mr. and Mrs. Hall," he said. "I will be on the grounds if you need me."

"Thank you, Darrel. Let me know if you need anything," Pam answered. She was always the perfect hostess, Tim thought once again. Even to the help.

"Any reason why you have this much security, Pam?" he asked.

"Oh, it's not really that much. Darrel comes around a few times a week. I am rather isolated up here.

Of course, if we have guests, we have more."

What Pam meant by "guests" were the various types that the Agency needed to house temporarily. In other words, Pam's home was what was also known as an Agency safe house, and Pam was known as a hostess. Occasionally, people in need would show up in the middle of the night, but that did not happen as much as it did back in the old days during the Cold War. In fact, it happened so infrequently that Tim had to wonder if he was the reason Darrel was even on duty. Perhaps Sebastian and Pam thought that he would change his mind about helping them and hightail it out of there.

"Pick up your drink and come into the dining room, Tim," Pam ordered.

Tim got to his feet and followed Pam. The dining table was beautifully set with two candles lit. "Sit at the head of the table, dear," Pam told him.

It was not lost on Tim that Pam's "dear" wasn't nearly as sarcastic as Tim's had been earlier.

After he obeyed, Pam disappeared into the kitchen and came out again with a small roast beef surrounded by potatoes on a platter. "Why don't you start carving, Tim?" she asked as she went back for two bowls of green vegetables and a bottle of a red wine. She filled her own and then Tim's glass, turned on the classical radio station, and sat in a chair to the left of Tim's.

"Mrs. Robinson, I think you're trying to seduce me," Tim joked, referring to a line in the film *The Graduate.*

"You would be so lucky," was Pam's response.

The meal was delicious, probably the best that Tim had enjoyed for several years. At least, for the years he'd been in Baltimore...which were becoming the elephant in the room. Tim still hadn't asked Pam why she'd decided to desert him there.

Well, there was no time like the present. "So, tell me, Pam, why did—"

"Why did I leave you in Baltimore?" Pam interrupted.

Tim blinked. "Since you bring it up... Yes, why did you?"

"Did Sebastian tell you what happened in China?" Pam asked.

"He did, but I'm interested in your side of the story." Tim knew that Pam would know that this was his big chance to trip her up. Tim seriously doubted that Pam would let that happen, but he thought he should give it a try anyhow.

Pam took a sip of her wine and gently dabbed her lips with her napkin. "The plan was for me to make a sexual advance on Ms. Lin, which I did, but instead of being receptive, which you said she would be—" Pam paused to collect herself. "Anyway, Ms. Lin slapped me across my face and produced a gun, which was unexpected. She aimed the gun at you and appeared to have every intention of shooting you. That's when I pulled out my 9mm and shot her in the neck."

“I have no memory of any of that,” Tim interjected.

“Yes, we know, Tim.” Pam now sounded discouraged.

“But why dump me in Baltimore?” Tim wanted to know.

“Because it was the safest option for you.” Pam picked up her wine glass and finished it in one gulp. “Agency management was furious, Tim. Some of the higher ups were apparently willing to disavow us and send us back to China to face prosecution for murder. However, cooler heads prevailed.”

“That usually does happen.”

Pam gave Tim her patented stare, which warned him that he was about to get it. “You know, Tim, I am not exactly happy being the fucking den mother to the idiots who come to this house for refuge,” she said, referring to her job operating the safe house. “I would probably be a Station Chief by now in a nice country like the UK or France, but instead I’m running a hotel for losers. Why do you think that is?”

Tim did not really want to know, but he knew that his wife was about to tell him anyway.

Pam didn’t disappoint him. “It’s because my husband miscalculated the situation in China some years ago,” she informed him. “But hey, guess what? He can’t remember shit.”

Pam got up and poured herself a shot of bourbon,

drank it, and continued her rant. "But you know what? I am very fucking lucky I have what I have, and now I have a chance to redeem myself and maybe even redeem you in the process. That's why I don't need you to screw this one up."

"Pam?" Tim answered softly after a pause. "Do we have dessert?"

Tim figured that the shot glass Pam threw at him missed by about a quarter of an inch. It didn't break, but it did leave a dent in the dining room wall.

"Chocolate cake," Pam said, walking back into the kitchen.

Pam cooled down dramatically after her rant. Both Tim and Pam ate cake and drank coffee with brandy after dinner while having a very enjoyable conversation. They talked about old friends, and Pam shared the latest Agency gossip. Tim was again surprised by how much he now remembered about his former work, but he was also concerned that he was becoming the man that he used to be again. Tim wasn't sure that he liked that person. The fact that Tim had experienced a certain amount of satisfaction that afternoon when he discovered that he probably would be able to poison someone by simply giving them some tainted silverware bothered him. Why would that make someone happy?

This was what Tim was thinking about as he began to fall asleep when he heard his closet door slowly open. He watched as the figure of a woman quietly entered his room. Yes, it was Pam. Tim would have wondered if she'd entered his bedroom in order to murder him in his sleep, but he didn't see any weapons.

Pam silently removed her nightgown and climbed into bed with Tim, putting her hand down the front of the sweatpants he was wearing. She pulled Tim's pants off and began to kiss his belly button, then worked her way down from there.

"Oh my god, Pam," Tim moaned as he released himself.

Pam came back up and kissed Tim passionately. "If we end up getting back together," she whispered in his ear, "then that slut Mary Ann has to go."

Tim placed his right hand between Pam's legs and began to reciprocate. "This is all I need," he thought to himself.

CHAPTER 17

Tim woke up alone the next day. He looked around to see if there was any evidence that Pam had been there, but there wasn't. The only think that had changed was that Tim was now naked. His sweatpants were on the floor, his t-shirt under the pillow. Tim did smell bacon being cooked, so he assumed that Pam was making somebody bacon and eggs.

By the time Tim was dressed and made it downstairs, Toby and Sebastian had arrived and were seated in the kitchen.

"Coffee, Tim?" Pam asked.

"Please," Tim replied.

As Tim sat down, Toby got up. "Don't leave on my account, Toby," Tim said as the other man headed for the door.

"Oh, he has plenty to do today," Sebastian remarked as Toby went outside. Through the window, Tim saw Toby get into the SUV and drive away. He wondered where he was going.

"Would you like some eggs and bacon, Tim?"

Pam was certainly playing the role of the dutiful wife, but Tim was not buying it, despite their love making the night before. Tim knew that Pam would do anything to get what she wanted.

"So, Tim, did you make any progress on you poison device?" Sebastian asked once he was sure that Toby had cleared the room.

Tim figured that Pam had already told him something, but now that they were together, he might as well bring them both up to speed. "I think I have a working prototype." Tim paused and looked down, seeing the fork that he had been working on the night before placed in front of Sebastian. Tim had discussed his progress on the device with Pam after her post-dinner rant. She had apparently brought the fork up from the basement to try it out on Sebastian.

"So?" Sebastian wanted to know as he picked up the fork.

"And it simply needs to be tested." Tim watched Sebastian put a forkful of scrambled eggs into his mouth, thinking about how fat and stubby his fingers were.

Sebastian did not appear to notice the two small needle pricks, but he soon began to rub his numb fingers. Tim looked at Pam, who was smiling. "Fingers a little numb, Sebastian?" she said as Sebastian began to examine his right hand.

"Excellent," Sebastian said as he continued to look at his hand. "Assuming that you indeed have not poisoned me, and this numbness will go away at some point." Sebastian was now shaking his hand vigorously. Pam must have applied a lot more Xylocaine than Tim had.

"No, you have not been poisoned, but I'm beginning to wonder about the numbness," Tim said, half joking.

Sebastian picked up the fork and looked for the two small needles. "I just don't see them," he commented.

"They are actually bigger than you think, but the lacquer does a good job of obscuring them," Tim remarked.

"Well, I'm impressed," Sebastian proclaimed. "Pam?"

"I'm impressed as well, Sebastian. I believe it's time to call Bob Ajacks."

The name Bob Ajacks was a pseudonym the three had used over the years for the man or woman in charge of the operation. This was the person who made the major decisions. Most of these individuals held a public position with the Agency, which meant that everyone in Congress and the news media knew that they worked for the CIA, so it was important not to casually mention their names when discussing any operation. Usually, only the case officer knew the real identity of Mr. Ajacks.

"That's great, guys, and I hope it all works out for you. In the meantime, I would like to get home." Tim knew that this was probably a little too much to expect, of course, since Toby had gone off somewhere and he doubted that Pam would give him a ride to Baltimore. Tim typically liked living without the expense of owning a vehicle—but he sure wished he had one now.

"Tim, why don't you plan on spending a couple more nights here with Pam?" was Sebastian's very nice way of telling Tim that he was not going anywhere. "Toby may not be back for a day or so."

Tim was beginning to think that all three of them would be hanging out together for an undetermined amount of time. Just like back in the old days, he thought.

Pam began to speak. "Tim, I feel that it is important that you hear the entire purpose of the operation, and then perhaps everything will begin to make more sense. Ajacks will tell you about that tonight."

Wow, what a big-time spy operation, Tim thought.

Well, at least it didn't seem like Pam or Sebastian were planning to kill him anytime soon. But Tim did firmly believe that one or two of the three would be dead by the time this was all over, and he had no intention of being the dead guy.

Mr. Ajacks was scheduled to make an appearance after sunset, which figured to be between 7 and 8 p.m. These types of managers almost never came over to your house or office in the daytime. "Democracy Dies in the Darkness" was the new slogan of the *Washington Post*. He'd originally thought it was silly, but it was beginning to make sense, at least in a literal kind of way. Everything decided in Washington seemed to occur in the dark of night, and it certainly was not a democratic process. In addition, the concept was not limited to the confines of Washington, D.C. Geographically speaking, it included the entire state of Maryland, the District of Columbia, and everything in Virginia north of the Rappahannock River. Within this area, you had (in no particular order): the NSA, the US Naval Academy, Camp David, the CIA, the FBI Training Academy and Laboratory, the DEA, the Quantico Marine Base, Fort Detrick, Fort Belvoir, Fort Meyer, the Pentagon, and Mount Weather.

The list of facilities went on and on, as did the secret deals made there. Deals that affected US policy worldwide, all occurring within a 50-mile radius of where Tim was developing his killer fork. And no one voted on any of this, he thought.

Tim had returned to the basement to continue his work on the fork and gain some distance from Pam and Sebastian. He had not been around other spies for five years now, and he was finding that he really did enjoy his new life.

The basement television was turned on, muted, and Tim looked up to see the President in a photo op with the leader of North Korea. It seemed like just months ago that the *New York Times* had reported that North Korea had developed an ICBM capable of carrying a nuclear warhead to the US continent, or at least to the west coast, yet here were these two leaders sitting side by side, smiling. Tim certainly did not have any new trust for North Korea, but at least the two sides were talking with one another, which was a vast improvement...yet, to many in the media, something was wrong. Although the media had a hard time explaining exactly what was wrong with the President having a summit, it did not stop them from criticizing it. However, no one seemed to be too worried about North Korea at this point.

Tim had no problem with the media, although it did appear that most outlets had become rather one-sided. The current President was certainly different than the usual politician, and he could understand why many found him so objectionable. He seemed to lack the usual filter of professional politicians. It was not that the other politicians did not have similar views as the current President, but they knew when to shut up. What made that even worse to many in the press was that the President did not seem to care about their opinions. In fact, he seemed to relish their condemnation and disapproval. That in itself was somewhat history-making, but also dangerous. Each time the President disregarded some new media outrage, the press would up the ante. To Tim, this made Nixon and the sixties seem like a picnic.

At 6 p.m., Darrel came down to the basement and opened the gun safe. "Hey Darrel, what's going on?" Tim asked.

"Hi, Mr. Hall. Nothing much," Darrel answered. He pulled out two M16 rifles and four clips, and Tim heard the familiar sound of the bolts being pulled back to make sure they were operational.

"Extra help coming over tonight?" Tim asked.

"No big deal," was Darrel's response.

The fact that Darrel was a man of few words was

not surprising to Tim. Most good security guys didn't say a lot, which was really what you wanted. Talkative people were easily distracted.

Darrel grabbed the two rifles and headed back upstairs as Pam yelled, "Tim? Ajacks will be here soon, so you need to get ready."

"Okay, be right up," Tim answered.

He'd almost said "Be right up, honey"—but he'd caught himself just in time. It amazed him how easy it was to fall back into married life.

Tim grabbed a can of aerosol fingerprint powder that he'd found while he was rooting around in the chemical cabinets the day before. He walked over to the gun safe and sprayed the powder on the combination keys. It was apparent that only the keys 4 and 5 had been entered, which meant that any combination of those two numbers could be pressed. He knew that typically you had only three tries to get in. A fourth try would lock you out. To make matters worse, one or two wrong passcode attempts would alert Pam that someone was screwing around with the safe. Therefore, Tim figured that he had one try. If that was wrong, then he could just confess that he was playing around with the safe. Pam would probably accept that explanation, but she would become suspicious if it happened more than once.

His best guess was that Pam was using 5454 since that would be the easiest for her to remember. He was correct. The safe beeped, and the door opened. Tim took a quick look at the guns, closed the safe, and headed upstairs to meet Mr. Ajacks.

CHAPTER 18

Although Tim was officially retired and no longer employed by the CIA, an Agency head coming over to visit was an occasion. Tim wondered if he should wear a tie but decided instead on a suit without a tie. He found one of his old suits in his closet along with a pair of black shoes and a belt. He took a quick shower, shaved, and dressed. He stood in front of the full-length mirror and decided that, considering everything, he didn't look too bad.

Tim descended the stairs and headed to the library.

Pam looked immaculate as always, although she'd chosen to wear a red dress. Tim thought that Pam's outfit was a little too showy, but he figured she had her reasons. Pam usually did. Anyway, it was certainly a very sexy dress.

Pam had laid out some hors d'oeuvres on the coffee table and also on a small table in the corner to the right of the bay window. Tim assumed that this was for Mr. Ajacks. The unspoken rule was that Mr. Ajacks was not to be looked at. He would come into the room and watch the presentation shown by Sebastian and then either give a go ahead or an order to kill the operation. Tim was actually pleased that Mr. Ajacks would at least be aware that he was part of the operation. If he were an unknown contributor, the more likely it was that Sebastian or Pam would get rid of him after he'd served his purpose.

Tim really did not know why he was so sure that the other two might want him dead. After all, they were all old friends, and old friends didn't kill you... did they? For a minute, Tim almost convinced himself that he was just being paranoid; but then he reminded himself of the subterfuge he'd experienced in the last two months. It just did not add up that Sebastian and Pam needed him and only him to develop a killing apparatus. The Agency was full of people who could do a much better job, so why find a guy like Tim who everyone had forgotten about?

Tim saw a pair of headlights shine against one of the bookcases, which indicated that a car was coming up the driveway.

Pam turned to him. "What can I get you to drink, dear?"

Wow, she was really laying it on, Tim thought. Maybe Ajacks believed they were still together. That could be a reason the two needed him...but it was unlikely to be the only reason.

"Vodka tonic, honey," Tim answered casually. He was trying very hard to play the game. "Do you have any idea who this Mr. Ajacks really is?" he added.

"No, only Sebastian knows. But I have a couple of guesses," Pam said as she bent over to fill Tim's glass from the ice bucket.

This did not go unnoticed. "By the way," Tim remarked, "that's a beautiful dress you're wearing."

"Why thank you, Timothy," Pam replied, giving him a kiss while handing Tim his cocktail.

Pam only called him Timothy at special moments, and she did seem pleased that he'd commented on her dress. Tim wondered if this would result in another midnight visit.

Sebastian had gone out of the house to meet Ajacks. Pam dimmed the lights, then sat on the couch with her back turned and indicated that Tim should sit next to her. Tim heard voices from outside and two car doors closing. Mr. Ajacks had either brought a friend, or his driver was getting out to stretch his legs. Pam picked up a small remote control from the coffee table and pressed one of the buttons. A movie screen began to descend from the ceiling.

"Honey, I wish you would tell me when you spend this kind of money," Tim joked, trying to ease the tension. Pam slapped his knee and told him to behave. Tim heard Mr. Ajacks and Sebastian enter the room.

Sebastian first made the big boss a gin and tonic, then returned to the back of the room. Next, Sebastian turned on his laptop, and a PowerPoint presentation appeared on the screen entitled *The Adults in the Room.* There was no discussion.

Sebastian's presentation began with a picture of the White House and a picture of the President conferring with various members of the House and Senate. Sebastian began to speak.

"Since the inauguration in 2017, most agree that the Executive Branch of our government has not operated in a professional manner." The next slide is a picture of a White House Press Conference that shows a number of reporters with their hands raised. Sebastian continued.

"Although the media has portrayed the President as not very intelligent, our analysis tells us just the opposite." Next, there is a picture of the President looking out of his office window.

"In reality, the President is a very intelligent man with many unique ideas. However, most members of the House and Senate simply do not take the President very seriously."

Sebastian next displayed a slide of the Vice President speaking with the President. "Now, the Vice President has for the last two years encouraged the President to govern in a more traditional manner. As a matter of fact, we have made a number of suggestions through the Vice President on how the President could better handle his critics in the Democratic Party as well as his own party, but to no avail."

We, meaning the Agency, have made a number of suggestions? Tim thought. Well, so much for staying out of domestic issues.

Sebastian now displayed a slide of the United States Capital Building and the Supreme Court. "Both the Legislative and Judicial branches have essentially stopped operating. Any legislation which does make it to the President's desk is vetoed and, to date, Congress has failed to override any of these vetoes. Meanwhile, the Supreme Court has refused to decide any new cases. The nine justices are essentially on strike."

All true, Tim agreed, but so what? Just wait for the next elections. But Sebastian's presentation had an answer for that. The next slide was a picture of a woman voting.

"Despite predictions to the contrary by the media, our internal polling indicates that the current administration has a better than 80% chance of being reelected. Here are the data points that indicate this to be true." Sebastian then began to review five different charts on how the Agency had determined that the President would be reelected.

At this point, Tim began to zone out and look over to Pam to see how she was taking in Sebastian's data points. Pam appeared to be hanging onto his every word. Tim, on the other hand, might have ended up tuning the entire presentation out if Sebastian did not begin to speak of the 2016 election.

"Now, although we were successful in the last general election, the general feeling is that the pendulum has swung too far the other way."

What? Tim almost said it out loud. What the hell did the Agency have to do with the last election? Tim elbowed Pam and mouthed this question, but Pam just held her finger to her lips for him to be quiet.

"Now for the X, Y, and Z factors," Sebastian said. "The movements by the groups we refer to as X, Y, and

Z are predicted to gain momentum if the President is reelected. If these movements are successful, then the United States of America will divide into three separate and independent nation states."

To Tim, this had about as much chance of happening as California had of becoming their own country, but apparently the Agency had a different opinion. Tim was aware of these so-called movements, but he never took them very seriously. The X, Y, and Z movements were started in order to give ethnic groups better representation. This effort, which was supported by the progressive wing of the Democratic Party, was intended to make up for years of past discrimination. However, Tim mostly considered it to be a power grab.

The next slide indicated where the borders of these three new nation states might be. For the most part, the East and West coasts would become two separate nations, with the Midwest making the third. Tim wanted to ask if the citizens of the new Midwest nation state would take the name "The United Flyover States," but he did not think the joke would be appreciated.

"In addition, a number of southern states led by Texas are in discussions for creating their own fourth nation state," Sebastian reported, and he spent some more time discussing the possibility of a fourth group of states breaking away. Although Tim was sure that many would be interested in the subject, he still did not understand how it related to them and the Agency. Tim reminded himself once again that the Agency was not concerned with domestic issues or policies—unless Sebastian was planning on taking out the governor of Texas. Perhaps the target was in Mexico, Tim thought.

Sebastian continued. “Although these new nation states would still act in concert with one another, it is our analysis that the entire arrangement would be an unmitigated disaster and quite frankly would result in the breakup of the United States of America, which would threaten the stability of the world. Countries such as China and Russia would make serious attempts to take control of the west and east coast nations, and their economies could experience collapses like that of the country of Venezuela. This would result in a vast migration of citizens from both coasts to the Midwestern states. It is certainly possible that the entire situation could result in World War III...but, in the short run, the United States of America would cease to exist as we know it.”

Sebastian clicked on the next slide, which simply said in bold letters,

It’s time to take the country back.

Under that came the words,

It’s time to bring the adults back into the room!

If there had been a group of likeminded people in Pam’s library, then perhaps the room would have burst into applause at Sebastian’s proclamation—but it certainly left Tim Hall feeling speechless and underwhelmed.

Tim looked over at Pam to see that she was nodding in agreement. Well, she was certainly on board.

The picture on the screen now showed the Vice President and many current and former cabinet members. There were also a good number of women and a few African Americans, the usual number of African Americans that the Republicans attracted to their events. There was no picture or mention of the current President. What were their plans for him?

Tim did not have to wait long find out.

"The President needs to become sick, incapacitated, and die," said the voice belonging to Mr. Ajacks, who was speaking from a darkened corner of Pam's library. Tim smelled smoke and turned to see a glowing cigarette tip in the corner. Agency heads apparently did not need permission to smoke.

"Of course, becoming sick and then dying too quickly will arouse a great amount of suspicion, especially with the President's base and the media," Mr. Ajacks continued, "so it is critical that the President does not pass away too quickly."

"How long should the President live after he's poisoned, sir?" Sebastian asked respectfully.

"I would say that the President should not live for any longer than six to eight weeks," Ajacks replied.

Tim was now in a state of disbelief. They can't be serious, he thought; yet no one seemed to be laughing.

"So, just to be clear..." Tim interrupted. "...we are planning on assassinating the President because we do not feel that he is acting like an adult?"

Tim could feel the stares of Pam and Sebastian burning into him. Speaking directly to Mr. Ajacks was not allowed.

Ajacks stepped a little to his left so his line of sight was directly focused on Tim. "Well, we can't just blow his brains out like JFK. That would start a constitutional crisis. We could end up in worse shape than we are right now. We have considered other methods to speed up his demise. The President is a 78-year-old man, after all, but he does have his fans, and we need them to be on our side. This is why we feel that he deserves a slow, painless death which will go unnoticed by the public—at least at first."

Ajacks paused to take one more drag off his cigarette and a sip of his drink. "The Vice President would step in to handle the day-to-day operations and slowly bring in his own staff to help him. These would be men and women that the public already knows, and by the time the President peacefully passes away, the adults will already be on the job."

Mr. Ajacks raised his voice. "Everyone, meaning both Democrats and Republicans, will feel safe for the first time in three years. What we need from you, Mr. Hall, is a slow acting but deadly poison. Something that will be hard to trace and easily covered up. Something that will kill a 78-year-old man in 50 to 60 days. Do we have such a compound, Tim?"

"Working on it, boss," Tim answered, but he knew right away that this was not what Mr. Ajacks wanted to hear.

Pam then spoke up. "My husband is a little shy. We have developed a working prototype that will deliver the poison. It is a type of fork. A killer fork."

"A killer fork, you say?" Ajacks sounded impressed.

"Yes sir," Pam agreed, "one that could be substituted at a state dinner. But, of course, placing the fork at the dinner has not been worked out yet."

"We can take care of that, Pam," Ajacks reassured her. "When can you deliver your killer fork?"

"Next week, sir."

"Next week when?" Ajacks shot back.

"Thursday?" Pam asked.

"Wednesday," Ajacks replied.

"Wednesday it is."

Pam was finished, and Ajacks was ready to go. "Well, it does appear that at least most of your team is on the same page, Sebastian, so if there are no more questions, I will be going. It was a pleasure to meet you, Pam," Ajacks remarked as he ignored Tim and turned for the door.

Sebastian got in between Tim and Ajacks, which partly blocked Tim's view of the man, although Tim was pretty sure about Ajacks' identity. Ajacks hadn't gone out of his way to hide that from Tim, after all.

As Sebastian walked Mr. Ajacks outside, Pam gave Tim one of her looks. "I feel like I have a fucking teenager in the house," Pam said as she began to gear up for her admonishment. "If you have any questions about the operation, you ask me or Sebastian. You do not ask Ajacks."

Tim turned and began to walk away, but Pam caught up to him and lowered her voice to a kind of mean whisper. "Listen to me. I am trying very hard to give these assholes a reason to keep you around after all of this is over, but you have not been helping. Why is that?"

"Oh, I don't know, Pam," Tim began, "maybe it has something to do with me being pulled into a plot to assassinate the President of the United States."

Pam was getting ready to respond when Sebastian came back into the house. Tim ignored Sebastian and headed down to the lab.

Pam started to go after him, but Sebastian stopped her. "Let him cool off. I'll speak to him later."

"I just want to make sure he doesn't do anything stupid like destroy the prototype fork," Pam said as she heard the basement door close.

"Not to worry," Sebastian reassured her. "I have the killer fork right here, safe and sound."

CHAPTER 19

Tim's first thought was to destroy the fork, but maybe he could use it as some kind of leverage. *"Let me go or I'll kill the fork!"*

As he looked around it, though, it became apparent that the fork had been taken. Oh well, Tim thought. It would not have been too difficult for them to make a new one, anyway. Or would it?

Maybe that was the real question—and the reason that Tim was here in the first place. Tim's training had taught him that when a group decides to kill a head of state, the less people who knew about it, the better. So how many people knew about this plan? 10? 20? It was hard to say, but it was most likely no more than 20. The three of them and Ajacks made four, but then there had to be some management types and a couple of agents in the Secret Service who were aware of the plan, plus some people at the FBI. There was certainly no love lost between the FBI and this administration, Tim thought. So, there would be a total of between 20 to 25 conspirators involved, and Tim was being used simply for economic reasons.

Like many occupations, the modern-day Agency had become a company of specialists, i.e., men and women who performed one particular task and only that particular task. Tim, on the other hand, was an old school spy who knew how to do a lot of different things. In the modern-day Agency, developing the fork might have taken 10 to 20 employees at the minimum. Engineers to design it, mechanics to put it together, chemists to test the poisons, testers to make sure it all worked, with meetings, meetings, and more meetings. The inclusion of Tim simply bypassed all of that red tape.

Although he no longer had the fork in his possession, Tim had determined that Sebastian and Pam still needed him, which would give him some more time to figure things out.

Tim pulled out his cell phone and checked both his voicemail and text messages. Nothing from Mary Ann. He had texted her yesterday, and it was a little unlike her not to at least leave some kind of message, even if she was pissed off at him. It was also not lost on Tim that Toby was not around. Somebody had brought a car around for Sebastian during the day on Friday, and he had indicated to Pam that he would not be spending the night.

None of this meant anything, at least in regard to Mary Ann and her safety. Sebastian must also have a life somewhere, and maybe he just wanted to take the weekend off from his work. The work of planning assassinations.

The door at the top of the steps opened, and someone began to descend down to the basement.

Tim thought it would be Pam coming to yell at him some more, or perhaps even to apologize—with

Pam, you never could guess. Instead, it was the deep and British voice of Sebastian Oak that called out. "Tim? Are you down here? I need to speak with you before I leave."

"Sure, Sebastian, come on down." Unintentionally, Tim's tone had sounded like the announcer on a television game show.

Sebastian entered the laboratory and saw Tim sitting on a stool at one end of the granite worktable. Sebastian sat at the other end, made himself comfortable, and began to speak. "Tim, I feel that I owe you an apology. It was me, after all, who suggested to Pam that we bring you back in, and it was me who tricked you into traveling to the Dominican Republic."

"Yes, that's a good place to start, Sebastian. Why did you lure me to Santa Domingo?"

"We were attempting to reverse your amnesia, my friend."

Tim and Sebastian were far from friends at the moment, but Tim was very interested in finally finding out the purpose of his so-called medical vacation. "Reversing my amnesia, Sebastian?" he asked. "My doctors at Johns Hopkins told me that could not be done."

"The FDA has not approved any drugs or treatments involving drugs for amnesia. However, that does not mean that no treatments exist. There are actually quite a lot of things that can be tried," Sebastian said.

"Things that can be tried?" Tim repeated skeptically. "What kind of things?"

"Well, I'm not a medical man, Tim, and you know that, but I think that we can both say that your treatment was something of a success."

This was, of course, a rhetorical question. Tim could not deny that whatever treatments were performed had achieved a certain amount of success. At one point, he'd determined that he had lost around four years of his memory, but now it was maybe just a few months. He could not be sure of that, but Tim now recalled most of his life up until the trip to China. That was supposed to be his last assignment before retirement—and, in a sense, it had been.

"If you arranged all of this, Sebastian, why did you insist on collecting $17,500 from me?"

"I said that unapproved methods were applied, Tim. I did not say they were free." Sebastian was almost laughing now. "Besides, the doctors and locals had to be paid. But if you're so concerned about the money, I'll pay you back personally. Will you take a check?"

Tim could not believe that Sebastian had the gall to offer this, but he also somehow wasn't surprised. "Sure, Sebastian, a check will be fine."

Sebastian produced a checkbook from his suit jacket and began to write. Both of the men knew what a senseless gesture this was, since Tim's fate had already been sealed. Wising off to the department head certainly did not endear him to anyone, but that probably did not make any difference. Tim figured that he had perhaps until Wednesday, the day of delivery, or maybe a day or two past that. As soon as everyone was convinced the fork would work, Tim was a dead man.

Sebastian pushed the check across the table and over to Tim. Tim picked it up in order to examine it.

Sebastian and Molly Oak, the check read in the left corner. 2365 Eagle Cir, Bethesda, Maryland 20819. Pay to the order of Tim Hall, Seventeen thousand and five hundred dollars and no cents. In the memo line was written, "For Services Rendered."

Tim's curiosity got the better of him. "Have I ever met your wife Molly?"

"Oh no, my wife has no idea what I do for a living. She thinks I'm in the import-export business."

"Yes, aren't we all?" Tim replied, and both men had a laugh. That was often how these kinds of things went, Tim thought. Nothing personal, this is just part of my job; it was just the standard line people in intelligence gave to one another.

"So, Sebastian, I haven't seen your friend Toby for a day. Where has he gone off to?"

"Oh, I meant to tell you," Sebastian said with some excitement in his voice. "Toby and Mary Ann have decided to get back together, and Toby requested some time off in order to make that happen. Toby sent me a picture of the two lovebirds." Sebastian produced his iPhone and showed Tim a selfie. In it was Toby with his arm around Mary Ann's shoulder, but it looked a little like a chokehold, and Tim could not see Mary Ann's hands.

"Now, look at this one. I have to agree with you

about Mary Ann, Tim. She is exceptionally beautiful," Sebastian said as he showed Tim the picture. It was a close up of Mary Ann, and Tim saw what appeared to be a bruise below Mary Ann's right eye, partially covered up by makeup. Sebastian turned his phone off and placed it back in his pocket.

"Toby wanted to be sure I let you know that there is no longer any reason for you to text, call, or email her. In other words, it's over between you two." Sebastian got up to leave, adding, "Maybe Pam will take you back."

When he started heading for the basement steps, Tim was on the other man's back before Sebastian knew it. Tim took Sebastian by the shoulders, turned him around and shoved him against the stone basement wall.

"Look, you fuck," Tim's nose was about two inches from Sebastian face. "Mary Ann doesn't know anything about any of this, so why don't you leave her alone?"

Sebastian just smiled at Tim. "That is totally up to you, Tim," he answered pleasantly. "Yes, Mary Ann and Toby do not know anything about any of this, and my intention has always been to allow both of them to return to Las Vegas. I am not a murderer, no matter what you may think; but I am also not about to sabotage my operation because you have the hots for some Las Vegas bartender. Now, please let go of me before Darrel gets here."

At that moment, the basement door opened and

Darrel, Pam's security, came down the stairs with his pistol drawn. He had obviously been watching everything on the security cameras.

"Step back, Mr. Hall," Darrel commanded, and Tim took both of his hands off of Sebastian and raised them in the air. He knew the drill.

"Place your hands behind your head and lace your fingers together."

"Everything is okay, Darrel," Sebastian interrupted. "Mr. Hall and I were just having a difference of opinion." He casually began to straighten the lapels on his suit jacket. "You can leave us; I'm sure that Mr. Hall will behave himself now."

"Okay, Mr. Oak, as long as you're sure." Darrel turned and headed back upstairs.

When he was gone, Sebastian smirked at Tim. "As you can see, Tim, I'm holding all of the cards. All Pam and I want from you is just to cooperate, and who knows? You may even get the chance to cash my check. So, think about it."

Sebastian turned and headed back upstairs while Tim brought his hands back down to his sides. He certainly did have a lot to think about.

CHAPTER 20

Tim decided to go to bed. It had been a very long day and an even longer evening. He climbed up the basement stairs and into the library to look for Pam but couldn't find her. He looked in the kitchen, but she was not there either. She'd probably also gone to bed.

Tim wondered what room Darrel was hiding in. He had to be somewhere close by. Tim wondered if Pam had a secret room somewhere that she'd failed to show him during the initial tour of the house. Besides, as far as Tim knew, Pam was sleeping with Darrel. That thought had crossed his mind.

Tim climbed the steps and started down the hall for his room. He saw that the door to Pam's room was closed, and he had no intention of knocking.

Tim had removed his clothes and climbed into his bed when he heard a soft knock on his own door. The door opened, and in came Pam, dressed in a floor-length silk robe. Her hair, which had been tied in a bun earlier, was now down to her shoulders. In her right hand was a pair of metal handcuffs, and not the kind you might buy in a sex shop. Real ones that the cops would use.

Pam sat on the edge of Tim's bed. "Sebastian and Darrel have both advised me to handcuff one of your wrists to the bedpost just to make sure you don't get any ideas about leaving during the night, but I really thought that was an overreaction, don't you think?"

"That is probably not the correct method of entertaining your house guests," Tim joked.

"Oh, I totally agree," Pam remarked as she opened her robe to reveal the black garter belt and bra she was wearing. "And who knows?" she continued. "You might just turn the tables and handcuff me to the bed."

Pam dropped her robe and panties to the floor and climbed into the bed with Tim. She closed the end of the handcuff around her left wrist, then pulled the other through the headboard and secured her right wrist. It was quite the trick, but Pam had done it all before. This had been a part of an ongoing game of spy versus spy that Pam and Tim had played with each other over the years. It usually involved Pam playing the victim, although she would also occasionally be the aggressor. Tim had found this out one morning when he woke up hogtied with Pam's Hermes scarfs.

"If you're worried, I might make noise, you can always put something in my mouth," Pam purred.

Tim virtually lost it at this point and was now all over his wife. He began kissing her, first at the top of her head, then working his way down until he reached her feet. He then worked his way back up, stopping here and stopping there. He ended by finishing inside of Pam. Exhausted, he fell asleep on top of her.

The next morning came earlier than Tim would have liked, with the March sun shining through the windows facing east. Tim got up to pee, but he did not get very far. Pam had handcuffed his right wrist to the bed after all. He began to yell for her, but then saw that she was lying right next to him. At least she didn't leave me, he thought.

"Hey, honey, would you take off the handcuffs? I have to pee."

Still half asleep, Pam raised her left hand and reached for the end of the handcuff attached to the bed. She gave it a hard pull, and the handcuff opened right up. They were phony handcuffs after all.

"There you go, dear," Pam mumbled, falling back to sleep.

It was eight on Saturday morning, so Tim decided to let Pam sleep late. He made his way to the kitchen, where he found Darrel drinking a cup of coffee.

"Good morning, Darrel. How was your night?"

"Pretty slow, Mr. Hall, after I had to break up you and Mr. Oak."

"Yeah, I'm sorry about that Darrel. Sometimes Mr. Oak just rubs me the wrong way." Tim was guessing that Darrel was not in on the assassination plot. He was just the hired muscle doing what he was instructed to do.

"That's not a problem, Mr. Hall," Darrel said, getting up.

"Don't leave on my account, Darrel," Tim said.

"Oh, I have paperwork to catch up on—but thanks."

Darrel started walking toward the back of the house. Tim leaned back to see if he could see exactly where Darrel was headed, but lost sight of him as he rounded a corner. Tim heard a door closing, but not like a door that rested on hinges. More like a sliding door.

That must be Pam's secret security room. Most likely, it was behind a hidden door made to look like a bookcase or wall. Tim made a mental note to look for this room later on.

Tim opened the refrigerator, found the eggs and bacon, and began to make breakfast. He was aware that Pam preferred her eggs sunny side up, but he only knew how to scramble them. It took a very long time for Tim to like any kind of eggs, as he never ate them as a child. It was not until Tim was at Berkeley that he even tried an egg. In his freshman year, he ate all of his meals at the college cafeteria, and sometimes scrambled eggs and bacon were the only things available for breakfast. Tim was forced to learn to like them. He smiled at that memory, thinking that he'd been forced to like many things in his life.

Tim made a tray for Pam that included orange juice and coffee along with the bacon and eggs. If he could have located some kind of flower, he would have included that as well. Although he would never admit it to Pam's face, he did enjoy the little sexual fantasy game, including the part where Pam had somehow slid out from under him and handcuffed him. But that also spoke to Pam's desire to always be in control. Sure, Pam got off on being dominated, but at the end of the day, she would let you know one way or the other that she was running the show.

When Tim entered the room, Pam was sitting up with her back against the bed board, looking at herself in the mirror across the room as she brushed her long blonde hair.

"Oh, my darling, what a sweet thing for you to do," Pam said, smiling as Tim placed the tray in front of her.

Tim took his cup of coffee from Pam's tray and walked over to the window. He saw two men in military fatigues speaking with each other. "Exactly how much security do you have, Pam?" he asked.

"I can't tell you that, Timothy." Pam took a bite of her eggs. "But enough. Why do you need to know?"

"Well, it would be pretty difficult for me to walk out of here. It's really a long walk back to Baltimore," Tim said, half joking.

"Well, first of all, the security is not here because of you. And by the way, you are not a prisoner here. If you want to go home to Baltimore, then just say so. I can arrange for a ride." Pam took another bite of her eggs. "I was hoping that we could spend the weekend together and talk over some things. Last night's meeting did not really go as planned, and you should have been better prepared. That's on me."

"Yes, I agree," Tim responded. "If you had told me

that the entire purpose of our reunion was to assassinate the President," Tim paused to make sure that he had Pam's attention, "then perhaps I would have moved to Canada."

"If Sebastian and I had not brought you back Tim, you would still be wandering around Baltimore. But that's another subject." Pam finished the food on her plate and began to drink her orange juice.

"Anyhow, I really do not see this operation as a plot to assassinate the President. It is much more than that. It is a chance for the United States to take correct-ive action. Historically, this country has always taken corrective action when faced with adversity, starting with the Civil War of the 1860s. And believe me, we are on the verge of another one right now."

Perhaps Pam was right about that. Tim could not recall a time when the country was so divided, and many people, especially the younger ones, no longer had faith in the electoral process. Maybe laws should be changed where the winner of an election would have to receive at least 60% of the popular vote or a run-off election would be required. However, that probably would not completely satisfy everyone. The losers would still whine like always.

"Sebastian said last night that the Agency predicted that the President would win in 2016 and not the woman? How did you know?" Tim asked Pam.

"First of all, people lie, so you have to include that in your calculation, and anyone conducting an honest poll would know that. The problem is that the poll takers already have a bias. Most pollsters really wanted her to win so they would be on the right side of history, and they were looking for any data to support that."

Gunshots sounded somewhere in the woods, and Pam turned her head for a second before continuing. "Hell, I wanted her to win, but I was 90% sure she would not."

Pam did appear sorry that a woman had not yet been elected President, but in her mind, the first woman to hold the office would most likely be a Republican. Men just would not trust a woman Democrat.

More shots sounded outside, and Tim was beginning to get concerned. "Pam, is there any chance we're being attacked?"

"Oh, that's just the boys playing some type of war game in the woods. It's one of the disadvantages of living here. The Agency likes to have these training exercises, and our woods here are very similar to the ones in Eastern Europe."

"Don't the neighbors complain?"

"We don't have any neighbors for five miles in any direction. You don't remember much about living here, do you, Tim?"

"Well, I certainly don't recall any paramilitary training happening in my backyard," Tim replied, laughing.

"That is something new, and I admit it's a pain in the ass, but it's also part of the deal."

"The deal" Pam was talking about was that she did not own the house. It belonged to the Agency, although it was listed in Pam's name for tax purposes.

Pam finished her breakfast and got out of bed. She gave Tim a kiss and thanked him again for providing breakfast, then headed to her bathroom.

"Tim? I have to go into Leesburg and do some grocery shopping. I thought you could come with me and get out of the house for a while. Interested?"

"Yes, I would love that," Tim replied.

"Okay, give me thirty minutes. Maybe we can have lunch."

"Yeah, that would be great," he answered, still looking at the men in fatigues.

It did cross Tim's mind that he could probably ditch Pam in town and make his way back to Baltimore, but why bother? It would be easy enough for Sebastian and Pam to find him again. He could, of course, go to the police, but who would believe him? He no longer knew anyone at Langley or the FBI. At one point in his career, Tim had been badged into the FBI at both Headquarters and Quantico, meaning he could walk right into the buildings and speak to almost anyone, but those days were long gone. On the other hand, both Sebastian and Pam most likely still had contacts at the FBI, and a phone call would be all it would take. *"Hello FBI, this is CIA Agent Pam Hall, and my husband thinks he's invented a killer fork which will be used to assassinate the President."* Tim had to laugh at the absurdity of his situation.

Pam came bounding down the front steps wearing a very tight pair of blue jeans with brown boots and a white cable knit sweater. "Ready to go?" she asked cheerfully.

"Lead the way," Tim responded, following her out of the house.

"I can't wait to show you my new car," Pam said.

Darrel came around to the front of the house from somewhere in the back. Pam saw him and waved. "We're going to Leesburg, Darrel. Do you need anything?"

"No, ma'am, but thank you for asking."

"He's such a nice kid, don't you think, Tim?"

Tim did not know how nice Darrel was or was not. All he knew was that, like Toby Wheeler, Darrel was built like an NFL linebacker and could most likely tear Tim into two pieces.

"I guess, Pam. How long has he been around?"

"Oh, not long. Maybe about a week now. We never know who we're going to get. Langley just sends me a profile before they get here so I can make sure they're legitimate."

"So, where's the secret security room?" Tim thought that he might as well ask just to see how Pam would answer.

"It wouldn't be a secret room if I told you where it was," Pam answered with a laugh. "But I'll tell you what: if you can figure out exactly where it is, I'll give you a tour."

"You know, Pam, when things slow down, you and I could start hosting Spy House Weekends and sell tickets."

For a second Pam seemed to take Tim seriously, but then she started to laugh again. "Tim, you're such a funny guy!"

CHAPTER 21

Pam's new car, a black Mercedes S560, was more like a 4-star hotel than a regular automobile. In order to be polite, Tim had planned to ask Pam if she would like him to drive. Now, Tim was happy he had not. In all honesty, Tim didn't believe that he could figure out how to drive the S560. At least not at first. The car did almost everything short of driving itself.

"I feel like a queen driving this car," Pam explained as she turned right onto US Route 15 to Leesburg, and Tim knew that she was telling him the truth. Pam began to describe each of the car's features. The ventilated and heated front seats, KEYLESS-GO, active parking assist... Yes, the car would park itself, and Pam even demonstrated this feature by stopping at the elementary school parking lot in Luckett, Virginia.

"Nothing like falling in love with a car, is there, Pam?" Tim said, but Pam freely admitted it to be true.

Tim had Googled Pam's S560 to see that the MSRP was in the vicinity of one hundred and eleven thousand dollars. Where the hell did Pam come up with that kind of money? Tim wondered,

but then he thought about it. Pam was probably pulling down somewhere around $140K to $150K a year at the Agency, and she did not have a house payment. Pam had also earned a fair amount of danger pay over the years, which she most likely put away. So sure, he guessed she could afford it and was not being paid off by the Russians.

The Aldrich Ames incident in the '90s really woke everyone up at Langley, and management started paying close attention to everyone's lifestyle. Pam and Tim hadn't known Ames personally, but they did know a lot of people who did. One friend of Pam's who worked in the Russian section told her about how Ames would always come around to her desk and ask what she was working on. He apparently did that to many people. That in itself did not arouse any suspicion, but Pam's friend felt that Ames must have used something that she had unintentionally revealed. People died because of Aldrich Ames, and Pam's friend quit the Agency soon after Ames was convicted. She just couldn't take it any longer.

Pam and Tim, on the other hand, had always lived rather cheaply. After they were married, they lived in an apartment in Falls Church. Next, they rented a house in Vienna, Virginia. They never considered buying because they were never at home. They never bothered to have children because neither Pam nor Tim would give up their jobs in order to be together. In the 1980s and '90s, married agents could not be assigned to the same overseas office. This was the reason why many of the women Pam had trained with gave up their careers. They married their Agency husbands and started families.

So not only were Pam and Tim never home, but when they were away, they were at different locations around the world. Management finally began to relax the married rule, but by then both Pam and Tim were working stateside. Pam and Tim did go on missions together, especially after 9/11, but they were never posted overseas again. Tim recalled thinking that running a safe house would be a great way of ending his career, but Pam thought it was a dead-end assignment. There was just one more job to do, something in China regarding intellectual property. That was the last thing Tim remembered.

Pam was still talking about the new Mercedes. "Look at this, Tim!" she called out as she let the car momentarily drift toward oncoming traffic. All sorts of bells and lights began to sound as Pam guided her vehicle back. "Now that's what I call a safety feature," Pam almost screamed with excitement. She was certainly having a good time, Tim thought.

As Tim and Pam drove closer to Leesburg, the two-lane Route 15 became a four-lane highway. Tim had observed that there were now many more new homes on each side of the road. Big 5,000 square foot houses that must cost at least $700,000 each. When Tim first started coming out to this part of Northern Virginia in the 1980s, there was maybe 50,000 people in Loudoun County. Now, there were 60,000 in Leesburg alone, and it was still growing.

Pam took the exit from the Route 15 bypass to Route 7 east. They were heading for Wegmans, a high-end grocery store. It was noon on a Saturday. The place would be packed.

Wegmans was similar to Whole Foods, except Wegmans carried more stuff. A lot more stuff. It was the kind of place where one could spend an entire day, and a few people actually did. You could shop there, eat there, and shop some more; and although items would be on sale from time to time, it was in no way cheap.

At one time, the entire DC area was dominated by basically two grocery stores: Safeway, which was headquartered in Oakland, California, and Giant Foods, which was once locally owned. That all began to change in the 1990s, as other grocery store chains from the South and Northeast expanded into the region. Not that the increased competition lowered food prices. To the contrary, food prices actually rose in the DC metro area, especially in the District of Columbia. This all made Tim feel that the price of food did not follow the normal rules of economics. It was not supply and demand pricing, it was "how much are they willing to pay" pricing, and the citizens of Leesburg and Loudoun County appeared to be willing to pay a lot.

They could pay a lot because they made a lot of money working for companies that contracted with the U.S. government. Defense contracting, to be precise. Many homes boasted incomes of over $200,000, which in turn gave Loudoun County the highest median household income in the United States. Yet, Loudoun was not the only county in the DC metro area. At least eight other counties in Maryland and Northern Virginia were in the top 20. The other counties with high median household incomes were clustered either around New York City or San Francisco, which included Silicon Valley.

However, it was not the amount of income that impressed Tim, but the contrast with the other places in the world that he'd visited. In some countries, a paved road was something to behold, and Tim often wondered what would happen if he could transport a group of citizens from one of these poor counties to Loudoun County for a day and bring them over to Wegmans. These people might first faint at seeing the quantity and quality of goods available, then ask why they didn't have the same.

For decades, consumerism was part of the foundation of US foreign policy, with the US sending messages like, "Increasing consumption of goods is economically desirable," or "If you behave yourself and reject your form of government, all of this can be yours." But it never seemed to work out that way. The citizens of Cuba, for example (or at least the ones that were still holding on to the dream), appeared to love their leader Fidel until the day he died and apparently still embraced that particular brand of socialism. To Tim, it seemed like the Cubans were saying, "Sure, life sucks down here, but making life better is not our job, it's the government's job."

Pam's voice brought Tim back from his daydream about the economic inequities of the world. "Now watch this, Tim." She had lined up to a parallel parking space. Although there were plenty of open parking spots where she could have simply just pulled in, Pam pressed a button, and the S560 dutifully began to park itself.

When the car had finished, it beeped as if to say, "all done." "Thank you," Pam answered.

"Have you given it a name yet?" Tim asked.

"Given who a name?"

"The car. Have you given the car a name?"

"It's a car, Tim. It doesn't need a name. Quit being silly," Pam teased as she pressed the auto lock button.

The M560 made three different sounds as it was locking, but, to Tim, the car also sounded as if it were saying, "Quit being silly."

Pam grabbed a discarded shopping cart and handed it over to Tim. "Take this. There probably won't be any inside." And she was right.

The first section they visited was produce, and Pam went right to work examining various fruits and vegetables. Tim thought about how casual she was. Have a meeting about assassinating the President the night before, do the week's shopping the next day. Pam had an amazing ability to compartmentalize almost everything in her life.

For that matter, so did Mary Ann. Maybe that was the one thing that Pam and Mary Ann had in common. Maybe it was what had attracted Tim to these two women in the first place. Tim was what his late grandmother used to call a "worry wart." As a child, Tim's grandmother would often come over to watch Tim while his parents were at work. Tim would always be fretting about money, since it was the one thing, he heard his parents constantly discuss. These discussions would filter down to Tim, and he would then express his concerns to his grandmother by saying, "I hope we have enough money for the mortgage payment" or "I hope we have enough money for food."

Tim's grandmother never directly addressed her grandchild's concerns; if she had, she might have solved what would become a lifelong problem. Instead, all she would say to Tim was, "Don't be a worry wart," or "You're being a worry wart, Timmy." She never simply said, "Tim, your parents make lots of money, so there's no reason for you to worry about losing your house or having nothing to eat."

Most adults did not have those kinds of discussions with their children back in the 1960s. If a child had concerns about the family income these days, on the other hand, some parents would probably arrange a meeting between their children and their accountants in order allay any concerns. That was just how life seemed to roll...from one extreme to the other.

Pam had now entered the meat, chicken, and fish department and was trying to determine how fresh the precooked shrimp was. "Would you like some shrimp before dinner tonight?" she asked Tim.

"Sure, honey," Tim replied.

"I think the flounder looks good. You like flounder, don't you?"

Tim thought that most fish, including flounder, tasted about the same, but Pam seemed to be enjoying the whole shopping experience with him, so there was no reason to disrupt the vibe. "Yes, I love flounder. Are you planning on frying it?"

"Yes, with breadcrumbs," Pam said but she had

become interested in another kind of fish on the ice and began to ask the fish man questions about it.

Pam was behaving a lot like Mary Ann would if the two of them were to go grocery shopping, which Tim thought was rather peculiar. Speaking of Mary Ann, maybe this would be a good time to try calling her. Tim pushed the shopping cart over to Pam. "Where are the restrooms in this place, Pam?"

"Up front by the check-out lines," Pam replied, pointing in the general direction.

"Okay, thanks," Tim said as he began to walk to the front of the store.

"Tim?" Pam called after him. "I'll be over by the frozen foods."

Tim waved and began to walk. When he was sure that he was out of Pam's sight, though, he pulled out his iPhone and told it to call Mary Ann.

She picked up on the first ring. "Where the fuck are you, Tim? You told me that you would be back by now!"

Ordinarily, Tim would have tried to say something funny in order to ease the tension, but there was no time to screw around. "Are you okay, Mary Ann? Where is Toby? Did he hurt you?"

"Well, the short answer is yes, I'm okay. Toby is out, and yes he did hurt me—but again, I am okay."

Tim felt sick to his stomach. It was one thing for him to get into a jam, but he never intended to bring

Mary Ann down with him. If he could have just kept his dick in his pants, she would probably be back in Las Vegas by now.

"You have to get away right now," he told her. "Do whatever it takes, but just get away."

"I would do that if I could, but I don't know exactly where I am. I'm locked in a shipping crate."

"A shipping crate. What kind of shipping crate?"

"Well, it's more like a shipping container. The kind they put on ships."

Tim now knew exactly what Mary Ann was in, and he knew that finding her would be a problem. Spies calling the police anywhere in the world was a big no-no and should be avoided, but this was an exception.

"Mary Ann, call 911 and tell them what's going on. They should be able to locate you using the GPS in your phone."

"Toby was able to deactivate that in my phone, but besides, GPS can only track you to a general area. There are thousands of these things, and Toby will see the cops long before they find me. If it's the same to you, I would prefer not to be beaten and tied up again."

Tim was at a loss for words. He was over 50 miles away from Baltimore, but even if he was there, he'd have no clue where to start looking for Mary Ann. She could be in several places.

Tim was about to say something to Mary Ann to comfort her, but she spoke first. "Tim? Now listen to me. I've been in tight spots before...even worse than this... but I've always gotten out of them. I can handle Toby, and he has no intention of leaving me here. So please don't worry. I know what I'm doing. But you need to be careful. I'm not exactly sure what Sebastian, Toby, and your wife are up to, but I know it's not good, so you need to just get along with everyone until we can figure something out."

Tim was very surprised how calm and professional Mary Ann was sounding and acting, but he reminded himself that she was a private investigator and had dealt with some very bad people over the years, so it was silly to feel that she could not handle herself. Tim even considered telling Mary Ann about the plot, but that would be a sure way of getting her killed. No. It was better for her not to know about it.

"Okay, Mary Ann, yes, it does sound like you have everything under control, but you do need to get away from Toby and out of town as soon as you have the chance. This situation is more dangerous than you can imagine."

"What's going on?"

"I can't tell you—but no matter what happens, I just want you to know that I love you."

Tim's last statement was met with a pause, and Tim heard what sounded like a metal door opening. Toby was back and coming in.

"I love you too, Tim," Mary Ann said as she hung up the phone.

By the time Tim made it back to Pam, she had made it through the frozen food section and was now looking at the dry goods. Tim considered this section to be the weakest part of Wegmans. The aisles were short and didn't seem to have the same large selection of items as an average grocery store, such as Harris Teeter.

"You took your time. Is everything okay?" Pam asked.

This was decision time for Tim. If he chose to lie and not tell Pam he'd been on the phone with Mary Ann, it could become problematic. It was very possible that Pam had someone in the store with eyes on him who would report to her later that he'd made a phone call. Getting caught in a lie would destroy any trust he had developed with Pam over the last two days, so Tim decided to be straight with her.

"I just called Mary Ann, and she told me that Toby has her locked in a shipping container somewhere at the Port of Baltimore. Do you know anything about that, Pam?"

Tim's question seemed to catch Pam off guard. Pam had probably figured that Tim would lie about making any phone calls. Now, she had to address the Mary Ann and Toby situation.

"We should talk about this in the car, not in the middle of Wegmans," she hissed.

"We can talk anywhere you fucking like, Pam, but if anything happens to that girl, then you are going to have to kill me too, because I will do everything in my power to take down you and your pal Sebastian."

Tim was aware that he really did not have much to bargain with, but there was some reason that Pam and Sebastian were keeping him around. They must still need him for something, since Pam was going out of her way to be nice to him. Both needed Tim to be calm and cooperative, and right now he was anything but.

Pam began to speak in a low voice. "Tim, I'm sure Sebastian has every intention of sending Toby and Mary Ann back to Las Vegas safe and sound. However, since you decided to become romantically involved with Mary Ann, it has just complicated everything." Pam paused and looked Tim in the eye to make sure she had his attention. "It has complicated our operation because you are behaving like some lovesick teenager."

Pam was attempting to turn the argument around and make it Tim's fault that Mary Ann was being held hostage. "Hey," he answered with a glare, "back in January, I was a retired government employee who happened to ask a woman out on a date. Not a covert agent involved in a plot to—"

"Don't say it!" Pam interrupted loudly enough to attract attention from a couple behind them.

She was right. They really should be discussing this in the car.

Pam and Tim both stopped speaking after that, and Tim wandered over to the candy aisles. Pam walked up behind him and whispered, "Would you like some candy, little boy?"

Making a joke out of the situation was one of the methods Pam and Tim always used to apologize to each other, but Tim was not going for it this time.

Pam began to look at the bins of candy sold in bulk. She soon started to speak again. "Sebastian and I hired that girl to engage you, Tim, not to fuck you. So as far as I am concerned, it's her fault that she's locked in a shipping container." Pam paused to look at the Lemonhead candies, deciding to buy some. "But if it will make you feel better, I'll call Sebastian and make sure she's released."

"And how will I know that, Pam? How will I know she's okay?"

"How about I invite her and Toby over for dinner on Sunday?"

Tim turned and looked at Pam to see if she was serious. If Pam was wearing a big grin, he would know it was all a joke.

He couldn't detect a hint of humor in her expression, though, which meant he'd have to ask. "You're joking, right? You want to invite Mary Ann and Toby over for dinner?"

"Yes," Pam agreed, "Mary Ann, Toby, and Sebastian. Sebastian will have to be there as well; there will be no way around that. Would that be satisfactory?"

Pam's offer was certainly an unexpected move on her part, and Tim really wasn't comfortable with the idea; but is would at least prove to him that Mary

Ann was all right. Otherwise, Tim would just have to take Pam at her word.

"Yeah, that would be great," he eventually replied.

Pam could obviously hear the reluctance in his voice. "Hey, it's up to you, babe. If you want to make sure your girlfriend is okay, what better way than to see her in the flesh?"

"She's not my girlfriend," Tim protested, although he knew he was lying.

"Okay, so she is not your girlfriend, but do you want to see her or not?" Pam was really selling the deal now.

"Yes, yes. I would," Tim finally said.

"Great. But one rule: if you say anything to Mary Ann or Toby about the operation, they will not leave the house alive."

Pam made this statement so casually that it sent a chill down Tim's spine. He had no doubt that she was 100% serious.

"So, what kind of food does Mary Ann like?" Pam asked.

"Italian," Tim answered automatically, thinking back to their first date.

"Then she will love my lasagna. Now go away while I call Sebastian."

Tim felt like he had been dismissed by his

mother. He obeyed.

CHAPTER 22

Tim wandered far away from Pam and her pending phone conversation with Sebastian. Although it may have been helpful for him to hear how his wife actually interacted with Sebastian, he really didn't feel like listening. He knew it would just piss him off.

He found himself in the section of the pharmacy where sleep aids were sold. There were certainly several different kinds of sleep aid products that did not require a prescription. Tim's philosophy about insomnia was that, if you stayed awake long enough, you would certainly go to sleep at some point. The fact that so many people brought sleeping pills indicated to him that they would rather be asleep most of the time.

On Tim's right, he could hear two women having a conversation about filling out forms. Not just one form, but several forms. From what Tim could tell, the woman that needed to fill out the forms was some kind of doctor. At least, that was how the pharmacist was addressing her. "You will also need to fill out the back page as well, Dr. Lockwood."

Tim didn't think he knew any doctors by that name, but there was something familiar about the woman's voice. He moved to the other end of the aisle for a better look, but she was still bent over, filling out the back page of the form.

When Tim was in school, there were not a lot of women doctors, but now they were all over the place. He was not a big fan of women doctors, mostly because he could never get any of them to write prescriptions for anything good (with "good" meaning opioid pain killers or benzodiazepines). But, of course, these days, no doctors would give you any decent painkillers unless your broke your back—and sometimes not even then. Tim placed the blame for that at the feet of the pharmaceutical industry for the invention of oxycodone.

Oxycodone was a long-acting and extended release painkiller that had been advertised to doctors as having a low rate of addiction, or at least that's what Tim had read. But whoever made the low addiction claim must have been a lunatic—or at least an idiot. If these pills had been taken as directed, then perhaps the addiction rates would have remained low, but when do Americans do what they're told? Oxycodone would get patients addicted very quickly, and addicted very quickly they became, in epidemic proportions. The government's reaction was to pressure doctors to no longer prescribe anything with any relation to an opioid, and those that refused because of a silly notion that they knew better than the government (and the media) were rewarded with suspended medical licenses and jail time. The media and government demanded scapegoats, since someone had to be blamed. The opioid crisis, as the media had come to call it, was still a major problem, but the story had played itself out. The election results of that November night in 2016 had changed the conversation.

Tim was still thinking about opioids when he heard a cheery voice say, "All done!" and finally discovered the identity of Dr. Lockwood. She was Nurse Jennifer, Dr. Justice's nurse from Santa Domingo. Tim circled around to try and get another look. Yes, definitely her.

Nurse, now Doctor Jennifer had said little to Tim during his few days in Santa Domingo, but he could not forget her voice. She had a girlish-sounding voice that was kind of high and squeaky—a voice that might turn some men on, but others off. As Tim watched (now from a distance), Jennifer continued speaking with the pharmacist. She did seem to know everyone behind the counter, and they appeared to all be joking about something, since they were laughing.

Tim next looked back over his left shoulder to see if he could find Pam. He spotted her at the back of the store, having an animated conversation on her phone. Pam's right arm swung around as she seemed to be making a point. Tim had determined that it was imperative that Pam did not meet Nurse/Dr. Jennifer by chance. It was possible that Pam did not know Jennifer, but it was more likely that she did.

Meanwhile, Jennifer had finished her business at the pharmacy and started for the exit. Tim followed her until he was sure that she'd left the store, then turned around and headed back to the pharmacy. The pharmacist was still at the register.

"Hi. Was that Dr. Lockwood standing here a second ago?" Tim asked.

The pharmacist eyeballed Tim for a minute, considering what she should say. "Yes," she finally answered.

"Is she still in the medical building next to the old hospital?"

The knowledge that the hospital in Leesburg had two campuses, one in Leesburg proper and the other two miles east of the town limits, was a good indicator to many that you were a true local.

As soon as Tim made this known, the pharmacist opened right up. "Oh no, they've moved to the new office next to Lansdowne." Lansdowne was the new hospital outside of Leesburg.

"With Dr. Justice?" Tim added, guessing that Dr. Justice had not changed his name for this charade.

"Oh, I just love Dr. Justice," the pharmacist exclaimed. "He's just the funniest man."

"Yes, he certainly is," Tim said, agreeing with the pharmacist for an entirely different reason.

"Tim?" Pam called, coming up behind him. "What in the world are you doing?"

"Oh, I'm just checking to see if they are giving away any free samples of Vicodin."

The pharmacist did not find Tim's joke funny whatsoever. "Vicodin is only available by prescription," the pharmacist sternly informed him. "And we ask for identification as well."

"As you should," Tim answered as he walked away.

"Are you still taking codeine, Tim?" Pam sounded concerned.

"I wish, but you can't get it anymore."

"You don't need it anyway," Pam said as they pushed the shopping chart to the checkout lines.

$450 was the total grocery store bill, and Tim paid for it with one of his credit cards before Pam could stop him.

"Tim, I appreciate your generosity, but it was totally unnecessary. I expense account most of this as a business cost."

"You mean you write off your groceries as a business expense?"

"Well, yeah, because they are," Pam agreed defensively.

Pam and Tim loaded the groceries and began to drive home.

"Do me a favor and drive me by the new hospital," Tim said. The new Loudoun Hospital was on the north side of Route 7.

"Why?" Pam seemed a little suspicious.

"Just want to see my tax dollars at work," Tim answered.

Pam took the exit out of the Wegmans parking

lot and crossed over Route 7 to the new hospital. Pam drove around, and Tim saw the office building where the pharmacist had told him Nurse Jennifer's new office was. There were also a number of low-rise senior citizen assisted living centers, which Tim thought were very conveniently located. Maybe it was an unmentioned selling point, as in, "Hey, we're right next to the hospital!" Thinking this made Tim laugh for some reason.

"What's so funny?" Pam wanted to know.

"Oh, I was just thinking about being a senior citizen and living right next to a hospital," Tim confessed.

It really was not all that funny. Tim had now reached the age where living in an adult community probably made sense, but he found the mere thought of doing so extremely scary. Perhaps Tim's laughing was a response to this fear.

"Well, I guess it works for some people. But not for me," Pam said.

Pam was almost six years younger than Tim and had no thoughts of retiring, which was a big reason she wanted out of her job managing the safe house. Pam had her sights on landing a Station Chief position somewhere in Europe. Tim knew this but did not believe Pam had much of a chance. Over the years, she'd pissed off too many people.

"So, have you seen enough?" Pam wanted to know, referring to the hospital campus.

"Yes, and thank you. You know me. I was just

curious what all was back here."

"Yes, I do know you," Pam replied while laughing. "By the way, I did speak to Sebastian about inviting Mary Ann and Toby to dinner on Sunday night, but he doesn't think it's a good idea."

"In other words, no," Tim said.

"In other words, no," Pam agreed. "He is willing to let you speak with her or even Skype her if you want. Anything to prove that she's not locked in a dungeon somewhere."

Tim hated Skype or any system where your face appeared on a screen. Although it sounded like a good idea, most people apparently did not enjoy seeing themselves live on camera. The technology for viewing a person you were speaking with on a telephone had been around for decades, but it just never took off.

"No, I think letting me speak with her in private will be enough."

"Tim, I trust you, but Sebastian does not. He feels that if you and Mary Ann are together, you will do something crazy in order to escape with her. I told him that you are not that dramatic, but he's not buying it."

"Pam, you really need to stop this crazy thing," Tim said, referring to Operation Poison the President, which was what he'd decided to name it.

"It's too late to stop it, Tim. There are just too many people involved now, and the plan is moving forward."

Tim took that to mean that the other conspirators had decided on a time and a place for the poisoning. Tim still believed that he might be able to stop it, but he needed to get Pam back on his side.

"Besides," Pam continued, "No one likes this guy, and most Americans will be glad when he's gone. Even if he were to lose the election next year, the President will remain a powerful force."

"But it's not a matter of if you like or don't like the man," Tim protested. "Removing a duly elected President by means not stated in the Constitution is illegal."

"Gosh, Tim, let me find you some marching band music I can play while you say that again," Pam answered sarcastically.

"Well, if you only read the *Washington Post* and the *New York Times*, then you might believe that no one likes the President, but you know that is just not true. There are a lot of people who like him."

"Really, Tim? I think you like the President, don't you?"

Pam was trying to back Tim into a corner. Tim did not like or dislike the President. He did feel that the President was treated unfairly by most of the media.

"The President could cure cancer and the *New York Times* would find a way to criticize it," Tim would often say, but a lot of the progressive Democrats had drawn a line in the sand. If you said anything positive about the President, then you must support him, and supporting a racist and homophobic President must mean that you were also a racist and homophobe.

"I don't hate him because my friends told me to," Tim finally responded.

That was a shot directed at Pam and at some of Pam's girlfriends. When Tim and Pam were together, Pam belonged to a couple of women-only groups, which was how Tim referred to them. Basically, these women would get together, have lunch, and bitch about their husbands or boyfriends, provided they had one to complain about. Tim found that harmless and even kind of funny until the most famous woman in the world decided to run for President.

"I tell you what," Pam said. Tim could tell she was getting mad. "If they did not stop her from winning, we would not be in the situation we are in today."

"No one stopped her from winning; she simply became overconfident and lost."

This of course was a simplistic explanation of the election results voters woke up to on that Wednesday morning. The reasons behind why the woman lost the election had taken on almost Kennedy-esque conspiracy proportions. There were now countless theories about who was behind it all, and the Agency was a prime suspect, of course.

"Well, Sebastian feels that the Agency stopped her," Pam said, trying to defend her statement.

"Really?" Tim asked Pam. "I didn't know Sebastian had reached that level of management."

The CIA, like other government agencies, was a top-down organization, meaning that decisions were made at the highest level, which was usually the Executive Branch or Presidential level. The notion that the U.S. government was full of rogue department heads willing to deviate from official policy for their own political gains was just not true, but that did not stop many from believing it. Believing that there was some unseen hand controlling everything seemed to be a comfort to many. Closer to home, Tim feared that Sebastian was preying on Pam's conspiracy fears.

"Pam, I really do not feel that it would have been possible for anyone to rig a national election. Not the Russians, not the Chinese, not the Agency. Sure, it's possible that someone might want to try, but the fact that the United States does not have a uniform system of voting for the President in a way protects that from happening."

Pam had stopped at a traffic light, which gave her the chance to turn and give her husband a look that said, "Are you crazy?"

But Tim continued his explanation. "Just about all the states have a different method of voting, counting votes, and reporting vote counts. In other words, there is no central database of votes that can be hacked and manipulated. The worst thing that could happen would be a switch to internet voting. Now, those results could be easily manipulated."

"In your opinion," Pam reminded him.

"Yes, in my opinion."

"Well, in my opinion, Tim, this election was rigged, and the simple fact that she won the popular vote tells me that."

"She won the popular vote because the entire state of California voted for her," Tim exaggerated. "And if this country were to dump the Electoral College in favor of the popular vote, then only the states with the highest populations would decide the Presidential election."

"I think you're using Tim math." This was what Pam called Tim's somewhat dubious calculations. "What you're saying might be true if the entire state's electorate voted for one candidate over another, but when would that happen, Tim?"

Pam had a point, and since a President had only been elected by not winning the popular vote two or three times, there was probably no good reason why the Electoral College system could not be dropped. It bothered Tim that states with small populations would lose more of the little clout they had, though.

US Route 15 began its winding descent down to the Potomac River and the Point of Rocks Bridge. Pam would have to make a left turn onto Lovettsville Road into the oncoming traffic. It was a tricky driving maneuver, not to mention that drivers making the turn also had to be aware of the possibility of being rear-ended.

"They really do need to improve this intersection," Pam commented as she successfully made the left turn.

"There is a lot of traffic heading in from Maryland," Tim observed.

"And it's the weekend," Pam replied. "You should come down here during rush hour. Commuters coming to Virginia from Maryland, commuters driving from Virginia over to Maryland. The traffic is just insane."

Nothing like two states divided by a river, Tim thought to himself. Maryland and Virginia, New York and New Jersey, New Jersey and Pennsylvania. Everyone always seemed to be fighting over some land use issue or, in this case, building a new bridge and improving a dangerous intersection. But the area was still nothing short of beautiful, and even Tim would not be happy if it was disrupted.

Pam took the hard-left turn into her driveway like a pro. To begin with, the driveway was difficult to see, which that was done by design. The last thing anyone needed was weekend sightseers asking for directions. The first 25 feet of the driveway was gravel and appeared uninviting. That was also done on purpose to hopefully deter any motorist who may have accidently taken a wrong turn from proceeding any further. Those who did were met by the safe house security detail. Tim did not know how many men and women were on the property or even where they were located exactly, but he knew they were there.

Pam was not happy about what the driveway was doing to her new S560, and she told Tim about how she tried to get the Agency to pave the driveway all the way down to Lovettsville Road, but they refused. Pam had very little influence over safe house security.

"Does the Loudoun County Sheriff's Office know about this place?" Tim asked Pam as the S560 made the slow climb up the hill to the house.

"Oh, they are aware we're here," was all she would say about it.

Darrel was waiting to greet them as Pam pulled up in front of the house. "How was your shopping, Mrs. Hall?"

"Just the usual headache, Darrel. Would you be a dear and take the groceries into the kitchen?"

"Not a problem, Mrs. Hall," Darrel replied as Pam headed straight for the house.

"Do you need any help, Darrel?" Tim offered.

"No, Mr. Hall, we got it."

Tim was not sure who Darrel meant by "we," but a young woman in fatigues appeared out of nowhere and began to help Darrel with the bags of groceries. Where do they all come from? Tim once again thought to himself as he followed Pam through the front door.

Pam had disappeared somewhere in the large house. Tim looked in the kitchen, but he only saw Darrel and the young women in fatigues, who were now putting away the groceries. Tim thought about telling Darrel that he and Pam would take care of that but changed his mind. Tim hated putting groceries away.

Thinking that Pam had gone to the secret security room, Tim decided to see if he could catch her coming out. Tim walked to the sunroom, which was the last room in the house. It only had a door that opened out to a patio and a swimming pool that had been covered for the winter, so Tim turned and walked back to the dining room. The door to the security room had to be somewhere in between.

Tim heard what sounded like a vacuum starting, then Pam's voice. "It's over here, Tim."

He walked back to the sunroom. "Over here," Pam said again, and Tim turned around.

There were two bookcases built into the wall. In between the two bookcases was a small table with a vase on top of it. Tim had checked the two bookcases, but neither of them appeared to be doors. That was because the actual door was behind the small table, opening inwards. The vase was glued to the table.

The doorway made a small opening, and it would have been difficult for anyone with a waist greater than 45 inches to fit through. "Pretty cool, huh?" Pam exclaimed. "I designed this myself."

"But not for the overweight," Tim replied.

"No, not for fat people." Pam was only politically correct when she wanted to be.

The secret room was not very wide. Only about six feet, Tim estimated. On one end of the room, Tim saw a ladder which appeared to lead to the second floor and then to the roof. There was a metal desk and a filing cabinet with combination locks on each drawer. At the other end of the room was a metal door that Tim assumed led to the outside of the house. The locks on the door appeared to be very sophisticated.

On the wall, there were 15 video monitors showing the rooms in the house and parts of the grounds around the house. Below that, there were four telephones that Tim figured were direct hardlines to someplace. Most likely the central security station at Langley. There were also three laptop computers that controlled the entire system. Below that was a mini refrigerator. Tim opened that, saw some cans of Coke Zero, and took one.

"Don't be spraying Coke all over my monitors," Pam warned, but Tim ignored her.

"So, show me how it all works."

"Well, first we have the property." Pam had her hand on a joystick, which moved from one camera to the next.

Tim could see the traffic on Lovettsville Road and then at the intersection of Lovettsville Road and US Route 15.

"See, still quite a lot of traffic," Pam remarked.

Next, Pam moved back to the safe house property. For the most part, all they saw were woods until she came upon two members of the Security Detail, who were leaning against a tree smoking a cigarette. Both were dressed in armor and armed with M16 automatic rifles.

"I will have to speak with Darrel about these two. I've caught them fucking off before. However, speaking of fucking, Tim, check this out."

Tim looked to his right and saw two figures in bed. "Let's get a close up," Pam said, laughing as she zoomed in.

It was a video of Pam and Tim from the night before. Tim was somewhere between Pam's legs, which she seemed to be enjoying.

"I need to make you a DVD of this in case I'm not around, honey. Do you think your girlfriend would like a copy?"

"She's not my girlfriend," Tim repeated. He did not comment on the video.

"Don't worry, dear, all of these are password protected," Pam remarked. Tim took that to mean that Pam had videotaped both times they had made love.

"Why, Pam? Were you planning on posting them on YouTube?"

"No, but now that you mention it..."

Pam placed her hand in Tim's lap and began to unbutton his blue jeans. "You know, Tim, this is the one room in the house where there are no cameras."

At that point, they both stood up without saying a word. Tim took Pam by the shoulders and pushed her gently against the other office wall, so she was facing him. He began to kiss her as he reached down to her waist and pulled her knit sweater over her head, throwing it on the workstation.

"Be careful," Pam giggled, whispering, "That's a

couple of hundred thousand dollars," into Tim's ear.

Pam was wearing sports bra, which Tim removed by lifting it over her head. Tim began to work his way down by kissing both sides of Pam's neck until he reached her breasts, which he began to kiss one at a time. He then placed his head between them. Meanwhile, Pam reached down to undo her jeans. They were extremely tight-fitting, and she needed Tim's help removing them. With Pam's jeans now down to her ankles, Tim began to work his way back up, kissing Pam's inner thighs as he moved. Pam just about lost it at that point and almost demanded that Tim get inside her right now.

The floor was covered by industrial-grade carpet, but someone had left a blanket on one of the chairs. Pam grabbed the blanket with her free hand. Her other hand was on Tim's member to make sure he was as hard as possible. "Godammit, Tim, take me!" she demanded.

"How do you want it?" Tim was now teasing her.

"Any goddam way. Just do it!"

And they did.

Like many guys, Tim had given up trying to determine if a woman had an orgasm or not. They were very good at faking it, after all. However, Tim was pretty sure that Pam had reached that magical place.

The entire room smelled like sex afterwards, and the blanket was big enough that both Tim and Pam were able to wrap themselves up in it.

"I think I may have made a mistake, Tim," Pam said.

"What kind of a mistake?"

"I'll tell you later. Right now, let's take a nap."

That was an excellent idea, Tim thought as he began to fall asleep.

"Mrs. Hall, are you okay?" Someone was yelling this in Tim's dream. Were they talking about his mother? What the hell was his mother doing here?

Tim opened his eyes and at first had no idea where he was. Then he saw the glow of the TV monitors and realized that he was still in the security room of the safe house. Pam had already risen from the floor.

"Yes, yes, I'm fine, Darrel. Mr. Hall and I will be out in a minute."

"Okay, Mrs. Hall, just checking," Darrel replied.

"So how long have you been Mrs. Hall?" Tim asked.

"I don't know what you mean, Tim. I was Mrs. Hall the day we were married."

"When we were married, you kept your maiden name, Atkins. Why change it now?"

"I don't know, Tim. I guess I thought that going by Mrs. Hall instead of Ms. Atkins gave me a bit of legitimacy."

"Legitimacy? What's that supposed to mean?"

"Well, I guess what I mean is respect. We get some very creepy guests staying in this house, Tim, and not just people from the Agency. During the slow periods, we contract with the US Marshal Service, and they bring all kinds here. Insisting on being called Mrs. Hall creates a kind of separation between the guests, the security details, and me."

"So, you should thank me for giving you legitimacy," Tim pointed out.

"Tim, does this have something to do with me and Sebastian leaving you in Baltimore for the last two years?" Pam wondered.

So, it was two years now. Tim had originally thought that he'd been in Baltimore for four or five years, but now Pam was telling him that it was just two. Now that Tim was thinking about it, he really could not be sure how long he'd been in Charm City. It was like he had been semi-conscious or in a daze the entire time. Tim did recall that anytime he did think that he may have been recovering his memory, he would wake up the next day back in a daze. Dr. Gray, his neurologist, had told him that the retrograde amnesia would often have that characteristic of feeling on the cusp of recall, only to fall back into the abyss. "It's your brain protecting itself," Dr. Gray had told him time and time again, but Tim could no longer be sure about that.

"I'm sorry, Pam, it's all just this thing with my memory. Sometimes, I feel like I am on the verge of remembering everything—but then poof, it all goes away." Tim made a gesture to illustrate this with his hands.

"It's not a problem, dear. You had a horrible experience."

Tim almost believed that Pam was being sincere, but then he remembered yet again that this was Pam, a woman ruthless enough to kill her own mother if it meant getting what she wanted.

Tim and Pam were both now dressed, and Pam opened the door that led outside the house. The door was on the west side of the safe house, and the March sun was beginning to set. Tim figured that it must be around 6 p.m. and would be dark soon.

Darrel came around from the front of the house to meet them. "Darrel?" Pam began. "Please tell your two guys on the east side post to quit smoking cigarettes and fucking off. A troop of Girl Scouts could take them out. Tell them to pay attention to their surroundings."

"Yes, ma'am," Darrel answered. Tim was a little surprised that he didn't salute her.

As Pam and Tim began to walk away, Darrel called back, "Mrs. Hall? I think you better see this."

Pam turned and walked back to Darrel, who had his iPhone raised to show a text message from one of Darrel's contacts. "POTUS ill, taken to BNH," it said.

"Holy shit!" Pam swore under her breath.

She started for the house, and Tim followed.

CHAPTER 23

"Where the fuck is my cell phone?" Pam yelled as she walked in the front door. "Tim, ring it, would you?"

Tim did not believe that he had Pam in his contacts, but when he looked, there she was—Pam Hall. Tim selected the icon next to Pam's name, and a number with the area code of 571 appeared, but nothing else. "Figures," Tim said to himself.

Tim could hear a cell phone ring from the dining room. Pam was back in the sunroom but came running when her phone began to ring. Tim could only laugh now. "Even secret agents misplace their phones, but there's an app to prevent that," he thought. He may have even said that to Pam, but he could tell she wasn't in the mood to joke around.

In the dining room, Tim found Pam staring intently at her phone screen. Tim started approaching her, but she raised a hand to stop him. "The President has taken ill and been admitted to Bethesda Naval Hospital for observation," Pam said, but she appeared to be in a trance.

Tim recognized that the wheels were turning in Pam's brain as she tried to decipher what this could mean. He'd turned and started for the library when he heard Pam's voice again. "They've started to move. They've started to move without me. I have to call Sebastian."

Tim continued to the library.

When he reached it, he opened his phone, went to Google News, and started to scroll down the page. The President becoming ill and being admitted to the hospital would certainly be the top story, but all the news Tim found relating to the President was about China and tariffs. Tim checked the other news outlets such as CNN, the *Washington Post*, and Fox News, but could not find anything about the President becoming sick. Tim was sure that the news was true, but it hadn't reached the media yet.

It soon would. He wondered which outlet would report it first and guessed CNN, since they had sources (sometimes known as stringers) all over the DC metro area. Tim continued to scroll until he found a news item that did catch his eye. It was from TV Channel 2 News.

Prominent neurologist found dead in Fell's Point alleyway.

"Prominent neurologist Felix Gray was found dead this morning in an alley next to a well-known gay bar, the Pink Flamingo. Police are investigating a possible hate crime."

Tim thought that all murders involved a certain amount of hate, but the fact that his own doctor was apparently murdered was just a little too much of a coincidence. Tim was not aware that Dr. Gray was gay, but that really did not make any difference. There were lots of gay people out of the closet these days, so what was the big deal?

What bothered Tim was the conversation Dr. Gray and Tim had had during their last appointment. It did appear to Tim that Dr. Gray perhaps knew a little too much about the covert world Tim and Pam inhabited and knowing too much about any secrets could end up getting you killed.

"Sebastian." It was Pam voice coming from the rear of the house, but it sounded like she was speaking to a recording. "Sebastian, I have tried to call and text you on all of the phone numbers I have. Please call me and tell me what the hell is going on!"

Pam was sounding desperate now—and worse, panicky. That was one of Agent Pam Atkins-Hall's weak points. She did have an inclination to panic and had shown that years ago at spy school. As a matter of fact, it almost resulted in her being tossed from the program, until Tim had helped her work on it. Tim, strangely enough, never did panic and had always felt that panicking was a waste of energy—energy that otherwise could be used to figure out what to do.

Pam came into the library and headed straight for the bar. She poured herself a shot of Jack Daniels and drank it in one gulp. She poured herself another and sat down directly opposite Tim. Her head was bowed, and she appeared to be staring at the brown drink in her shot glass. She then swallowed that as well and looked at Tim.

"What does it all mean, Tim?"

"Well, it's possible that the President has not

been poisoned and is really sick...but if that were the case, Sebastian should be on the phone with you right now telling you so. But he's not."

"No," Pam agreed, "he's not."

"So, let's now assume that the President has been poisoned and that the other conspirators have decided for one reason or another to cut you out of the plan. In other words, Pam, they have decided to move forward without any input from you; and that might be a good thing, because once you go down this road, there's no turning back. You would be looking over your shoulder for the rest of your life."

"Yes, Tim, but the thing is that I have already gone down the road."

"Tell me how, Pam."

Tim watched Pam lift her head and stare at the ceiling. She sniffled a little, and for a second Tim thought that his wife might be crying. As she brought her head back down and looked at him, though, Tim could see that she was not.

"It was my idea to bring you back from the dead, Tim. I sold it to Ajacks and to Sebastian. They were not for it, but I felt that you could be useful. You were always very good at making things happen, and I thought you would be a good asset."

An "asset" in the world of espionage was not a particularly good position to hold. Assets did supply critical information and perform important functions, but, at the end of the day, they were usually expendable. Tim had thought from the beginning that Toby and Mary Ann were assets, but he'd never realized he was one as well.

He did not show his disappointment to Pam. "Okay, so you brought me back in. What else?"

"Well, I think that I could probably take credit for the entire idea of poisoning the President."

This was what Tim had been afraid of hearing. Pam was in too deep, which probably meant that this was not the end of her (and, for that matter, Tim's) involvement. The other conspirators were keeping them around, but for what purpose?

Tim thought he had a pretty good guess. "Pam," he began, making sure he had her attention, "when a president is assassinated, the public usually wants to know two things. How did it happen, and who did it?"

Tim looked Pam squarely in the eyes. "When the President dies, they will tell the public how, but next they will need to tell them who, and I'm afraid that will be you and me."

Pam sat for a minute as she let Tim's words sink in. Then she calmly got to her feet, walked over to the bar, and made two vodka martinis. She handed one to Tim and sat next to him again. "So, what do you think we should do about that?"

"First, I think you need to fill me in on some missing information. What do you know about the treatment I received in the Dominican Republic?"

"Well, I know what Sebastian told me. He

thought that perhaps your retrograde amnesia could be better treated in Santa Domingo."

"Assuming that I am suffering from retrograde amnesia."

"And what makes you think that you're not suffering from amnesia, Tim?"

"I will get to that in a second. First, do you know a woman doctor named Lockwood and a fat guy named Justice?"

"I assume that the fat guy named Justice is also a doctor?" Pam asked.

"Yes, both are doctors. Lockwood and Justice, and they have a practice in the medical building next to Lansdowne Hospital."

"No, I don't. Why do you ask?"

"I saw Dr. Lockwood at the Wegmans pharmacy this afternoon, except in Santa Domingo she went by the name Nurse Jennifer."

"And?"

"And, what were these two doing in the Dominican Republic? Why would two doctors from Leesburg, Virginia, pretend to operate an embryonic stem cell research center in a foreign country?"

"For fun and profit? How the hell am I supposed to know?"

"It just doesn't pass the commonsense test, Pam. There would be thousands of doctors in the Dominican Republic who would do anything you paid them to do. Why bring these two down from Virginia?" Tim paused. "Unless they already knew something about me. Something about my case. They have answers, Pam. Answers that you and I need to know."

"So how do we get these answers, Tim?" Pam wondered.

"I need to have an after-hours conversation with both doctors, but I will need your help."

"Sounds like a gun and duct tape job," Pam pointed out. "Do you have any other felonies in mind? Perhaps we should knock over a bank on our way back home."

Despite Pam's sarcasm, Tim could tell that she was beginning to consider how to best proceed. Pam got up from the couch and walked over to the computer, tapping some keys and then moving the mouse around.

"Well, they are both internists—and according to their website, they are open Monday until four o'clock. There is a picture of the practice, Tim, and it looks like there may only be one other person. A receptionist nurse type. It looks like we could take and control the office, but not for longer than for ten to twenty minutes. It's a big office building with too many variables. We certainly would not want to hang around for too long."

"Too many variables" was Pam's way of saying that too many unexpected things could happen. Friends and family dropping by...UPS drivers delivering packages...anything that could result in Tim and Pam losing control of the situation.

"Why don't we arrange for a home visit, Tim? We could get them as they walked in the door."

"I guess it depends if they have kids. I really don't want to do a home invasion and traumatize any kids," Tim said.

"That's what I love about you, Tim. You're so fucking considerate. Our lives are on the line, but you're worried about giving some kid a nightmare." Pam was laughing as she said this, but she was completely serious.

"Let me see if I can find out where these two live, assuming they do live together," Pam added as she typed more information into the database. As an active agent, Pam had access to personal information that a marketing executive would die for.

"Wow!" she exclaimed after a few seconds. "These two live in a really exclusive community. A gated one, but that should not be a problem. Perhaps we should get them before they head out for work."

"No, we get them as they're going into their office. That way, no one gets suspicious."

"Shit, Tim, now that we know where they live, let's just drive over there in the morning, knock on the door, and walk right in."

Pam's plan was so simple that Tim felt stupid for

not thinking of it before.

He was about to start making plans for the Sunday morning visit when Pam's iPhone began to ring. Pam had left the phone on the coffee table, and Tim picked it up before Pam could reach it. The phone indicated that Sebastian was calling.

"Give me my phone, Tim!"

"Cool down, Pam, and think for a minute. I guarantee you Sebastian will call back."

"Think about what, Tim? I need to know what's going on!"

"What's going on, Pam, is that Sebastian is setting a trap for us. He will first apologize for not picking up the phone when you called, then tell you that everything is okay. He will invite himself over tomorrow and offer to take us out for lunch or something, but as soon as we leave this property, you, me, and most likely Mary Ann, assuming she is not already dead, will be murdered. The three of us will be blamed for poisoning the President, and they will use that goddamn fork I made as evidence."

"Well, you have it all worked out, smart guy, but has it occurred to you that just maybe you're wrong about everything?"

Tim was getting frustrated. "All I know is that the President of the United States is in the process of being murdered, and the perpetrators are going to need someone to blame. I am just a retired Agency drunk... but you, Pam, you are a star. And they are going to need a star to blame all of this on."

Pam's iPhone rang again, and Tim handed it back to her. "Go ahead, answer it."

Pam took the iPhone from Tim and walked to the back of the house. "Sebastian? Where in the hell—"

That was all Tim heard as Pam entered the sunroom and closed the door behind her. Two minutes later, she returned and sat down next to Tim.

"Sebastian said almost exactly what you said he would, Tim. He told me that everything was okay and that Ajacks had decided to start the plan sooner than he expected. He told me that the President has been admitted to Bethesda Naval Hospital. Next he said that he wanted to come over Sunday and take you, me, and Mary Ann out to lunch."

"And what did you tell him?"

Pam laughed. "I told him that you and I would be spending the day in bed and for him not to come over until Monday. He really did sound disappointed and next suggested dinner, but I held firm and told him Monday."

"You know he may come over anyway."

"Yes, that did occur to me...but you and I do have a date with Lockwood and Justice."

Tim's iPhone began to make sounds suddenly, alerts as to some kind of news event. Tim looked down at his phone and saw that CNN was reporting that the President had been admitted to Bethesda Naval Hospital for an unknown condition. Next, Tim received a similar alert from the *Washington Post*. And ones from the *New York Times*, Fox News, NBC, ABC, and CBS. Then the BBC reported. Pam was receiving similar notifications. She looked at Tim.

"Well, I guess the news is out there now."

CHAPTER 24

Neither Pam nor Tim was particularly hungry, but they knew that eating was important. They both decided on BLTs, so Tim started to fry up some bacon. Meanwhile, Darrel came into the kitchen to ask if everything was okay. Pam said that it was, but she did need to speak with him, and they both walked outside. Tim wondered what Pam might need to tell Darrel that she could not say in front of him and asked her about it when she returned.

“Darrel takes orders from me, Tim, and me alone. If I started giving him orders in front of you, then he might become suspicious I was being coerced.”

“Okay, I get it. So, what orders have you given Darrel?”

“I told him that we’re on total lockdown until Sunday morning, which means nobody gets in.”

“Or out?” Tim asked.

“Now why would you want to leave here on such a dark and stormy night?”

Pam was kidding, since it was a very pleasant evening for the first week of March. But it showed Tim that she was getting her sense of humor back, which meant that Pam was beginning to relax.

Pam stuck her head in the refrigerator and began to remove items, then started chopping some lettuce and tomatoes for the sandwiches. "So, Tim, you mentioned a while back that you were beginning to have some doubts about your retrograde amnesia diagnosis?" she asked.

"Did you ever meet my neurologist, Pam?"

"I remember a little skinny man who seemed to have lots of nervous energy hanging around your hospital bed. Was that the guy?"

"Sounds like him. Anyways, he was found dead over in Fells Point Friday night."

Pam stopped chopping the lettuce for a second and looked at Tim. "When was the last time you had an appointment with him?"

"The day Sebastian revealed himself. As a matter of fact, Sebastian and Toby met me in the hallway outside his office."

"What did you and your doctor..."

"Dr. Gray," Tim supplied.

"What did you and Dr. Gray speak about during your appointment?"

"I made the appointment mostly because I was concerned about my mental state. I was apparently behaving rather bizarrely but had no memory of it."

"Oh, was that the time you ended up in the Johns Hopkins Psychiatric Ward?"

"You heard about that?" Tim asked in surprise.

"I heard that they caught you running up and down some street in Baltimore screaming your head off. I thought that you had finally gone around the bend, honey," Pam said with a sigh.

"Hey, I was afraid I had dementia like your father, Pam."

Pam's father's illness was a very sensitive subject. She'd never visited her father after he had been diagnosed, which was a sore subject with the rest of Pam's family. Pam was also terrified that she would also develop the disease one day. Tim, of course, knew all of this and was aware that he needed to tiptoe around the subject.

"But Dr. Gray did not see any evidence of brain damage," he continued. "As a matter of fact, he commented that I appeared to have the brain of someone in their late 30s."

Pam continued to make dinner but appeared otherwise lost in thought. Tim thought that his wife was most likely revisiting her father's illness, beginning when he simply began to repeat himself. Pam's father's mental capacity quickly began to decline after that.

Tim knew that thinking about dementia would send Pam into a funk and was mad at himself for even mentioning it. "Earth to Pam, Earth to Pam," he said.

Pam looked at him. "I'm with you, Tim. Dr. Gray said you had the brain of a teenager."

"A thirty-year-old, Pam, but yes, that's what he said. He also said that people's brains tend to shrink over time, but my brain had not. But who knows? Maybe it was all complete bullshit."

"Okay, but I still don't get your point. You went to your neurologist, and now he's dead. What's the connection?"

"Who told you about my amnesia, Pam?"

"Sebastian told me when I visited you at Johns Hopkins. You had no clue who I was. You had no clue who Sebastian was. You also had no clue who you were." Pam pointed her finger at Tim as she said this.

"Pam, what happened to me in China?" Tim asked.

"You were in an automobile accident, Tim."

"How do you know that, Pam? Were you there when the accident happened?"

"No, I had gone ahead."

"So how do you know I was in an accident?"

Pam frowned. "Sebastian was able to get a message to me."

"What kind of message? I mean, what did he say, Pam?"

"He said that you and he had been in an accident. He said that you were driving."

"I did not have an international driver's license. I

was not supposed to be driving."

"Well, it would not have been the first time you broke the rules, Tim," Pam answered sharply.

"True, but not this time," Tim answered. "But you did shoot Ms. Lin, didn't you, Pam?"

"Yes, but only because I was not planning on spending the rest of my life in a Chinese prison."

"And Sebastian told me that you were saving my life, Pam."

"Well, she did have the gun pointed at you, darling."

Pam had finished putting together the lettuce and tomato and bacon. "The sandwiches will be ready in ten minutes," she announced as she placed some slices of bread in the toaster. "Let's have another drink in the meantime."

Tim mixed two vodka martinis and sat down opposite Pam in the library.

"So, Tim, cut to the chase," she demanded. "What are you trying to tell me?"

"What I'm trying to tell you, Pam, is that I was not in any traffic accident in China. I was drugged by Sebastian. As a matter of fact, I have been drugged for the last two years. I have been drugged since I returned from China by the late Dr. Gray. He was giving me Propofol without my knowledge."

"What is Propofol?" Pam asked.

"It's a drug used to put people to sleep, but a recent drug test found that I appeared to have quite a lot of it in my system. Apparently, Dr. Gray was administering it to me in timed-release capsules. Propofol also has quite the effect on the memory, Pam. Almost like amnesia."

Pam looked at Tim incredulously. "I'm not sure if I like your tone of voice, Tim. Are you suggesting that I had a role in this plot?"

"I don't know, Pam. You'll have to tell me. I was told that you were dead. Why?"

"Because I wanted you out of my fucking life, Tim. You and your constant whining and complaining. You were holding me back. No one would give me a chance for any station manager position because they all knew that if they hired me, they also got fucking you."

Tim was very surprised at Pam's outburst. He'd been hoping that Pam was not part of the conspiracy to keep him drugged, but he never suspected that she was responsible for telling Tim that she was dead. It had never occurred to Tim that he had been any kind of drag on Pam's career. Tim viewed Pam's lack of success at upper management as her own fault, but perhaps she had a point. Tim's lack of seriousness on and off the job certainly did not endear him to anyone. He remembered one of his performance reviews. "Tim is an exceptional case officer," the comment read, "but his lack of seriousness does not help him or his team." At the time, Tim had been proud of that trait, but he'd never thought about the negative effects it might have had on his colleagues or his wife.

Pam continued. “So, Sebastian and I thought that if you were told that I was dead, you would just accept it and not bother trying to find me. Trying to find a wife you didn’t remember anyhow… I thought that I deserved a new start.”

“What about the Agency, Pam? Do they think I’m dead as well?”

“No, as far as the Agency is concerned, you transferred to the Social Security Administration and retired from there. You are just another retired federal employee under the jurisdiction of the Office of Personnel Management. You are only dead to me.”

“Dead to you, Pam? You know, I had forgotten what a sweetheart you could be. If that old Land Rover outside still runs, then just give me the keys and I’ll be out of here in ten minutes. It’s been fun playing house for the last couple of days, but maybe it’s time I get back to Baltimore.”

“Tim, we are way past that now. If what you say about Sebastian is true, then you will not make it to Monday morning, and that goes for me, too. Come on. Let’s get something to eat.”

Pam got up and headed back to the kitchen, taking the bread out of the toaster. Tim figured that Pam’s outburst was most likely related to his mentioning Pam’s father’s dementia, but he also knew that Pam was telling him the truth about wanting him out of her life. She was not the type of woman who would make such a statement, only to take it back an hour later.

Tim walked into the kitchen and sat at the table. Pam handed him a plate with a perfectly made BLT on it, just like one he would expect to be served at a restaurant. Pam never did anything half-assed.

They both ate in silence. Tim tried to let go of Pam's comments but found that her words still stung. He really did just want to leave and return to the life he had been living for the last two years.

Finally, Pam spoke. "So, you believe that Dr. Gray was administering drugs that resulted in amnesia? How would he be able to do that?"

Tim was not sure if Pam was interested in his hypothesis about how Sebastian and Dr. Gray were able to keep him dazed and confused for the last two years or if she was just trying to restart the conversation. As far as Tim knew, Pam may have been in on it as well.

"Dr. Gray wrote me prescriptions that he had me fill at a compounding pharmacy. He told me that a regular drug store like a CVS would not carry the medication and that it had to be made up special."

"What's the name of the pharmacy, Tim?"

"Kelley's Pharmacy, which is right down the street from Johns Hopkins. It's the pharmacy that makes the compounds used in lethal injections."

"That's appropriate, I guess," Pam said, but Tim felt that she was still just trying to make conversation and wasn't all that interested.

Tim continued anyway. "So, like a dummy, I just had it filled each month. Dr. Gray told me that the medication was to prevent seizures and headaches, plus it would help me sleep."

"And it worked?" Pam asked.

"Yeah, it worked great. I couldn't remember shit."

Pam and Tim went back to eating in silence. When they both finished, Tim collected the plates and glasses and placed them in the dishwasher. Pam stood up and motioned for Tim to follow her.

Pam headed down to the basement and asked Tim to take a seat at the worktable. Next, she walked over to the gun locker and entered the combination. She removed what appeared to be two pistols and four magazines of ammunition, then placed the items in front of Tim.

"I was hoping that we would not get to this point, but it appears we have," Pam said as she picked up one of the two weapons. She double-checked that the pistol was unloaded before handing it to Tim along with the two magazines. "Have you been certified on this weapon, Tim?"

It was Tim's nature to make a joke about everything, and guns were no exception, but Pam's outburst about Tim's lack of seriousness had changed the tone of their relationship. "Yes, Pam, I've qualified on the range," he said.

"That's not what I asked you, Tim. Are you certified to handle this weapon?"

There was a difference. Qualified meant that you scored over 70% shooting at a fixed target, whereas certification meant that you had a complete understanding of how to operate the firearm. The GLOCK G19 9mm was the last weapon that Tim had trained on. The first weapon that Tim had ever handled in his life was a Smith and Wesson .38 caliber revolver, which everyone trained on at spy school, but it was years before Tim needed to carry a weapon on assignment. As a rule, spies did not carry guns. Only the ones in the movies did. Getting caught packing a gun by the local cops in many countries would get you thrown in jail and then deported, which would defeat the purpose of you being there in the first place. Plus, the old saying of "never pointing a weapon at someone unless you intend to use it" was very true, so the gun play was always best left to the contractors who had experience in shooting at and killing people.

With all this said, there were occasions where a firearm was required. Tim and Pam were in one now. He picked up one of the magazines and closed his eyes as to try and determine its weight.

"They're 24s," Pam remarked referring to the number of bullets in the magazine.

Tim was about to push the magazine into the handle of the luger when Pam stopped him. "I would prefer that you did not have a loaded firearm in the house, Tim."

"An unloaded gun is kind of worthless, Pam," he

said. But he placed both the gun and the clip back on the table.

“Well, assuming we will be okay for today, before we do anything else, let’s go over to the range and get some practice.”

“Where is the range?” Tim asked, thinking that they would have to drive to Leesburg.

“Just behind the house.” Pam pointed in the general direction. “We will need to get up early, so don’t stay up too late.”

Pam had pulled back and released the slide on her Glock 19, and it made a distinct click. She turned and headed back upstairs.

“Don’t worry, mom, we’re going to bed right now,” Tim replied, but Pam was already out of hearing range. Just as well, he thought. She probably would not have found Tim’s comment particularly funny.

CHAPTER 25

Despite Pam's wishes, Tim loaded the Glock after she had gone to bed, then walked through the house to make sure all the doors were locked. There was no reason to make it too easy for anyone coming in, although he did agree with Pam that it would be unlikely for Sebastian and Toby to try anything tonight. As far as Sebastian knew, Pam did not suspect that she had been double-crossed, so any planned assault on the Lovettsville Road safe house could wait until Sunday or Monday.

Satisfied that all the doors were locked, Tim sat in the library and switched on the TV. The channel was on CNN, which had apparently decided to call the President's illness "The Crisis in the White House." CNN must have had ten different reporters on the story, plus another six talking heads to comment. Fox News was also offering wall-to-wall coverage, but they did not seem to have to the same number of reporters and talking heads as CNN. MSNBC was doing one of their usual "the President should be in jail" shows but were suggesting that perhaps he was only pretending to be sick so he would not have to go to jail. MSNBC was making it loud and clear to their audience that they were going to make sure that the President would not get away with that. On the other hand, the four networks did not see any reason to interrupt their regularly scheduled programing in order to stand at the front gate of the Bethesda Naval Hospital and repeat the same information repeatedly.

Tim heard the outside door to the kitchen open and figured that it must be Darrel, but he picked up his gun from the coffee table and put it in his pocket anyway. He headed to the kitchen, where Darrel was making a pot of coffee.

"Hi, Darrel. Is everything okay?"

"Yes, Mr. Hall. Everything is fine."

"How is the President doing?" Tim asked, figuring that Darrel must have some inside information.

Darrel laughed. "My understanding is that he has a tummy ache. That's why everyone is so excited."

Oh, I bet he has one hell of a tummy ache, Tim thought to himself. The real problem for the doctors would be determining which poisons were used. Different poisons had different antidotes and treating the President for one but not the other could have deadly consequences.

"Is that why we're locked down, Mr. Hall? Is that why you have a Glock 19 9 in your pocket?"

"Right now, Darrel, no one is sure about anything or anyone, and that includes Mr. Oak. I get that you don't know anything about me, Darrel, but Mrs. Hall is calling the shots, and I think you know that above all else, you can trust Mrs. Hall."

Darrel nodded to indicate that he understood.

"You can tell Mrs. Hall that no one will penetrate the perimeter tonight or any night that I am here."

"I will, Darrel, and thank you."

Darrel poured his thermos full of black coffee and headed back outside as Tim watched.

"I just wish I could trust Mrs. Hall," Tim said to himself.

Tim walked back to the library and opened his iPhone. There was a text message from Mary Ann, but all Tim saw when he opened the message were three question marks. Tim decided to call her, but, at that moment, his cell phone rang.

"Tim?" It was Mary Ann's voice.

"Mary Ann, where are you?"

"I'm back at your condo. Toby brought me back here just now."

"Are you okay?" Tim wanted to know.

"I'm fine, Tim, but I'm confused. What's going on?"

Tim was at a loss about what to tell Mary Ann. He was happy that she was away from Toby and Sebastian...but for how long?

"Mary Ann, in the freezer of my refrigerator, I have some money hidden. Take it and get out of town."

"I'm not leaving without you," she protested. "I know you are in trouble, but you need to tell me what's going on."

"Where is Sebastian? Is he in the room with you now?"

"No, Sebastian and Toby have both gone off. I don't know where, but Toby told me that when he comes back, we are going to go back to Las Vegas. He said that Sebastian told him that our work is just about finished here. But I'm not leaving without you, Tim."

"Can you get your hands on a car?"

"I already have a car, Tim."

It hadn't occurred to Tim to wonder if Mary Ann had a car or not. He'd never thought to ask.

"Really? What kind of car do you have?"

"It's a red 2012 Toyota Camry, and neither Toby nor Sebastian knows that I have it. I keep it in a garage over by the hospital."

"That's fantastic. Anyway, if you look in my freezer, you will find about ten thousand dollars in cash and some gold coins. Take that and head for Leesburg, Virginia. There is a Red Roof Inn right off US Route 15. Check in under the name Mary Ann Sky Horse."

"Mary Ann Sky Horse?" she repeated doubtfully.

"Yes, that's your new Native American name."

"Well, okay, Tim." Mary Ann still sounded unsure.

"And Mary Ann, ask for a room around back and off the road."

"Okay, Tim," she agreed again. "Anything else?"

"Yes. When you leave my condo, leave the lights on and go out by the loading dock area. We must assume you're being watched. Do you know how to get from Baltimore to Leesburg?"

"No, not really, but isn't it close to Dulles Airport?"

"Yeah, about fifteen or so miles. Stay on the interstates and toll roads. When you get here, send me a text."

"Okay, Tim, I got it."

"Wonderful. Now, please be careful."

"I will, Tim."

"Okay. Love you."

"I love you too, Tim."

Tim put down the iPhone and turned his attention back to CNN. Although the sound was turned down, he could tell what the four talking heads were discussing. What happens if the President were to die? For Christ's sake, Tim thought, some of these assholes just can't wait. He recalled the day that John F. Kennedy was shot in Dallas, and how some of his second-grade classmates were happy about it and said as much. As Tim became older, he understood that these children were just repeating their parents' opinions of the man; but it still gave him a creepy feeling that any American would celebrate the death of their President, no matter what their political persuasion.

Tim's phone beeped, letting him know that he'd received a text. It was from Mary Ann. "On my way," it said, followed the three hearts.

Tim figured that he would get Pam to drive him to Leesburg to find Lockwood and Justice. After that, he would ditch Pam and hook up with Mary Ann and take off to Canada or Mexico. Of course, that all depended on whether Mary Ann was indeed by herself and it wasn't a trap.

"Tim?" Pam was calling to him from upstairs. "Are you coming to bed?"

"Do you care?" Tim responded.

"Yes, I want to speak with you."

Tim turned off the TV, grabbed his phone and Glock, and headed upstairs.

Pam was waiting for him on the landing. "Is that a loaded gun?" she demanded.

"Yes, Pam, I have loaded my firearm, and I hope you've done the same."

Pam seemed to let the no-loaded-guns-in-her-house issue go. Tim continued to his room, knelt by his bed, and placed the gun between the top and bottom mattresses.

"Well, I just hope the safety is on," Pam said as she stood in the door.

Tim turned around to face her. "So, what do you want to talk about, Pam?"

“Us. I would like to talk about you and me.”

Tim wanted to tell Pam that, as far as he was concerned, there was no “us”—but that sounded too much like a line in some movie. “Okay, Pam, let’s talk about us,” he agreed.

Pam pulled up a chair and sat down. “Tim, I believe that our marriage was over a long time ago, and that you and I were just going through the motions of being married. So, I was planning on asking, or suggesting, I should say, that you and I call it quits when we returned from China.”

“Yes, China,” Tim repeated. “It funny to me how China keeps coming up.”

“I guess it was the tipping point. Do you remember anything about that operation now?”

“No, Pam. All I know is what you and Sebastian have told me.”

“You and I were meeting Lilly Lin at her house. She was going to tell us who in the United States was passing on the source codes to a number of computer programs, but you also thought that perhaps I should come on to Lilly in a sexual way.”

“If you say so, Pam, but I remember none of this.”

“Well, you did, and that’s not the first time you’ve suggested that I start lesbian affair with a woman we needed as an asset. I think it turned you on.”

"Pam, I'm sorry if any of this made you uncomfortable, but we were there to do a job, not to party. You've been playing this game for too long now to all of a sudden decide that the Agency has exploited you sexually but please finish your story."

"You are missing the point, Tim. I have laid my body and soul out for this company, and all I get is a nice house to live in rent-free as long as I'm willing to babysit a bunch of creeps."

Tim wondered for a second if Pam also considered him a creep but thought that he'd better not ask. He now had a clue what was bothering his wife. "So, this is all about you not getting a station assignment at an embassy?"

Most US embassies had a CIA station that was known to everyone, and the station chief was a known member of the Agency. No more covert or undercover work, everything right out in the open. To many, it was a plum assignment, provided you were in a relatively safe country. On the other hand, Tim knew a Chief of Station who was assigned to a country that was so unsafe he was forced to sleep in a cage.

"It's just not fucking fair, Tim. I shot and killed Lilly Lin to save us, and management is holding that against me."

Pam was becoming visibly upset, and Tim knew he had to calm her down. "Pam, look at me," he said, and Pam looked up. "Tell me how it all happened."

"I took Lilly's hand and told her that I would like to get to know her better. She stood up and walked to the door. Next thing I know, she's holding a gun on you, Tim, and demanding that you get down on your knees. She then says that we are under arrest for spying and starts to make a phone call, but she is looking at you, not at me. I had a Glock 19 strapped to my ankle, which I pulled and shot Lilly. The bullet hit her in her neck, and blood was everywhere. Sebastian then came running in from outside. You were still on your knees, but you should have seen your face."

"Pam, you say that Sebastian came running into the apartment. Are you sure about that?"

"Positive. He took us downstairs and put me in a car with one of our Chinese contacts. You and Sebastian jumped in the other car, which is the one you had the accident in."

"But was I driving?"

Pam had to think for a second.

"I'm pretty sure that Sebastian was driving."

"And you said Sebastian came into the room after you shot Lilly?"

"Yes, but why are you asking?"

"Because Sebastian told me that you and I came running out of the building and jumped in the car. He said that I shoved him over and demanded to drive. Maybe it's a small detail, but then again, maybe not."

"What are you getting at, Tim?"

"What if there was no accident, Pam? What if the China trip had all been for something other than to determine who was leaking intellectual property? Perhaps I was drugged in China and remained drugged."

"Well, that's an awful long time to stay drugged, Tim."

"Yes, it is, and Sebastian would need a lot of help and cooperation to make that happen."

"Which is why you think I was in on it."

"Yes, Pam. I don't want to believe that about you, but..." He trailed off.

"But you wouldn't put it past me," Pam finished. "Is that what you're trying to tell me, Tim?"

"I don't want to think that you dislike me enough to do something like that to me, Pam."

Pam paused for a second, then began to speak. "I don't dislike you, Tim, and the last two days reminded me how much I enjoy having you around. You are very good company, and I always liked having sex with you because you really care about me getting off, and a lot of guys don't even try."

"So why do I feel like I'm about to get a big 'but'?" Tim joked.

"Because you are, Tim. When you and I were both assigned to Langley, everyone used to refer to me as your mother. The other women would say things like, 'What has your boy Timmy done now?' Or 'Go home and take care of Timmy.' And then there were the 'Your husband is just wonderful' comments. I mean, I was living in your shadow, but what really pissed me off about you is how easy you made everything look."

Tim had been semi-aware of how competitive Pam could be, but he never thought that she was jealous of his career. What was really stupid was Tim's beliefs that Pam had been proud of some of his accomplishments. He supposed he'd been wrong.

"So why the hell did you marry me, Pam?"

"Because I wanted a guy, and I wanted to be married. Just about all women want to be married to somebody, Tim, but in this job, it's hard to find someone to be married to. I dated a lot of guys before I ran into you again at Langley, but they all wanted me to quit the Agency."

"Until I came along."

"You're a real good guy, Tim."

Somehow, being a real good guy did not sound the same as being the love of someone's life, but Tim let it go.

"Look, Pam, I'm sorry. I truly am. I had no idea I was doing any of this to you. I was just trying to get along in my career the best way I knew how. I had no intention of trying to make you look bad or, maybe more importantly, feel bad."

Pam walked across the room and kissed Tim on the forehead. "I guess that's all I really wanted to hear," she answered. "An apology. Would you like to lie down with me here on your bed?"

"Sure, Pam," Tim replied as he kicked off his shoes and lay down. Pam climbed onto the bed next to him and placed her head on his shoulder.

What a bunch of bullshit, Tim thought to himself. Why should he be expected to shoulder Pam's career as well as his own? But his apology had seemed to satisfy her for the time being.

Tim found himself drifting off to sleep and thought about waking Pam so she could return to her own room but decided against that. If someone broke in intending to kill them, they would at least be easy to find.

CHAPTER 26

Morning came, and Tim woke up to see that Pam was still asleep next to him with her head on his shoulder. This was his wife, he thought. This was the woman who he had been married to for twenty-five years.

The fact that Tim had been away from Pam for the last two years was really not of any consequence. During their years at the Agency, they'd been apart for as long as three years. Since married agents could not be assigned to the same location, they were usually thousands of miles apart. Sure, they would meet up from time to time in romantic locales such as Paris and Rome, but they never seemed to live with each other for more than a few months at a time. Tim had thought that the safe house assignment would finally give them a chance to be together, but that was before China, the accident, and Sebastian Oak. It had never occurred to Tim that Pam did not love him until the previous night's conversation, but now that he thought about it, Pam had rarely said that she loved him. Sure, there would be a "love you" here and a "love you" there, but never a conversation about what they thought of one another.

Tim heard a noise in the kitchen, which meant that the security detail was about to change. Tim figured that he should speak with Darrel before he left for the day. He gently elbowed Pam. "Hey, wake up. You slept in your clothes."

Pam opened her eyes, turned, and looked at the clock. "Oh, my goodness. It's seven."

She got up and ran to her room. Tim heard the door to the bathroom shut and figured that Pam would be in there for a while.

He reached between the mattresses and pulled out the Glock 19 9mm, then laid it on the bed. He did not have a holster for the weapon and thought about asking Pam for one, but he decided that it would fit in his jacket pocket along with the two ammo clips.

Tim found some of his old clothes to put on. He placed the Glock in his jacket and yelled, "Pam, I'm going downstairs to speak with Darrel."

After hearing Pam say something that sounded like "Okay, honey" in reply, Tim headed down to the kitchen.

Darrel was seated at the table filling out some paperwork. "Good morning," Tim said. "How is our Commander in Chief today?"

"As far as I know, he's doing okay. Nothing is happening at the hospital that would lead us to believe otherwise," Darrel answered.

If the President had passed away, then there would be all kinds of movement at Bethesda Naval Hospital as well as around the city, so the fact that everything was quiet said a lot.

"Any more rumors about what might be wrong

with the President?" Tim asked.

"No, apparently it's still just something with his digestive system. I understand that the best gastroenterologists in the country have landed at Andrews Air Force Base."

Tim was impressed with whoever Darrel was texting. Flying in world-renowned physicians to attend to the President would certainly be a huge piece of news.

"You could make some cash leaking that to the press, buddy," Tim remarked, wishing instantly that he could take it back.

"We don't speak or leak to the media, Mr. Hall," Darrel said rather coolly. "We have integrity."

"And I wish more people did in this town, Darrel. Please accept my apologies. I often try to be the funny guy in the room, which just ends up getting me into trouble."

"Not a problem, Mr. Hall. I just wanted you to know that our guys don't leak information, and if I ever catch a member of my team speaking with a reporter, that will be the last reporter they speak with."

Tim was not sure how serious Darrel was, but decided not to pursue it. "So, Darrel, was there anything worth noting last night? Lost drivers looking for directions? Vehicles driving by the house slowly?"

Darrel frowned. "Are you and Mrs. Hall expecting an attack? I'm only asking because Mrs. Hall instructed me to look for the very same things."

Tim thought about how to answer this, then asked, "How old are you, Darrel?"

"Twenty-seven, Mr. Hall."

Tim nodded. "Mrs. Hall, I mean Pam and I, were in school together," he explained. "We call it spy school, but that's really not the official name or anything."

"Sure, Mr. Hall." Darrel was beginning to sound a little patronizing, as if he was speaking to his grandfather about the 1970s.

"Well anyhow, part of the training was about detecting threats, so they took a bunch of us to Richmond and paired us up. Pam and I were a pair. They placed us in this house and told us that we may or may not be attacked in the next 48 hours. Our job was to prevent that from happening. Pam and I were the only two students who passed. Everyone else did not."

"So, what happened, Mr. Hall?"

"There was this old lady crossing the street. Not in front of our house, but down at the corner. Well, there were these kids who seemed to hang out there every day, and two of them grabbed the old lady and started beating her. I mean, it was the most real beating you ever saw. I was about to go out there and do something—what, I don't know. But Pam told me to stop and take a position at the backdoor. We did, and bam, the bad guys came in the backdoor."

"So, was there a moral to all of this, Mr. Hall?" Darrel wondered.

Tim had to think for a moment and wondered what point he was trying to get across to Darrel. "The moral, Darrel, is to do what Mrs. Hall tells you. She is a much better spy than I ever was."

Darrel just smiled at Tim and his pointless story. "Mr. Hall, we're off at 9 a.m., so if the attack happens after that, the Charlie Team will have to handle it," he answered.

Tim had hoped to convey some inspirational story about how things are often not how they appeared, but in reality, the reason Tim and Pam had passed that test was because Pam followed General Order number one, which said, *I will guard my post and will not quit my post until properly relieved.*

One of their instructors at Camp Perry was a retired US Navy Chief Petty Officer who was a big believer in the General Orders, and Pam also took them very seriously. The fact that Tim and Pam did not quit their post because of the old lady was the reason they passed the assignment.

Pam came bounding down the steps dressed in a different weekend outfit—or, at least, different from yesterdays. Boots, tight blue jeans, and a blue and orange sweatshirt from the University of Virginia, where Pam had received her MBA. Tim had not been back to school since his recruitment, but Pam was a big believer in continuing education. Tim began to wonder if it bothered Pam that he had a Ph.D. from Berkeley. Like other things, school was just easy for Tim, and it almost never occurred to him that school was very hard for some.

"Good morning, Darrel. Did anything noteworthy occur last night?" Pam asked.

Darrel gave Tim a look, then turned to make an exit. "Mr. Hall will explain it to you, ma'am," Darrel yelled as he closed the door.

Pam looked at Tim quizzically. "Is everything okay?"

"Basically, yes. The President is still alive, but Darrel and the A Team are getting off duty in about an hour and a new team will be arriving, perhaps with new orders from Langley concerning us."

"They wouldn't dare," was Pam's first response, but then she reconsidered her statement.

"Sebastian could easily countermand the orders from protecting the perimeter to securing the entire property, which would mean that nobody leaves, including us," Tim said. "Pam, we've got to question the two doctors. They can tie everything together, which makes them..." He paused.

"Which makes them a liability," Pam finished. "Goddammit! While you and I were sniping at each other about our relationship, Sebastian and Toby were heading over here."

"I'm not sure about that, Pam. Sebastian and Toby were still in Baltimore as of 11 p.m. last night."

"And you know this how, Tim?"

Tim hesitated for a second. "I spoke with Mary

Ann last night," he admitted.

Pam shot Tim one of her looks. "Oh, I get it. You have a little spat with the wife, and you're on the phone to the girlfriend. You're no different than all the other assholes I've met in my life."

"Said the woman who told everyone that her husband was dead," Tim sniped.

"I think you have that turned around, honey. I told you I was dead so you would leave me the fuck alone."

Tim looked at the clock. It was 8:30, and the new security detail would probably be there by 8:45. If the new detail had orders that the property should be locked down, that would start immediately.

Tim turned to Pam. "Pam, if we don't get out of here soon, the whole Tim and Pam are dead thing may well turn out to be true."

Without a word, Pam ran back upstairs, then came back with her bag and a piece of paper, which she handed to Tim. The paper showed a picture of the home where the doctors resided along with its address.

"Here, you navigate," Pam ordered, walking out the front door to confer with Darrel. Pam next unlocked the Mercedes 560, signaling that it was time to go.

"May I ask what you were speaking with Darrel about?" Tim wondered.

"I asked him to call or send me a text if the new

security detail has any plans to change the security of the grounds. That is something you and I need to know before we come back here."

Pam took a right from the safe house driveway toward US Route 15, turning on the GPS. "I need to go to 23456 Farwell Dance Road in Leesburg, VA," she said.

"Stay on James Monroe Hwy for 5 miles," the computer responded.

"Okay, thanks," Pam replied.

"I don't think the GPS needs to be thanked, Pam."

"Courtesy is free, Tim, and it never hurts."

Tim almost expected the GPS computer to agree with Pam.

"Here, Tim, open this bag and find what looks like a couple of cop badges."

Tim opened Pam's bag to find two rolls of duct tape and some coils of rope as well as handcuffs and what appeared to be leg irons. There were also two blue folders with the words United States Marshal Service embossed on the front. The first ID had a picture of Pam, but with the name Wanda F. Fairfax. He handed the ID to Pam. "Here you go, Wanda."

Pam laughed. "The other one is yours." Tim opened the ID to find a picture of a man with thinning blond hair. It did not look at all like Tim. The name on the ID was Robert C. Boiling.

"I don't think anyone is going to believe I'm Agent Boiling."

"You are Deputy Marshal Boiling, Tim, and I am Marshal Fairfax. Actually, I am a Special Deputy Marshal since I supervise a safe house the Marshals use from time to time, but that badge has my real name, which needless to say we will not be using today."

"What about all of the duct tape, handcuffs, and leg irons?" Tim asked.

"Well, the duct tape and rope is from Home Depot, but all of the metal items are from the Marshals."

"What about the whips and harnesses and ball gags and that kind of stuff, Pam?"

Pam quickly turned her head and gave Tim one of her looks. "I'm not a fucking weirdo, Tim."

Tim thought that was debatable.

"In a quarter of a mile, turn left on Evans Pond Road," said the GPS.

Pam made the turn, and Tim saw several large homes situated on two-acre lots. "It's back here someplace," Pam told him.

"Turn right on Farewell Road," said the GPS.

"Gosh, what a name for a street," Pam remarked. "If Sebastian and Toby got here last night, then we may be the ones to discover the victims."

The gatekeeper shack for the gated community

where the two doctors lived was ahead. A middle-aged man was inside, watching a small TV. He wore a rent-a-cop type uniform.

"Okay, Tim, let me do the talking," Pam ordered.

"What happens if he doesn't let us in?"

"Then the guy will spend the day in the trunk, Tim—but it won't come to that. You were a covert agent, right? I would have thought you'd done this before."

Pam pulled up to the gatehouse, saying, "Good morning. My name is Marshal Fairfax, and this is Deputy Marshal Boiling. We have a meeting this morning," Pam handed their phony IDs to the gatehouse rent-a-cop.

"Who are you going to see?" the man wanted to know.

"If I tell you that, it would not be a surprise. The United States Marshal Service is not required to inform fugitives that we will be visiting; in fact, it's against the law."

"Okay, okay, okay," the rent-a-cop said, opening the gate. "But that's a pretty nice car for a couple of feds to be driving around."

"A drug dealer forfeited this to us. It does make a very nice undercover vehicle," Pam agreed.

"Okay. Have a nice day," said the rent-a-cop, returning to watching his TV.

"That took more time than I expected, and that

guy came very close to getting arrested," Pam said as she looked in the rearview to make sure the rent-a-cop was not calling the real police.

"You have arrived," the GPS said.

Instead of stopping, Pam did a drive-by. "Only see one car. You don't suppose they've gone to church, do you?"

"Somehow, I doubt that," Tim said.

Pam drove back around and parked about 500 feet from the house of the two doctors. They got out and began walking toward the large brick home. "I'll take the front door, you cover the back, Tim."

Pam was behaving like a real cop, which made Tim think that perhaps his wife had joined the wrong agency.

"You did bring your weapon?" she added, and Tim patted his right pocket. "Well, you better take it out. I don't know what these two are capable of."

Tim took out his Glock and held it in both hands, just as he'd been trained to do. He walked to the right side of the house and stopped. From this position, Tim was able to peer around the corner. Then he waited.

He could hear Pam gain entry to the house and speak to someone. Pam then came to the back door and called, "Tim? You can come in. They're not home. The housekeeper says that they went to their office in Leesburg."

Tim walked toward the sound of Pam's voice

and found her standing on the back deck of the home. "Come in," she ordered. "I need you to speak with the housekeeper."

Tim found a rather nervous Hispanic woman standing in the kitchen by the sink. She was visibly shaken, but she did seem to calm down some when Tim spoke Spanish to her. Their conversation lasted for almost two minutes, and Tim could tell that his wife was bothered by the fact that she did not understand what Tim was asking the woman. Tim then thanked the woman profusely but told her not to call her employers under any circumstances. The woman thanked Tim for being so understanding.

"Okay, Pam, let's go. But the senora has been a big help, so you may want to thank her. Since courtesy is free."

"Stuff it in your butt, Tim," Pam remarked as she walked out the front door. Tim smiled at the housekeeper and followed Pam back to the car.

"So, what was your new friend telling you about her employers that you found so fucking interesting?"

"You just hate it when I can do something that you can't, don't you, Pam?"

"Cut the shit, Tim, and tell me what the maid told you."

"She said that she heard them arguing last night and that they're planning on leaving town. To where, she did not know, but they are apparently freaking out. They are at their office right now, but she didn't know for how long."

Pam had already started the car and was speeding to the gate. The rent-a-cop got out of the booth to say something, but he quickly retreated. Pam obviously had no intention of stopping.

"Slow down, Pam! The last thing we need now is a ticket," Tim cautioned.

The Sunday morning traffic was light, and Pam's speed was approaching 80 mph. For some reason, the Commonwealth of Virginia had passed a law that considered speeds greater than 80 mph to be reckless driving, which carried almost the same penalties as driving under the influence of alcohol. On the other hand, the speed limit on some of the state's rural interstate highways was 70 mph, so a mere 10 mph over the speed limit would get you cited for reckless driving. Tim was sure that the state legislators in Richmond felt that they were just trying to protect the drivers from excessive speeds. After all, it was easy to pass laws, and the voters thought it looked good. Yet they were also applying undue pressure to the state police and court systems.

"I have never received a speeding ticket," Pam told Tim, "but not because I've never been pulled over."

"What do you do, flirt with the cop?"

"No, I just mention the name of the county's liaison officer and say that I'm on official Agency business. Most of them don't even check."

Most of the local police departments in the District, Maryland, and Virginia had an officer, usually a captain, who acted as a liaison between the local and Federal law enforcement and intelligence communities. Although the CIA was not a domestic law enforcement agency, there were situations where an agent might find themselves in a compromising position. In these types of cases, the liaison officer would step in... but not for the purpose of fixing speeding tickets.

"You certainly do push your luck," Tim remarked.

"Oh, cut me a break. You would do the exact same thing if you could."

They stopped at a traffic light in front of the local outlet mall. Pam took a post-it note off of the dashboard and scribbled a name on it, then handed the note to Tim.

"Look, if something happens to us today and I'm not around, call this guy. He will at least listen to what you have to say and won't think you're some kind of nut."

Tim looked at the note. It read Captain Paul Henderson, LCSO. There was also a phone number.

"Thank you, Pam," he said. "I really do appreciate it."

And Tim did. The two of them had probably broken at least three laws already today, and it wasn't even noon yet.

CHAPTER 27

As Pam drove into the Lansdowne Hospital complex, Tim was thankful that is was not a Monday or any other weekday. The parking lot for the medical offices was no more than a quarter full, so finding a space would not be a problem. As a matter of fact, the problem was finding the right space. Pam wanted to park behind the building with her car at an angle, which would prevent anyone from parking to close to her new Mercedes. Tim, on the other hand, thought that parking in the middle of a vacant parking lot would attract attention. After considering this, Pam finally agreed that parking at an angle would be a little too conspicuous and decided to park with a group of other cars closer to the hospital.

At this point, Tim felt that this had to be the strangest operation he'd ever been involved in. He was keenly aware that the country was on the verge of collapse and that his and Pam's lives were in grave danger, yet they were arguing about where to park.

"So how do you think we should do this, Tim?" Pam asked.

"I don't know. I've never been a B and E guy," Tim replied as he looked around. Across the lot next to the medical building was an Audi parked in the Doctors Only spaces. "It looks like they're here. What do we do if the door is locked? I kind of doubt they will open if we knock."

"I got that covered," Pam replied as she reached into her bag and produced a set of lock picks. "I did take a course in this, but it's been a while."

"And locks change all of the time," Tim added.

"Fuck it, let's just get this done," Pam declared as she got out of the car and began to walk towards the building. Tim got out as well and had to hurry in order to catch up to his wife.

"I hope you still have your Deputy Marshal ID, Tim," Pam asked, but did not seem to care to hear the answer. She was focused on the building and the front door. "There may be security at the desk—"

"But yeah, let you do the talking," Tim finished. Although it was Tim who was really interested in interviewing the two doctors, it was apparent that Pam now wanted to as well. Tim could tell that she was angry at being double-crossed by Sebastian. This indicated to Tim that Pam would want to take the lead in the interview, which did scare him. Pam could be headstrong and was certainly capable of screwing this up. The last thing either of them needed was for the two doctors to clam up.

As they entered the building, there did not seem to be any security whatsoever, just an empty desk. Tim looked it over, but it did not appear that anyone had used it recently. The doctors' office was on the fourth floor, and Pam had already pushed the elevator call button.

A loud ding sound soon followed, and the two elevator doors opened wide. Tim pressed the button for the fourth floor. When the doors reopened, Tim and Pam stepped out slowly, since neither knew what to expect. The medical building was rectangular in shape, and suite 420 would be at the end of the hall. Tim and Pam both turned to the left and slowly walked to the office.

When they reached the office door, Pam placed her finger to her lips and pressed her ear to the wood. She nodded, indicating that she could hear that both doctors were in the office. Pam then motioned for Tim to produce his gun, placing her hand on her own pistol and slowly removing it from her holster. Pam next placed her hand on the doorknob and smiled when she discovered that the door was unlocked. She turned the knob and counted, "One, two..."

On three, Pam pushed open the door with her shoulder, and Tim followed in behind her.

Opening the door activated a chime, which the two doctors apparently did not hear. Pam and Tim stood alone in the waiting room.

The doctors were in separate offices but speaking to one another through an interconnecting door. There was also a television on, showing Meet the Press. The subject, of course, was the condition of the President. Tim motioned to Pam that he would enter Dr. Jennifer's office first if she covered Dr. Justice. Pam nodded to indicate that she understood the plan.

Tim silently counted it off, then raised his Glock

using both hands and kicked open Dr. Jennifer's door. Tim saw that her head was down as she read a document, but she quickly looked up and saw Tim.

"You!" Dr. Jennifer screamed, staring at him. "Richard, run!"

Tim heard motion in the next office and a door opening, but his attention and the Glock remained trained on Dr. Jennifer.

"Freeze, fat boy, or you're fucking dead," Tim heard Pam command from out in the waiting room. He then turned his attention back to Jennifer.

"I need you to slowly place your hands behind your head and lace your fingers together," Tim said as he paced around to Jennifer's left side. He did not see any weapons. He also noticed that Jennifer was sitting in an office chair with wheels.

He next looked at Jennifer's face to gauge how she was reacting. She did appear to be somewhat afraid.

"Okay, Jennifer, I need you to relax," he said once she'd complied. "We have no intention of hurting you or Dr. Justice, but if you do try anything, you may get seriously hurt. Now, I need you to slowly push your chair back away from your desk using your feet. Slowly, now."

Jennifer pushed her chair back until it was close to the window. Meanwhile, Tim could hear Pam speaking softly to Dr. Justice and next what sounded like handcuffs closing; then, the sound of duct tape peeling off the roll.

"Do you have everything under control out there?" Tim yelled to Pam, careful not to use her name.

Yeah, we will be in there in ten seconds."

Tim was still focused on Jennifer, afraid to take his eyes off her until Pam came in. He had to admit to himself that he just was not very good at this kind of thing.

"Okay, fat boy, let's go."

Tim moved aside as Dr. Richard Justice entered the room. His hands were cuffed behind his back, and Pam had wrapped duct tape around his head two or three times to gag him. Pam took Dr. Justice by the shoulders, turned him around, and pushed him onto the couch.

Pam next looked at Jennifer. "Okay, honey, it's your turn. I don't trust this one," she added to Tim. "If she tries anything while I'm securing her, shoot her. Don't worry about me. I'll get out of the way."

Pam pulled a pair of handcuffs from her bag and walked behind Jennifer, grabbing one of Jennifer's wrists to place the cuff on it. She then took Jennifer's other wrist and placed it behind the back of her chair, effectively handcuffing her to the chair. Pam then took a roll of duct tape and wrapped it around Jennifer's ankles five or six times. "You can lower your firearm," she assured Tim. "Neither of these two are going anywhere."

"How did you learn how to do all of this so efficiently, Pam?" Tim figured there was no longer any point to not using names.

"Oh, I had a day-long class with the Marshals, learning how to effectively restrain fugitives. It was a blast, and we all went out for drinks afterwards."

Tim once again thought that his wife had joined the wrong agency.

"So, Tim, pull up a chair and let's start talking," Pam said.

"I don't know what you two want, but just take what you need and leave," Jennifer interjected.

Ignoring her, Tim pulled up a chair and sat on the other side of Jennifer's desk. "Okay, Nurse Jennifer. Or is it Doctor?"

"It's Dr. Lockwood to you," Jennifer said, attempting to take control of the interview.

Tim looked at Jennifer for almost a full minute but did not say a word. Finally, he turned to Pam.

"You better make sure the door is locked, Pam. I think this is going to take a while."

Pam laughed and walked out to the waiting room.

"Jennifer, my wife and I are your last hope. Sebastian and his henchmen will be coming soon to kill you, but I think you've already figured that out. But when they do come, there will not be any talking. Just shooting."

"Fuck you," Jennifer said.

All of a sudden, there came the sound of a key entering a lock and then a door opening. Tim looked at Jennifer and saw a very worried look.

"Shut her up," Pam whispered, referring to Jennifer. Tim stepped behind Jennifer and placed his right hand over her mouth. Jennifer tried her best to bite it, but Tim held firm.

"Mom? Dad? I'm back with the Starbucks." It was a young woman, probably college age. And it was their kid.

She walked directly into her mother's office and saw Tim with his hand over her mother's mouth. She would have screamed if not for Pam grabbing her from behind.

Pam took the young woman's arm and twisted it behind her back. "Tim, get a roll of tape." When he obeyed, Pam quickly forced the young woman onto her stomach and tied her wrists with the duct tape.

"What's your name?" Tim asked

"Joanna," the young woman sobbed.

"Okay, Joanna, just relax," Pam told her, "and I promise you will not be hurt." She quickly finished tying and gagging the young woman.

"So, what do we do now, Pam?" Tim wanted to know.

Pam motioned Tim to follow her into a corner of the room. When he did, she hissed, "This is a stroke of luck, Tim. Those two weren't talking before, but I bet they'll start now."

"Yeah, I know, I know," Tim agreed.

Pam looked around and saw two keys hanging on the wall behind the receptionist's desk. Pam took one of the keys. "Tim, pick Joanna up and follow me."

Tim did as Pam ordered, following her to the office door and out into the hall. Pam then used the key to open the door to the ladies' restroom. She entered, and Tim followed with Joanna. Pam opened one of the stalls and placed Joanna on a toilet. Pam then took the roll of duct tape and wrapped the tape around Joanna's waist and the pipe, securing her to the seat.

Pam knelt down to speak with her. "Joanna, I'm sorry that we had to do this to you and to your parents, but everything will be all right. You will only have to stay here for an hour or so, and we will make sure someone comes and finds you, okay?"

Joanna nodded. "Okay," Pam said again, then walked with Tim back to the hallway.

"Tim, when we get back in there, I will question the fat man. You take Jennifer," she ordered. "Tell Jennifer that if she doesn't cooperate, she will never see her kid again."

"Yeah, sure," Tim responded.

Pam glared at him. "Look, Tim, I don't like doing this either, but it's the only way we are going to find out what we need to know. Do you understand?"

Tim nodded

"Then let's get this done."

Tim and Pam reentered the doctor's office to find Justice on the floor while Jennifer was struggling. Pam and Tim took it to be a good sign, since it showed that the two doctors were becoming desperate. Pam and Tim walked over to Justice and got him to his feet.

"Come on, fat boy," Pam told Justice. "You and I need to talk." Pam directed Justice back to his office.

Tim waited until they were gone, and then looked at Jennifer as if he were considering something. Jennifer spat at Tim, which landed on his pants leg. Tim raised his right leg and pushed Jennifer's rolling chair across the room. The chair hit the wall and then fell over to one side. Tim took his Glock out and pulled back the slide until it clicked.

"We have your kid now, Jennifer, and all it will take is one text from me and she's dead. Now start talking. Start at the beginning and tell me what happened in China."

"Sebastian Oak is behind it all," Jennifer gasped. "Please don't hurt my child!"

"That is fucking up to you, Jennifer. Continue."

"Sebastian has been moving intellectual property to the Chinese."

"Why?" Tim wanted to know.

"Money, just for money, but he needed to get you out of the way, so he came to us before he left and wanted some drugs that would make you lose your memory. He had us make up some syringes with Propanol, which he injected you with at some point. I don't know when."

"Okay, Jennifer. Now tell me what happened when I came home from China and what happened in Santa Domingo."

"Richard and I thought that we were done with all of this. I mean, we really never wanted to be involved in the first place, but we received an overseas call from Sebastian telling us that we needed to meet him at Dover Air Force Base in Delaware. So, we drive up there in the middle of the night, and we meet him at the front gate. Sebastian and these MPs take us to an airplane hangar for a private jet. Sebastian takes us on the jet, and we see that it's a medical transport plane with a patient. The patient is hooked up to monitoring devices and IVs, plus he is also wrapped in bandages. So, Sebastian orders everyone off the plane except me and Richard. He takes the bandages off the face of the patient, and for the first time we see that it's you. You appeared to be comatose, but all of your vitals looked good to me."

"What's your medical background, Jennifer?" Tim thought this might be good to know.

"I attended Harvard Medical School and did a residency in Emergency Medicine at Johns Hopkins and at Baltimore Shock Trauma."

"And you know Dr. Gray, my neurologist?"

"Yes, I know Felix, and I'm crushed that he's dead," Jennifer said, appearing to mean it.

"Just so you know, Pam and I are trying to make sure that you and your husband do not suffer the same fate. So, let's get back to the airplane."

"Yeah, so I checked your vitals, and you looked stable to me. Hey, would you mind picking me up off the floor?"

Tim looked to make sure that Jennifer was still secured to her chair. She was, but one of the handcuffs was beginning to cut into her wrist. Tim rubbed it to try to return some of the circulation.

"You know, that would be a lot easier if you removed these handcuffs," Jennifer suggested in a way that made Tim almost comply with the request.

"Forget about it, honey," Pam said. Tim turned to see her standing in the door.

"Tim?" Pam motioned him to come toward her and spoke to him in a low voice. "I can tell you're really out of practice. This woman is starting to play you. Remember, she is a mother, and the only thing she's thinking about right now is saving her daughter. We are making progress, so please focus on the task at hand."

Tim nodded to indicate that he understood. Pam was correct, of course, and he thought once again about how much better than him she was at doing this kind of work. When Tim was in the field, all he did was find out information, take that information to base, and talk about what it meant. Pam was more hands-on. In any event, Tim was happy that she was with him.

Tim walked back and sat opposite Jennifer again. He decided to change his tactics. "Okay, Dr. Lockwood," he began, "how is your wrist?"

"Fine, besides losing circulation. I didn't know your wife was such a bitch, Tim."

"Yes, she is, and I'm doing my best to make sure she does not murder your family. So, let's get back to me and the airplane in the hangar."

Jennifer looked startled by Tim's sudden change in tone, but she did continue the story. "So, you looked stable to me, and I asked Sebastian what this was about. He told us that he had administered the four syringes we had prepared and that he needed more, but both Richard and I told him that it would not be wise to just keep administering Propanol, and we asked what his intentions were. He asked us if there was any such thing as drug-induced amnesia. There actually have been some studies looking into that possibility using propranolol and a variety of benzos—"

"What kinds of drugs are benzos?" Tim interrupted, although he was pretty sure he knew.

"Well, originally there was chlordiazepoxide, better known as Librium, which was discovered by accident in the 1950s. That led to the development of diazepam, which is Valium, and alprazolam, which is better known as Xanax, but of course there are other kinds of benzodiazepines, such as Rohypnol, which you may know as the date rape drug."

"Okay, Dr. Lockwood, back to the airplane hangar."

"Well, we told Sebastian that yes, there were drugs which if administered over time could possibly induce amnesia for an extended period."

Tim finally felt that he was getting someplace. "So, what happened next?"

"We left you in the plane and sat at a table in the hangar, and Richard started writing prescriptions. I told Sebastian that we were going to need the cooperation of a neurologist, and that was when we decided to bring in Felix. Felix and I were in med school together. Sebastian said that he would take care of getting you transported to Johns Hopkins and transfer the case to Felix; I mean Dr. Gray. Richard and I then drove to Baltimore and checked into a hotel. I called Felix and we —meaning Richard, me, and Sebastian—met with him the next day. You had been transferred to Hopkins and were placed in a secure unit."

"Okay, I think I get it. Now tell me what the Santa Domingo trip was all about."

Jennifer looked over to the next room, where her husband seemed to be having an extended conversation with Pam. Earlier, Tim had heard Dr. Justice scream as Pam pulled the duct tape off his mouth, and Tim thought for a second that Pam may have enjoyed doing it. Pam had never tried to duct tape Tim when playing around in bed, and he made a mental note that he would never let her.

"Your husband can't help you, Jennifer, so why don't you just tell me what happened in the Dominican Republic," Tim said to redirect Jennifer's attention.

"Like I told you, we did not want to be involved with any of this, but Sebastian has been blackmailing us for years—"

Tim cut her off. "Just tell me what fucking happened in the Dominican Republic, Jennifer."

"Sebastian came to visit us and said that we needed to come up with a treatment for you to recover your memory, but we told him that it probably could not be done. After all, it had been over two years. How is your memory?"

It did seem like Jennifer wanted to know. "Pretty good now," Tim answered. "As a matter of fact, I'm beginning to remember just how big of an asshole I can be when I become angry." Tim said this while giving Jennifer a very cold stare.

"Okay," Jennifer answered, sounding more subdued. "So, Sebastian said that he needed you to recover your memory and that it had national security implications."

"Oh, I bet he did," Tim commented.

"So, I suggested that there were a number of things that we could try, and one was using embryonic stem cells to stimulate neuron functions in the brain. Of course, the other therapy we would need to do would be to induce a coma and flush all of the drugs out of your system. It's called a rapid detox. That could have been done anywhere, but the closest place for the stem cell implantation was in the Dominican Republic."

"So, all of this was arranged for a run-of-the-mill drug detox?" Tim asked.

"It was far from run of the mill," Jennifer protested. "Your body had become so accustomed to having several different kinds of benzophenones administered that the sudden discontinuation could be life-threatening—and believe me, in the 72 hours you were in the coma, you needed to be resuscitated twice. You owe your life to that man in the next room, Tim."

God, how many times had Tim heard that phrase? "Screw you, Dr. Lockwood," he answered. "You and your husband were the reason I needed to be resuscitated in the first place. You were just covering your asses. I only have two more questions. First, why the whole Nurse Jennifer bit with the chair and the straps, and why did you and your husband take seventeen thousand dollars from me?"

"Sebastian kept telling us that he would reimburse us for all the expenses we incurred setting up the phony clinic and everything, but he never did. We had to get some money for this—and believe me, it cost us a lot more than 17K."

"And the Nurse bit?"

"Oh, that's just this silly thing my husband and I do where I pretend to be a nurse, and he—"

"That's all I need to know, Jennifer," Tim said as

he cut Jennifer off. He really was not in the mood to hear any more sexual fantasy stories.

"One more question. The President has apparently been poisoned. Do you have any knowledge of what he has been poisoned with?"

"No, not a clue," Jennifer said.

"Has Sebastian ever discussed poisons with you, Dr. Lockwood?"

"In the years that I've known him, he's asked me all kinds of medical questions, Tim, and that started when I met him at Harvard."

"So, you two go back a ways?"

"Yes, but he has not asked anything about poisons recently."

"Tell me anything he has asked about poisons, Jennifer. It may be very important."

"Well, he did ask me once if one poison could mask another poison. In other words, could a doctor feel that he was treating one poison while missing another?"

"And when was this, Jennifer?"

"Oh, two or three years ago, I think. I figured he was asking in regard to some kind of CIA operation. That's why he usually asked."

Tim turned and walked out to the waiting room. Pam was waiting for him. "So, what do you think, Pam?" he asked.

"He basically told me the same story as your new girlfriend did," she answered. "He just told it quicker because I did not need to flirt with him."

Tim rolled his eyes. "Pam, why are you so fucking jealous? I mean, you apparently want me out of your life, but then you get angry if I have a civil conversation with anyone of the opposite sex."

"Because you belong to me, Tim. I picked you. I married you. You're mine until death."

Tim thought that this was a little crazy, given the circumstances—but it had been a stressful day, so he was willing to let it go.

But Pam was continuing. "You just have this way of flirting with women. I don't even think you know you're doing it. But we do."

By "we," Pam was referring to women in general. They'd talked many times before about how women had innate powers to figure out what men were thinking.

"Well, did your fat man reveal any clues about what the President may have been poisoned with?" Tim wanted to know.

"As a matter of fact, he seemed to think that it was thallium masked by arsenic. If that is the case, then the President would have about three weeks or less; but the longer it goes untreated, then the chances of recovery decrease."

"So, what now?" Tim asked, hoping that Pam

would provide the correct answer.

"Well, we need to get a message to the doctors at Bethesda telling them that there is a good chance the President has been poisoned with a thallium-based compound. That may be harder than it sounds."

Tim was pleased with Pam's answer, since he half expected her to say, "Fuck it, let him die," but it was good to know that she was using her head instead of her heart.

"We need someone who is not involved, someone who is innocent; but first, let's finish with the two doctors."

Tim looked into Dr. Justice's office and saw that Pam had bound and gagged the doctor to his chair using the duct tape.

"Okay, Pam, looks good. Let's bring in Dr. Lockwood."

Tim walked over to Jennifer's office to see that she was actively trying to squeeze out of her handcuffs. "Okay, Jennifer, let's join your husband," Tim told her as he began to push the woman and her chair through the connecting doors.

"Tim, it doesn't have to be this way. Maybe we can make a deal. We can certainly give you the money back from your trip to the Dominican Republic," Jennifer pleaded.

Oh my god, Tim thought. Do these two really believe this is all about a lousy seventeen thousand dollars? Tim's trip to Santa Domingo seemed like it was years ago, but what had it been, really? A few weeks, maybe? It really was only a few weeks back that Tim had been sitting at a bar in Baltimore flirting with a woman bartender who looked as though she was a member of a motorcycle gang. Now, he was deeply involved in an assassination conspiracy along with his wife. A wife who just a few weeks ago he'd thought to be dead.

This made Tim think of one more question. "Jennifer? Tell me again why Sebastian wanted so badly to bring me back into all this madness?"

Jennifer appeared to be trying to see if Pam was listening to their conversation. Tim saw this and knelt down in front of Jennifer so that they were on eye level.

"He said it was important to your wife," she answered. "As a matter of fact, he mentioned that she insisted."

"Have you ever met my wife before today, Jennifer?"

"No."

"Seen her around somewhere?"

"No."

"And I second that, Timothy," Pam said from behind him. "Let's finish this up."

Pam walked behind Jennifer and pushed her chair much harder than Tim had until it was in the center of her husband's office. Pam took one of the rolls of tape and wrapped it around Jennifer's midsection until she was tied securely to the office chair.

"These are mine," Pam remarked as she took the handcuffs off of Jennifer's wrists, momentarily freeing them. Pam then taped her hands and wrists, wrapping them almost to her forearms. Pam next pulled Jennifer's long red hair back and began to gag her.

"You don't need to do that, Pam," Jennifer said very nicely. "I promise to be quiet."

"Not a problem, honey," Pam replied as she grabbed Jennifer's nose. This resulted in Jennifer opening her mouth, and Pam shoved a piece of gauze in it. Pam then proceeded to wrap the tape around Jennifer's head four times.

"I think that's enough Pam," Tim said, suggesting that perhaps Pam was overdoing it.

Pam looked at Tim, then at the tape. "Yeah, I guess."

She turned her attention to Jennifer. "I'm sorry, honey, but my husband just can't help himself," Pam said, referring to Tim's tendency to flirt with every woman he encountered; but Jennifer just looked confused.

"I don't think she knows what you're talking about, Pam," Tim said.

"Oh, she does," Pam replied. "Now, let's go and get their kid."

The mention of Joanna startled the two doctors, as they both made sounds of protest. Ignoring this, Pam led the way out of the office and used the restroom key again to open the door. Joanna made a screaming sound as they entered.

"It's just us, Joanna, so calm down." Pam said, but Tim doubted that letting the young woman know that her kidnappers had returned would result in a calming effect.

Pam pushed open the door to Joanna's stall to find her just as they left her, although Tim could tell that she had been crying. Tim felt terrible and sensed that even Pam did as well.

"Tim, take your knife and cut the tape so Joanna can get up."

Tim did as Pam asked and cut the tape that was around the toilet fixture and Joanna's ankles. Tim then helped her to her feet.

"Now turn around, Joanna, and let me untie your hands," Pam said very gently as she peeled the tape from Joanna wrists. Pam next turned Joanna around so she was facing her.

"Now, Joanna, we are going to take you to see your parents so you can see that they are all right—but after that, we are going to need you to do something very important. So important that your parents' lives depend on it. Do you understand?"

Joanna nodded.

"Okay, then. I'm going to take your gag off—but no screaming. It's important for you to stay calm."

Joanna nodded again and did seem more relaxed. Pam slowly began to peel the tape away from her mouth. "This may hurt a little," Pam warned,

"Ouch!" Joanna said as the tape came off. "Who are you and why are you doing this to my mom and dad?" she demanded.

"Let's get one thing out of the way, Joanna: Tim and I are giving the orders and asking the questions. Your job is to answer the questions and do what you are told. If you do, then you and your mom and dad will have many more happy occasions. But if you try and cross us, then everybody dies. Understand?"

Perhaps it was the firmness of Pam's voice or something else that convinced Joanna to do as she was told, but her attitude completely changed. "Tell me what I need to do," she said.

The three of them returned to the doctors' office. "Okay, Joanna," Pam began, "we are going to see your parents now. They are both gagged and will not be able to communicate with you, but I just need you to tell them that you are okay, and everything will be fine. Understand?"

"Yes, I understand," Joanna replied.

Tim pushed open the door to Dr. Justice's office, and Joanna saw her parents bound and gagged. Both doctors tried to communicate with their daughter, but Pam held up her hand.

"Your daughter has something to say."

Joanna nodded. "Mom and dad? They are going to let me go, but I am coming right back. Everything will be okay. I just wanted you to know that I love you."

With the exception of Pam, everyone seemed to have tears in their eyes, including Tim. Pam simply shook her head from side to side and took hold of Joanna's arm to guide her back to the reception area.

Tim closed the door behind them. "Joanna?" he asked. "Do you go to school around here?"

"Yes, Georgetown Law."

"Really? Well, good for you. Do you live in DC?"

"Arlington, around Ballston, if you know where that is."

"Sure do," Tim replied almost a little too enthusiastically. "As a matter of fact, Pam and I used to live over by..."

"Tim, cut the shit," Pam said, sounding a little more flustered than usual. "Just get to the point."

"Okay. Anyway, Joanna, do you know where the CIA is in McLean?"

"Yeah, I guess I do. I've seen the signs for it."

"Like where, Joanna? Off of the GW Parkway?"

"Yes, there's a sign right when you take the exit off the Beltway before you cross into Maryland."

"Okay, great. What we need you to do is to drive there. Take that exit and follow the road until you come to the gate. Give them this note and tell the guards that you cannot leave until you speak with this man."

Joanna looked at the piece of paper and read the name. "Okay, but will he want to see me? Maybe they'll just think I'm crazy and arrest me."

"That's okay if they do," Pam interjected. "Just stick to your story. Tell them about your parents. Tell them that they are being held hostage. The important part is to tell them that the President needs to be treated for thallium masked by arsenic poisoning. You have to get that across."

"But why me? Why not you or my parents?" Joanna wanted to know.

"Because we would be killed before we had any chance to tell someone," Tim said.

"Look, this is a big deal," Pam told the young woman, "and I'm sorry that you just stumbled into all this. It certainly was not part of anyone's plan, but sometimes things like this just happen, and it's important that you are able to step up when called upon. Do you understand what I mean, Joanna?"

Joanna nodded.

"Then let me walk you downstairs. Tim, better stay here and watch Mom and Dad. "

Pam took Joanna by the hand and left the office. Tim walked over to the window and, in a few minutes, saw Pam leave the building with Joanna. Pam placed both hands on Joanna's shoulders and appeared to give them a squeeze. Then she watched Joanna get in her car and drive off.

Tim checked from his vantage point to make sure no one was following the girl. From what he could tell, no one did.

CHAPTER 28

Ten minutes had passed since Pam walked Joanna down to the car, and Tim was becoming a little concerned, but he felt that Pam had most likely gone to retrieve her Mercedes. He opened the door to Dr. Justice's office and found the two doctors exactly where Pam and he had left them. Dr. Lockwood raised her head and gave Tim a "please untie me" look, which he ignored, but he did feel an obligation to address the situation.

"I'm sorry that we have to leave you tied up, but we do have our reasons," he explained. "We've released your daughter, and she should be back shortly, most likely with the FBI. What you decide to tell them will be up to you. Pam and I are trying to stop the President from being assassinated, so any information you can give them about Sebastian Oak may be helpful."

Tim slowly shut the door and walked back to the window. Where the hell was Pam? Although it was possible that Pam decided to ditch him, he found that prospect unlikely. Despite their back and forth over Tim's alleged womanizing, they had been working well together.

Pam and Tim had always worked well together, and Tim never took Pam's allegations of womanizing too seriously. Tim just liked women, and he liked talking to women. He was sad about all of the platonic relationships that he was forced to give up because men were not comfortable with their wives or girlfriends having a relationship, even a non-sexual one, with another man. That sort of situation was unfortunate, but it was also a reality. Relationships were much more complicated than just romance and sex.

Twenty minutes went by, and no Pam. Something was wrong. It was now 4:15, and it was time to go. Tim also knew that there was a possibility that Joanna had disregarded their instructions and drove over to the Leesburg police station to report that her parents were being held hostage. Perhaps the town cops, sheriff's department, and state police were organizing a SWAT team and getting ready to storm the building. Maybe they'd already taken Pam into custody.

But something in Tim's gut told him that the young woman was still on her way to Langley. Hell, she was probably almost there by now, and the cops would be coming. Tim grabbed Pam's bag and headed out the door. He decided to take the stairs instead of the elevator.

He made it to the lobby in less than a minute, then slowly opened the door and looked both ways. It was all clear, so he walked to the front door and looked out at the parking lot. Nothing there either.

When he walked around the building looking for Pam's car, though, he noticed a loading dock where a van was parked. "Joe Smith's Plumbing and Heating" was written on the side. Kind of an odd name, Tim thought as he placed his hand on his Glock.

Tim never heard or saw Toby. He just seemed to come out of nowhere, but he had Tim on the ground before he knew what was happening.

"Hey, pal. I thought you were around here somewhere," Toby said as he grabbed one of Tim's arms, then the other. Tim felt the handcuffs closing on his wrists, and Toby made sure they were tight.

He picked Tim up by the handcuff chain and turned him around so that Tim was facing him, then reached into Tim's jacket. "What do we have here?" he asked as he pulled out Tim's Glock 19 9mm. "This is the second one of these I've found this afternoon."

Taking Tim by the collar in one hand, Toby began to push him toward the plumbing van. He opened the side door and threw Tim in—or, at least, it felt like being thrown. Tim landed on his knees and then his chest. He rolled to his side and could see a body lying beside him. It was Pam, but she appeared to be unconscious.

"What did you do to my wife, you asshole?" Tim said, but the wind was knocked out of him and he had a hard time getting the words out.

"I fucking hit her, Timmy, right below her nose, which is something I have wanted to do since I met her. You should thank me. I can tell you're the type of guy that lets women push you around." Toby slammed the side door, walked around the van, and got into the driver's seat.

There was a thick cage separating Tim and Pam

from the driver of the van. "I also gave her a hypo of some drug Sebastian gave to me for you," Toby added with a grin, "but your old lady was making a lot of noise, so I decided to use it on her instead. It put her right to sleep."

Tim was able to roll a little closer to Pam so he could examine her. Her upper lip was swollen, and there appeared to be bruising forming on each side of her nose. There was also a trickle of blood coming from one of Pam's nostrils, but nothing too serious—at least, Tim didn't think so.

"Where's the injection site?" Tim asked.

Toby was staring at the door next to the loading dock like he was expecting something to happen and was not paying attention to Tim. "Huh?" Toby asked.

"Where did you stick the hypo, Toby?"

"Oh, that." Toby was still not paying Tim or Pam any attention. "I stuck it in her ass. She was very surprised."

Tim could only imagine how surprised Pam had been.

Tim heard the passenger side door open. Mary Ann Layback got in. "All done," she said to Toby cheerfully.

Toby started the van and began to drive. "Let's see the gun, Mary Ann," he demanded.

"Oh, don't I get to keep it?" Mary Ann replied in her little girl voice.

"No, Sebastian is still not 100% sure about you, and besides, this is the gun we want the cops to find."

Mary Ann handed over the pistol to him.

Toby drove the van to the edge of the parking lot, where there was a line of trees and a drainage ditch. Tim could not tell exactly what kind of pistol Mary Ann handed over to Toby, but he could see that there was a silencer screwed to the end of the barrel. Toby placed the barrel of the weapon to his nose to confirm that it had been recently fired.

"How many bullets did you use?" he asked.

"Just two, like you told me to," Mary Ann replied.

Toby appeared to want more details. "And where did you put the bullets?"

"I shot the woman in the back of the head and the fat man in the temple." Mary Ann placed her fingers on her head to show Toby exactly where she'd shot the victims.

Toby stopped the van, opened the door, and tossed the pistol into the wooded area. "The cops should be able to find that easy enough," he said as he drove on.

Pam made a slight groan like she might be waking up, which resulted in Mary Ann turning around and seeing Pam and Tim for the first time. "Oh hey, Tim," she said. "Is that your wife? Is she asleep or something?"

"I think you need to ask Toby about that, Mary Ann," Tim replied. The fact that both Tim and Pam were handcuffed hand and foot in the back of the van seemed to go right over Mary Ann's head.

"Toby, what did you fucking do?" Mary Ann asked in the tone of a mother scolding a child.

"She wouldn't shut the fuck up, and I couldn't find anything to stick in her fucking mouth, so I used the hypo," Toby tried to explain.

Mary Ann rolled her eyes. "Sebastian wanted that for Tim later on, numb nuts. By the way, what's in the bag?"

Toby had apparently grabbed Pam's bag with all of the tape, rope, and handcuffs, and Mary Ann was now rooting through it. "Jesus, Tim," she said with a laugh. "What kind of party were you two having with those doctors?"

"I'll tell you one thing, though," Mary Ann continued with a smile. "You two didn't do a real good job tying those two doctors up. They were both about loose when I came in the room. Maybe I can show you how it should be done when we get back to your house."

Tim knew that there was no way the two doctors could have been close to escaping their bonds. Pam did too good of a job. It occurred to Tim that perhaps Mary Ann did not really murder the doctors, and this was all an act. He certainly hoped so.

"So, where did you find Mr. and Mrs. Hall, Toby?" Mary Ann asked.

"Well, she was on the other side of the building

speaking with some girl," Toby said. "But she got in a car and drove away."

"And who was this girl?" Mary Ann now asked Tim.

"Someone who came pounding on the door looking for Dr. Lockwood. Pam answered the door while I was holding a gun on the doctors. Pam must have taken her downstairs to get rid of her," Tim explained.

"What do you think, Toby?" Mary Ann asked.

"Who knows," Toby grunted. "She's gone, and there's nothing we can do about it now. But I wouldn't mention it to Sebastian," Toby told her.

"Sebastian is going to be mad enough when he finds out you used that hypodermic needle on Blondie down there," Mary Ann said, referring to Pam.

"Fuck him if he can't take a joke," Toby replied to Mary Ann.

"That's what I'm afraid of, honey," Mary Ann said to Toby.

Tim was unable to tell where they were at the present time since he couldn't see out the windows, but he imagined that they were on US Route 15, heading back to the safe house. Since Pam was effectively knocked out, Tim decided to try and make some conversation.

"So, Mary Ann," Tim began, "I take it you never checked into the Red Roof Inn."

"Oh, Tim," Mary Ann said almost lovingly, "you should have known that the three of us were sitting in your condo waiting for you to call. Sebastian had figured out that your wife had turned against him, so there was no use in anyone going over to the safe house. I was just waiting for you to call, but then Sebastian needed us to find you and your wife plus the two doctors. We did try their home, but only the maid was there."

"So, did you off her, too?" Tim asked.

"Tim, what kind of people do you think Toby and I are?" Mary Ann said defensively. "We do not kill indiscriminately."

"Unless we're paid to," Toby added with a strange sort of laugh.

Mary Ann glared at Toby for a second, then continued. "No, the maid is tied up in the garage. I suppose someone will find her eventually. Maybe the cops, after they find the two murdered homeowners."

"Do you two have any clue why Sebastian has you doing this?" Tim asked.

"As far as we know, it's just CIA work," Mary Ann replied.

"No, it's not CIA work," Tim countered. "The CIA does not operate within the borders of the United States. That is what the FBI, the NSA, and the ATF are for."

Toby and Mary Ann both laughed at Tim's statement, and Tim almost laughed at it himself. Yes, officially the Agency was not supposed to operate in the US, but there were numerous exceptions to that rule. If there was some kind of "Agency work" that needed to be performed within the borders of the United States, it was not like anyone at Langley threw up their hands and declared that they were powerless to act. They simply just sent some contractors out to handle the job and called it an internal security matter. Plus, it was not unusual to find people like Toby and Mary Ann to do this kind of work. There was a famous Agency myth that involved the Bobby Kennedy assassination and a private detective agency which Tim had recently read about in the *Washington Post*.

That said, Sebastian was really operating outside of the law, and Tim was sure that Sebastian had already arranged for Toby and Mary Ann's demise. Tim figured it was no harm to try again.

"Laugh all you want, you two, but I'm telling you the truth. After Pam and I have been murdered, you will go home to Las Vegas. You may even get there; but within a month, both of you will be dead. Maybe together or one at a time, but it will happen."

Tim's statement stopped both Toby and Mary Ann from laughing, and Tim felt that he may as well keep working on them.

"I can even tell you what is going to happen tonight," he added. "First of all, Sebastian is going to be real pissed off that you used the propanol on Pam instead of me. That drug is the same as truth serum, and yes, truth serum really does exist. Since I have been taking propanol for a couple of years now, it would work like a hypnotic. Sebastian was going to see if he could get me to murder Pam and then kill myself so they can blame everything on me."

"Blame what on you, Tim?" Mary Ann asked.

Tim suddenly understood that Mary Ann was anxious to know everything, whereas Toby just didn't seem to give a shit. Tim was now convinced that Mary Ann was playing on both sides of the fence, but for whom? Tim had known for a while now that Mary Ann played her dumb act a little too well—or, as he liked to put it, "She's too smart to be so fucking dumb."

It would be great if Mary Ann could come to his and Pam rescue at some point before Sebastian and Toby killed them, but that might be a little too much to expect at present. At any rate, Tim was still convinced that Toby was dumber than a bag of hammers.

"Mary Ann," Toby said in a whiny voice, "this guy is just fucking with us."

"Yes, he's right, Mary Ann. I was only a covert agent for over thirty years and supervised a number of operations, but what do I know?"

Tim had been hoping to divide Toby and Mary Ann's loyalties to Sebastian, but he was now pretty sure that Mary Ann had a different agenda. In any event, the fact that Toby had given Pam the propanol had most likely bought them some time. Plus, if Joanna had made it through and the President was now being properly treated, then Sebastian and his plan to place the adults back in the room would be falling apart. In fact, Sebastian may have already left the safe house—and, for that matter, the country—leaving Toby and Mary Ann holding the bag.

Assuming that assassinating the President and bringing back a bunch of old Republicans had been the plan all along. But what if that was not the plan? What if it was something else, something entirely different?

Tim closed his eyes and began to think. Dr. Lockwood had said that Pam had wanted him back for a reason and that she insisted on it. It would be silly to bring him back just so he could participate in some assassination, since there were hundreds of jokers who could design poisons. No, there had to be something else, something that only Tim knew, and it had to do with whatever happened in China.

Sebastian and Pam wanted me out of the picture, Tim thought, but now they need me back in. They need me back in because only I know something that they need to know... But what do I know?

Tim rocked to one side as the plumbing van negotiated the safe house driveway. Tim could feel the van round the circular driveway and then stop at the front door of the house. Toby and Mary Ann, who had been quiet for the last five minutes of the ride, got out and walked to the front of the house. Tim listened carefully, trying to hear Toby speak with Sebastian.

Tim heard Sebastian say, "You idiot, Toby," and then, "Toby, you are a fucking idiot!"

The voices grew louder as they approached the van and slid open the side door. Sebastian shone a flashlight directly at Pam and saw that she had a bruised upper lip.

"What have you done to her?" Sebastian demanded.

"I just had to rough her up a bit, boss—"

"Just shut the fuck up, Toby," Sebastian said, cutting him off.

He stood in front of the van door, apparently thinking about what to do next. Tim had never seen Sebastian this angry before. All that Tim could figure was that Sebastian must have also needed Pam for something and the fact that she was "dead to the world" did not help matters at all.

But Sebastian also needed Toby and could ill afford pissing him off—at least not for the time being.

"Okay, Toby," he ordered, "take the handcuffs off of Pam and Tim. Then you and Tim carry Pam down to the safe room in the basement."

Toby produced a key and quickly unlocked the manacles from the prisoners. Toby then grabbed Pam by the shoulders. "I can carry her myself, boss," he suggested.

Sebastian gritted his teeth. "And I said that you and Tim carry Pam down to the safe room. Now please do what I say."

Toby began to pull Pam from the van, then looked at Tim. "You grab her feet."

Tim got out of the van and waited until Pam's

feet were right on the edge. He then grabbed hold, and the two of them began to walk toward the house.

"Mary Ann?" Sebastian said. "You wait here and make sure nothing else happens."

"Can I have a gun now?" Mary Ann asked.

"Yes, as soon as Toby and I get back," Sebastian said as he followed Tim and Toby into the house.

Pam was heavier than either Toby or Tim expected, and they carefully walked down the steps to the basement past the gun safe and into the safe room. The door to the safe room was already open.

"Go ahead and put her on the bed," Sebastian ordered. "We're just going to have to wait until she comes to. Tim, call me if anything happens."

He turned to leave, but then stopped at the door. "Tim? You may be interested to know that the President is responding to treatment."

"Really," Tim replied.

"Yes, apparently a young woman drove frantically up to the Agency gate off the GW claiming that the President had been poisoned with thallium. She also said that her parents were being held hostage in an office building in Leesburg. When police arrived, they found the parents tied up but otherwise unharmed," Sebastian looked directly at Toby when he said the word "unharmed." Toby immediately turned and bounded back up the basement stairs.

"You see," Sebastian continued, "I was under the

impression that Drs. Justice and Lockwood were dead, but apparently that is not the case."

He sighed. "Oh well, sleep tight," Sebastian told Tim as he closed and locked the door.

At least the light stays on, Tim thought to himself. He began to laugh because it reminded him of a joke about a refrigerator light staying on even after the door was closed. Tim had this habit of laughing when he found himself in dangerous situations, but not because he was a brave man. To the contrary, Tim felt that he was a true coward. No, Tim Hall laughed in the face of danger because he was scared shitless.

CHAPTER 29

It bothered Tim that he still had not figured out what was really going on. Twelve hours ago, Tim was sure that everything was related to a conspiracy to assassinate the President so that a bunch of standard-bearing Republicans could be brought in to replace the present administration. Although there was indeed a plot, he was now convinced he'd been brought back and had his memory restored for some other reason.

Memory restored? Tim suddenly imagined a lightbulb turning on over his head. The reason Sebastian and Pam had gone to all of this trouble to restore his memory was that he had a piece of vital information that both of them needed to know.

But what in the hell could it be?

"What is going on, honey?" Tim heard Pam's voice, but she was talking in her sleep.

Pam had now been out for over two hours, and he was beginning to wonder what Toby had injected her with. He had assumed that it was just the propanol that he'd been given now for over two years, but perhaps it was something different. Since the shot was meant for him, that must mean Sebastian was going to make yet another attempt to extract whatever it was that Tim knew but would not tell him. To do that, one would need truth serum, better known as sodium pentothal.

Sodium pentothal was related to an entire family of drugs that were supposed to lower a subject's inhibitions or defenses, therefore resulting in a fountain of truth babbling out of the subject's mouth. The only problem was that it did not really work—not as you wanted it to work, anyway. Yes, it was possible to find out some basic information if you knew how to ask the subject the correct questions in the correct way, but it was not like you just gave a person some sodium pentothal and watched them spill their guts. Assuming that Pam had mistakenly been given the drug, Tim thought that he may as well see if Pam would tell him anything.

Tim got to his feet, walked to the sink, and filled a water glass for Pam. "The safe room in the safe house, a little redundant, don't you think?" Tim said, laughing at his own joke. Well at least it was not the secret room in the safe room of the safe house. Now that would really be confusing. Tim was really cracking himself up, he thought. His mind then turned to Mary Ann. Sebastian had most likely intended for Toby to shoot the two doctors, but Mary Ann, knowing this, probably talked Toby into letting her do it. Mary Ann then probably shot the couch a couple of times to prove to Toby that she'd actually completed the hit. Only a good person would take that kind of chance, so Tim's faith in Mary Ann was now restored. Hell, if she had been able to keep the gun, they would probably all be out of danger. Now, she was probably getting her ass kicked by Toby or worse. Sebastian and Toby would definitely kill her if they determined she was working undercover. Mary Ann might be able to convince Toby that she just felt sorry for the two doctors and could not go through with murdering them. She could also try and convince her ex that she was afraid to tell him she'd chickened out. Tim was sure that this was not the first time Toby had been suspicious of Mary Ann's motives, but she still might be able to trick him again.

On the other hand, she would not be able to fool Sebastian. Sebastian had certainly checked Mary Ann out to make sure she was who she said she was. That told Tim that Mary Ann must be in very deep cover, since it was expensive to give someone a complete backstory that could withstand scrutiny from a CIA agent. Possibly Mary Ann was originally planned to investigate Toby, but when Sebastian showed up, she was instructed to follow and see where it all led.

Pam made some more noise, which indicated to Tim that she would soon be waking up. If he was going to try interviewing the subject "under the influence" (as it was known in the interrogation business), then he'd better start soon. He pulled up one of the chairs in the safe room to the edge of the lower berth of the bunkbed. He took a paper towel and dabbed it in his glass of water, then wiped Pam's forehead.

"How are you feeling, honey?" Tim asked softly.

"Oh, okay," Pam replied as she laid her head in her hands and started to fall back asleep.

"Hey, honey, do you know..." Tim stopped on

the word "know" on purpose. He wanted Pam to think about the word "know." Tim had no scientific knowledge if this particular method worked or did not work, but it was the one he had used before to some success.

"Pam," Tim said again softly.

"Hi, Timmy," Pam replied.

"Hey, Pam? Why did you restore my memory?"

"Because."

"Because why, Pam?"

"Your PIN number, Tim."

"What about my PIN number, Pam?"

"The one that you won't give to me."

"I would give you anything, Pam."

"But you won't give me your PIN number, Tim."

"What PIN number, Pam?"

"The one for the..."

"The one for what, Pam?"

"The cryptocurrency, Tim."

"What PIN, what cryptocurrency, Pam?"

"My account, your account and, and..."

"Whose account, Pam?

"Fucking Sebastian. I want to sleep." And Pam did fall back to sleep.

Tim wanted to go to sleep as well. He knew that he could have continued the back and forth with Pam and may have even been able to retrieve some additional kernels of information about the cryptocurrency account that he was apparently part of, but he thought that he had come away with at least one answer. He, Sebastian, and Pam apparently had an account that involved Bitcoins, and the thought of that made him sick to his stomach.

In Tim's opinion, dealing with any kind of cyber or cyptocurrency was asking for trouble; but since 2010, it had gained a strong foothold in a number of markets, many of which were illegal. Cybercurrency was decentralized and unregulated, which always made it attractive to individuals holding large amounts of money. The Aldrich Ames scandal that rocked the Agency in 1994 forced CIA management to take an inward look at itself and its employees. No longer were employee lifestyles considered off limits. If management felt that you were living beyond your means, they called you in and asked you about it; but with cybercurrency, no one could tell how much money you had in the bank.

"Tim? What the hell is going on?" Pam was finally waking up from the sodium pentothal.

"How are you feeling, Pam?" Tim wanted to know.

"My head is pounding. What the hell happened?"

"You apparently ran into the fist of Toby Wheeler," Tim remarked. "But let me take a look at you."

Pam was still on the bunkbed, so Tim leaned over and checked her pupils. Pam did have a fat upper lip. "Do you remember what happened?" he asked.

"Yes. After I saw Joanna off, I was walking back to the building when someone grabbed me from behind. I did fight back the best I could, but something sharp was shoved in my butt. That's the last thing I remember."

Pam looked around. "So, we're in my safe room? Are we locked in?"

"Yes, it appears so," Tim responded.

"Did you try the door?"

Tim got up, walked to the door, and pushed hard. The door did not open.

"Am I missing something here, Pam? Is there another way out of here?"

Pam just looked at Tim, knowing that it was possible that Sebastian was listening to their conversation.

She obviously decided to change the subject. "So how long have I been asleep?"

Tim looked at his watch. It was after 8 p.m. "About four hours now."

"Wow. So, fill me in. What's happened?"

"Well, first of all, it now appears that the President is successfully being treated for whatever he was poisoned with. Seems like some young woman drove to CIA Headquarters and claimed her parents were being held hostage…"

"Okay, Tim," Pam interrupted. "I think we're going to have to assume that Sebastian is listening to everything we say. Why was I out for so long, and did that son of a bitch Toby hit me?"

"He did—and he also apparently shot you up with some truth serum. Truth serum which was meant for me."

"Truth serum?" Pam repeated.

"Sodium pentothal, to be exact. And although you and I both know how iffy the stuff is, I thought I might as well ask you something while you were under."

"Like what, Tim?" Pam smiled. "Did you want to know if I really have orgasms with you?"

"No," Tim responded, "but that would have been a good question. No, what I asked you was why you and Sebastian really brought me back in, and you basically told me because of my PIN number."

Pam just stared at her husband with no expression. "Is that all I said? A PIN number?"

"Well, a PIN number related to Bitcoins or some other kind of cyber currency, and you know what, Pam? I think you've finally told me the truth. I think that you and Sebastian have a significant Bitcoin account, and for some reason or another I have the PIN number to it."

"We all have PIN numbers, Tim. Just like we all set up the Bitcoin account. Me, Sebastian, and you. We set up the account using a PIN number that each one of us had a piece of. That way, we could not double-cross one another."

"But you did, Pam. You double-crossed me."

Pam placed her head in her hands and began to laugh. She then picked her head up and looked squarely at Tim.

"You are just fucking incredible, Tim Hall. You double-crossed us. It was you who said you didn't give a shit about all of the money. It was you who told Sebastian and me that you wanted out. It was you who just wanted to fade away. It was you who decided to live anonymously in Baltimore, and it was you who told us how to do it. All we wanted in return was your share of the Bitcoins, and you gave us your part of the PIN number. It even worked when we tested it, but it doesn't work anymore because you changed it."

"And how the fuck was I supposed to have changed a PIN number that I have no clue about in the first place, Pam?" Tim said defensively.

"We were told that you probably set something up in the blockchain program that changes your PIN each time you enter it, but that's just a guess. All we know is that it's in your head somewhere. We've certainly looked everywhere else for it."

"Pam is correct, Tim. We have done everything." It was Sebastian's voice coming out of a speaker in the ceiling. Pam was right that Sebastian had been eaves-dropping on their conversation.

"So, you and Pam are in this together?" Tim asked while looking up at the ceiling.

"Well, not exactly. Pam and I have each other's PINs, but whoever gets yours will control the Bitcoin account, which I might add is now well into the eight figures."

"And in the last two years, you haven't been able to figure my PIN number out?" Tim wanted to know.

"We have certainly attempted to figure out your PIN, but each time we enter a false PIN, the system re-sets. We now have to wait two weeks before each new attempt to enter the correct PIN number, and if we enter one more incorrect PIN, it will be three weeks be-fore we can try again. But time is running out."

"What Sebastian means, Tim," Pam began to ex-plain, "is that now is the time to exchange the Bitcoins for real money because there is information that the entire cybercurrency market is about to crash."

"Bitcoin is real money," Sebastian interjected.

"Yes, Sebastian, we know," Pam said in a condes-cending tone. Pam then whispered to Tim, "Sebastian is a real big fan of computer money."

"Yes, it does sound like that," Tim replied. "But what information tells you that the cyber currency market is about to crash?"

"Oh, Sebastian is up the ass of every economist

working at Langley. They tell him that the entire industry will be regulated by 2025, which is actually beginning to happen right now. That's what got us busted in China, or did you conveniently forget about that too, Tim?"

Tim had now heard so many variations of the "what happened in China" story that he'd stopped paying attention. "You did shoot Lilly Lin, correct?" he asked Pam.

"Yes, I shot and killed Ms. Lin, who by the way was an undercover agent for the Ministry of State Security," Pam said, sounding exasperated.

"Speaking of undercover agents..." It was Sebastian again on the speaker in the ceiling "Apparently, my own Ms. Layback is one as well."

"Told you so, you asshole," Pam said. "Who is she working for?"

"Toby is beating that out of her as we speak, but I do have to commend her: she's holding her own."

Tim knew it was Sebastian's move, but at least he now had a bargaining chip: the PIN number. And he was almost certain that he knew what it was.

"So, Sebastian, Pam and I are just dying to know what you plan on doing with us," Tim said sarcastically.

"That's up to you, Tim. If you can provide your part of the PIN number, then I may be able to see my way clear to let you return to your little corner of the world in Baltimore. Otherwise, we're still seeking those responsible for the attempted assassination of our President."

Tim of course knew that Sebastian had no intention of letting him and Pam go free, but he was interested in seeing if he would make the offer.

Pam, as expected, was completely against bargaining with Sebastian, and she let Tim know it. "If you give up your PIN number, Tim, I will kill you myself," she whispered.

Tim held up a hand to assure Pam that he had control of the situation. "And what about Mary Ann? Would you be willing to let her leave as well?"

"Not a chance, Tim," Sebastian replied. "Now, I suggest that you and Pam get a good night's sleep. You have a big day ahead of you in the morning." Tim and Pam heard the intercom turn off.

"So, what do you think, Tim?" Pam wanted to know.

"I think that Sebastian will still try to get me to tell him my part of the PIN number, but we are dead either way. What do you think, Pam?"

"I'm afraid that you're right. He will try and make a deal, but we're dead one way or the other. I think that Sebastian is ready to cut his losses, even if that means giving up all the Bitcoin money. He can't spend it if he ends up in a Super Max."

Most people who were convicted of espionage were sentenced to life in solitary confinement at a super-maximum-security prison, known as a Super Max. Many prisoners compared this experience to being buried alive.

"You know Sebastian has no choice but to kill your girlfriend," Pam added.

"Yeah, I know that, Pam. As a matter of fact, Sebastian will probably kill Toby as well—but Toby is too fucking stupid to figure that out."

"He will probably have Toby kill her and then dump the body in Baltimore. Then he will kill Toby or have someone kill Toby. Keeping his hands clean."

"Can we let that happen?" Tim asked.

Pam motioned Tim to come over to the lower berth of the bunkbed, where she was now seated. Tim sat, and Pam turned to him. "We still have to be quiet, Tim, Sebastian could still be listening," she whispered.

Pam looked up at the ceiling as she said this, but her attention was focused on something other than the speaker. "Do you see that smoke detector with the blinking green light, Tim? That just might be our ticket out of here."

"What do you mean?"

"When that alarm goes off, the door to the safe room automatically unlocks. I designed it that way in case I was trapped in here and someone decided to set the house on fire. It also brings the local cops and firefighters."

"What stops Sebastian from overriding the system?" Tim began to examine the smoke detector as he asked this.

"As far as I know, I'm the only one who has the code to do that." Pam paused. "But nothing is going to stop Sebastian and Toby from coming down here and shooting us. It takes the locals anywhere from 10 to 20 minutes to arrive, so they would have time to finish us off and make an escape. Sebastian may even be able to make it look like a murder-suicide. Those seem to happen all the time."

Pam was right. Murder-suicides did seem to be common out here in the suburbs. There were at least two or three per year, and the authorities just seemed to accept this. Pam and Tim would be murdered, Mary Ann would be murdered and dumped in Baltimore, and then Sebastian would have Toby killed and everything would be cleaned up.

"Tim," Pam began again, "I'm really sorry that all of this has happened. Sebastian and I should have stuck to the deal and just let you live out your life in Baltimore like you planned."

This was something that Tim had to think about. According to Pam and Sebastian, everything that had happened in the last few years was the result of a plan he'd devised. Or was this yet another fucking lie?

"So, Pam, you're telling me that my living in Baltimore was all part of a plan?" he asked incredulously.

"After Lilly Lin was killed, you had some crisis of conscience, and you wanted out," Pam explained. "You no longer cared about the money in the Bitcoin account and were willing to give it all to Sebastian and me, just as long as we left you alone. And we would have, if you hadn't double-crossed us by somehow changing the PIN number."

"But you said that number worked. You said you two tested it. Are you sure you just didn't fuck it up?"

"No, we did not fuck it up." Pam gave Tim an "Are you kidding?" kind of look. After all, Pam did not make mistakes.

"Well, I don't think I double-crossed you. That is something I would not do," Tim replied.

"That is exactly something you would do, Tim. You probably felt that what we did was wrong." Pam paused for a second and then continued. "You just decided that no one deserved the money, and I bet you thought you were so clever in changing the PIN; but you're just another fucking sanctimonious asshole, and you know what? I'm not sorry for destroying the little world you made for yourself."

Pam was really mad now, and Tim was glad that she did not currently have a firearm, since she might just kill him for the hell of it. He needed to get Pam to calm down.

"Pam, if I did do that, I'm sorry. And look, I know what the PIN is, and I will give it to you once we're out of here. You can have all the money, and I'll just head back to Baltimore."

Pam turned and kissed Tim on the ear. She then whispered, "Give me the PIN number now."

"No, Pam. I will give it to you once we are out of here and somewhat safe. As far as I know, this is all some kind of setup by you and Sebastian."

"Oh Tim, you're just being paranoid. If you want to wait until we are out of here, then we can wait. I only wanted to know the PIN number now because one of us may well be killed in the morning."

Tim doubted that Pam and Sebastian were still in cahoots with one another, but he may as well keep the PIN number to himself for the time being. It really was the only bargaining chip he held.

"So, tell me, what's the escape plan?" Tim asked in a whisper.

"You have to climb up on the top bunk and reach over to that smoke detector. There should be some lighters in one of the drawers, so we'll set something on fire. Once the alarm goes off, the door should unlock—but the trick is that we have to get to the gun safe, open it, and grab something. Maybe one of the shotguns. Someone will come running down the steps, and we are going to have to hold them off for at least two minutes. If they stay any longer, then they're going to have to deal with the fire and sheriff's departments. The sheriff's department knows that this is a safe house and will send some kind of SWAT team, who will arrest everyone until they can figure out who the bad guys are."

"What if everyone's a bad guy?" Tim asked, which resulted in Pam slapping his arm.

"Please be serious, Tim," Pam admonished, but added, "We are not going to be hanging around to explain why we were being held prisoner. We're going after Sebastian and Toby to finish this thing once and for all. They are not going to just get away, Tim. We have to finish it," she repeated emphatically.

"What are we going to chase them in, Pam? Your car is still in Leesburg."

"The Land Rover runs fine, and the keys are in the kitchen. We will use that."

The prospect of a firefight in the house and perhaps outside as well did not appeal to Tim. He had only been in one firefight, which had been several years ago in Central America. Tim had been working with some revolutionaries that the US was backing when they were attacked by government troops. Tim recalled firing an AK47 in the same direction that everyone else was firing, but he had no clue if he ever hit anyone. He and the other CIA types were quickly evacuated.

Now, Tim found himself wondering what happened to those guerrilla fighters. Maybe they were running the country now, but who knew? Like in many other professions, Tim had developed a detachment from the people he was sent in to help.

"So, what time should we do this, Pam?"

"I'm thinking about 6 a.m. Everyone should still be asleep, and it will take them 30 to 40 seconds to figure out what's going on. That should give us time to get to the gun safe. The weapons are all unloaded, so we're going to have to load and take cover. Realistically, that is going to take maybe a minute, so it will be tight."

Realistically. Tim thought about what that implied. Realistically, neither Pam nor Tim were in top shape, and by the time they fumbled with the gun safe lock, removed the desired weapons, found the correct ammunition, loaded that ammunition, and then found a place to hide...well, they would be lucky to do all of that within 5 minutes. Meanwhile, Toby and whoever else was around would be standing on the basement steps with their weapons trained on both Pam and Tim.

Some plan, Tim thought. Unfortunately, it was the only one that they had. They would need luck, a lot of it.

"What time is it, Tim?"

"It's almost 11."

"Okay. Is there any alarm clock we can set so you and I don't oversleep?"

That was a good question. Both of their iPhones had of course been taken away, and Sebastian had turned off or disabled all of the computers and phones in the safe room. Some safe room, Tim thought to himself, but he knew it wasn't designed to stop somebody from disabling it beforehand. The fact that the room had been turned into a prison cell was beyond ironic, though.

"I think my watch has an alarm feature," he offered. "I just need to figure out how it works."

Tim's watch was complicated, to the point that he could never remember how to set it ahead for Daylight Saving Time without first consulting the directions. There were three buttons on the watch that needed to be pressed in some kind of sequence, and

Tim never could recall how it worked. This caused him a certain amount of frustration, to the point where he didn't even want to wear a watch in the first place. However, he had always worn one, and he was glad that he had one now.

"Okay, I think I have it set. I just hope it's loud enough for me to hear it."

"Fine," Pam replied, now sounding like she was ready to fall asleep. "Do you mind if I put my head on you, Tim?"

"No, go ahead."

She did so, and they were quiet for a few minutes until Pam broke the silence again. "Tim?" she asked drowsily.

"Yeah, Pam."

"Tim, what's the PIN number?"

"5456," Tim whispered.

"5456? I thought we used that."

"That's the PIN number, Pam. It came back to me when I got in a cab at BWI."

"When you came home from the Dominican Republic?"

"Yes. All of the treatments used to restore my memory actually did work. It just took a little more time."

"What about Sebastian? Now tell me. Did you really not know who he was?"

"I knew who Sebastian was when I first saw him in Baltimore. But no, not in Santa Domingo. He did a good job of fooling me, but the day he drove up, yeah, I knew who he was. But remember, I thought he was there to kill me."

"Tim, we never wanted to kill you. At least, I never wanted to kill you. But I do want that money."

"What are you planning to do with all that money, Pam?"

"I plan on moving to Tahiti or perhaps Bali and living like a queen."

"What about becoming a Chief of Station somewhere in Europe? Was that all BS, Pam?"

"That train left the station back in 2012. This is as far as I'm going to get in the Agency," Pam said, referring to her job managing the safe house.

"And Sebastian, why does he need all this money?"

"I believe that Sebastian is in serious debt. He has the wife and kids and the house in Bethesda. I know his wife expects all of their children to attend Ivy League universities, which will cost a small fortune in itself."

Tim recalled Sebastian telling him that his wife did not know what he really did for a living. "I guess his wife assumes Sebastian is rich," he said.

"She does, and if he gets that eighty million, then I guess he will be; but it's really mine. I set it all up," Pam replied, giving no indication that she would offer Sebastian any kind of deal to split the money.

Tim thought that he probably knew where all of this money had come from, but he'd forgotten or erased the knowledge from his memory. If Tim's amnesia was truly self-inflicted, then it was perhaps the dumbest thing he'd ever done in his life. Losing your memory was extremely inconvenient. Yet, Tim also knew that it was exactly the sort of thing he would think of trying.

Tim had been haunted for most of his life by the things he had tried and failed, and he often fantasized about just forgetting everything and starting over fresh. Tim's work as an interrogator gave him a perspective on how memories were formed and recalled, but he was especially interested in how events were often forgotten. What happened to these memories? Could memories be completely erased, or were they still someplace in the gray matter? Tim was particularly interested in amnesia and retrograde amnesia, where traumatic events or injuries could result is severe memory loss. At one time, Tim had convinced himself that a type of retrograde amnesia could be drug-induced and had even thought about what drugs could possibly be used to achieve such a state.

But the big question remained: was Tim was really stupid enough to try it on himself, or had Pam and Sebastian cooked it up? Tim had decided that it was still Pam and Sebastian. Once again, they were lying to him, and from now on Tim would just have to assume that anything either Pam or Sebastian told him was probably a lie.

Tim now found himself falling asleep with his wife, the woman he had loved but could never trust, nestled against his chest and shoulder. Pam moved her hand down between Tim's legs. Before either of them knew it, they had removed each other's clothes and lay naked side by side, holding hands. Pam then climbed on top of Tim and looked into his blue eyes.

"You know I love you Tim. But..."

"There does always seems to be a 'but' in our conversations, doesn't there?" Tim remarked.

"Yes, there does."

"You do know that Sebastian may be watching us, Pam."

"I don't care. I just want you inside of me one more time."

Tim did not really know what Pam meant by "one more time," but he decided to let the question go. Tim was inside of her now, and he watched Pam's face as her hips moved up and down. Her eyes were closed, and Pam seemed to be fantasizing about something or someone.

Tim wondered if it could possibly be him, but he doubted he was worthy to be anyone's fantasy. Men really never knew what women were thinking, did they? That was, of course, a rhetorical question. No, men had no clue.

Tim Hall closed his eyes and enjoyed the moment. After all, it was his only choice.

CHAPTER 30

Beep, beep beep, beep.

Tim had been dreaming, but his watch alarm interrupted it. He opened his eyes and immediately had a feeling of dread, the type of feeling that someone gets when anticipating a very unpleasant or scary experience.

Tim recalled during some training class how one should not confuse the feelings of dread with the feeling of excitement. Dread and excitement were very closely related, and Tim understood that certain individuals actually became addicted to these kinds of feelings if they found a reward for them at some point later on. Perhaps this was what gambling addiction was about. Tim was not sure. All he knew was that he hated the feeling.

Tim turned off his watch alarm and nudged Pam, who was still resting against his shoulder. After their lovemaking, both had taken cover under a blanket. "Wake up. It's game time," he said, not really understanding why he'd used a sports metaphor.

Tim looked up at the smoke detector and how it appeared to be wired into the house's circuits. Tim hoped that when Sebastian was disabling the communications in the safe room, he hadn't also disabled the fire alarm—but what did they have to lose?

"I would kill for a cup of coffee," Pam grunted as she woke up.

Even if making coffee were possible, it would not be a good idea, since it might alert others to what Pam and Tim were doing. "I saw some cans of Diet Coke in the mini," Tim offered. "One of those should give you a caffeine fix."

Pam walked over to the mini fridge and grabbed a can. "Mm, nice and cold," she remarked, offering some to Tim.

"Yeah, that's good," Tim replied. It had been a long time since he'd had a Coke. He had given them up because he believed that they were making him fat. "My god, vanity is a real luxury," he mumbled.

"I guess, Tim," Pam replied, not knowing what her husband was talking about.

"So, are you ready to do this?" Tim asked.

"Yes, I'm ready," Pam replied.

"And we know what we're doing?"

"Well, I don't know if we know what we're doing —but I know what we need to do," Pam answered with a smile.

Pam had left a couple of lighters on the desk

along with some paper. Both Pam and Tim realized the value of having a cigarette lighter around, since you never knew when you might need some fire and absolutely no one carried matches any more. Now, Pam walked to the door of the safe room and placed her hands on it. Meanwhile, Tim lit the piece of paper and waved it under the smoke detector.

It did not take long for the alarm to respond. A high-pitched squeal sounded that almost made Tim nauseous. He jumped off the top bunk and toward the door.

There was a clunking sound, and Tim and Pam pushed the door open to find Toby sitting across the room. He had apparently been asleep but was quickly waking up. A body that appeared to be Mary Ann was lying at Toby's feet, her hands and feet bound with duct tape.

Tim jumped over Mary Ann and rammed into Toby, who was rising from his chair. This resulted in Toby, Tim, and the chair toppling over. Tim was now on top of Toby, and he threw a punch that landed on the side of Toby's skull.

Tim's punch did little to subdue the man, who grabbed Tim on both sides of his chest and threw him to one side. Tim landed on his left shoulder and looked back to Pam, who was now at the gun safe. Toby had lost the M16 that had been resting on his lap. As he bent down to get it, Tim jumped on Toby's back and wrapped his forearm around Toby's neck, trying to choke him—but the big man just wouldn't go down.

Toby was actually able to flip Tim off his back and onto the granite table. He looked to be deciding what to do next with Tim when the basement door opened, and Darrel appeared on the stairs.

Darrel looked truly confused as he saw Tim flat on his back, Mary Ann tied up on the floor, Pam in the corner holding a shotgun, and Toby holding an M16. Darrel was turning to Pam as to ask what to do when Toby shot him in his abdomen. Darrel dropped his weapon, grabbed his stomach, and fell down the stairs. Meanwhile, Tim rolled off the worktable and onto the floor. Tim looked at Pam, who had leveled the shotgun at Toby but had not yet fired. Tim turned to see Toby using the unconscious Mary Ann as a shield. He slowly walked up the stairs with Mary Ann in one hand while still holding the M16 in the other. The rifle was pointed at Pam, and Tim was convinced that Toby planned on shooting her very soon.

Darrel had dropped his Glock as he fell down the stairs, and the pistol had bounced about one foot away from Tim. Tim grabbed the pistol and yelled, “Hey numb nuts!” at Toby.

He fired.

The bullet hit the side of one of the steps and splintered the wood, which seemed to fly everywhere. Toby turned and fired a burst at Tim. The bullets bounced off of the granite tabletop, falling harmlessly around the room.

When Tim looked up once again, Toby was gone.

Tim looked at Pam as he walked over to check on Darrel. "Are you okay?" he asked her.

"Yeah, fine. How is Darrel?"

"Not good. It appears he's going into shock."

"Wait and watch that door," Pam ordered as she went back into the safe room and returned with a blanket and a first aid kit. "Do you remember if it's okay to administer morphine for stomach wounds, Tim?"

"Yeah, I think that's okay," Tim said as he watched Pam give Darrel an injection.

Meanwhile, they heard movement on the first floor and what sounded like the front door opening. "Sounds like people are leaving," Tim observed.

Pam took a marker and drew a large M on Darrel's forehead, signifying that he had been given morphine.

"I don't know if the kids know what the big M means, Pam, but they should get the idea if you leave the first aid kit out here."

"Yeah, I hope so. Do you still have Darrel's gun?"

Tim held up Darrel's Glock to show Pam.

"Okay, Tim. Here, you take the shotgun. I have what I need. We've got to go and try and catch up with Sebastian and Toby. We have to finish this."

Pam had treated Darrel for shock as best as she knew how, so now she stood up to leave. "Darrel, I'm sorry. I should have told you what was going on. I hope you can forgive me," she murmured. Pam then pushed open the basement door with the barrel of her Glock 19 9mm and motioned for Tim to follow her up the stairs to the first floor.

The house appeared to be empty, but the fire alarm was still sounding. "Tim? Do you have any idea how long we've been out of the safe room?"

Tim looked at his watch. "Over ten minutes, but less than fifteen."

"Okay," Pam said.

She stepped out into the hallway and yelled, "United States Marshal Service. You are on United States Government property! Make yourself known."

If there was anyone left in the house, they did not make themselves known.

"Why do all of that, Pam?" Tim wanted to know.

"It's possible that there are some contractors still here, and god knows what Sebastian told them. God only knows what Sebastian told Darrel. Anyhow, let's go—we might still be able to catch up to them."

Tim and Pam started toward the kitchen, where Pam opened a drawer and produced a set of keys while Tim looked out at the driveway. The plumbing van was still there, but not Sebastian's SUV.

"We need to check out the van, Tim. Can you do that while I start the Land Rover?"

Pam and Tim left the safe house by way of the kitchen door. The March air was colder than they had expected, but after a night in the safe room, it felt refreshing. Pam walked over to the Land Rover while Tim tried the doors to the plumbing van. All of the doors were locked, but Tim felt that the inside of the van needed to be checked in case Toby had dumped Mary Ann in it. He began to beat the passenger side window with the butt of the shotgun, but it didn't break. Tim next placed the barrel of the shotgun directly on the window and fired. The window shattered, setting off an alarm.

"Wonderful," Tim said out loud as he opened the door. Nothing; they must have taken Mary Ann with them.

At that point, Pam pulled up in the Land Rover, but stopped at the house's front door. She got out and stuck a post-it note on the door, then turned to Tim. "Anything?"

"Nothing," Tim replied.

"Then let's go!"

As Tim climbed into the passenger side of the Land Rover, he could hear sirens from somewhere down the road. That must be the Loudoun County Fire Department getting close. Pam reentered the driver's side, threw the Land Rover into gear, and headed down the driveway.

"Put your seat belt on," Pam told Tim as they bounced up and down. The suspension on the Land Rover was much tighter than Pam's Mercedes.

"What did that note say, Pam? The one that you stuck to the door?" Tim wanted to know.

"It just said 'victim in basement with gunshot wound to abdomen.' I just wanted to try and give Darrel a fighting chance."

Pam did seem truly upset that Darrel had caught a bullet in his gut. The paramedics might be able to save him if they got to him in time. Tim wondered why Darrel was not wearing a vest as usual and thought that perhaps he'd walked into the fight when he was just coming on duty.

Pam had now reached the end of the driveway and Lovettsville Road, where she turned right and headed to US Route 15. As she drove closer, they saw a line of cars at the stop sign. Beyond that was a line of cars backed up at the bridge that headed north across the Potomac River and into the state of Maryland. Sebastian's Mercedes SUV was the second vehicle at the stop sign attempting to turn left.

To confuse matters even more, a fire engine responding to the Safe House alarm was coming down Route 15 heading north but driving in the southbound lane in order to get around traffic. The siren and air horn from the fire engine were both blaring. It was able to make the left turn from US 15 to Lovettsville Road, a medic unit ambulance and some type of supervisor driving a Chevy Suburban soon following. After them came two marked Loudoun County Sheriff units and one Virginia State Police unit.

"Well, the gang's all here," Pam said. "And there will be more, especially when they find a victim."

One of the cars at the stop sign was able to make

the left turn onto US Route 15, and now Sebastian's SUV was first in line. Then Sebastian's turn signal went from blinking left to blinking right as Sebastian turned and headed south to Leesburg.

"Okay, here we go," Pam declared as she turned into the other lane of the narrow Lovettsville Road in order to go around the four cars in front of her. Pam leaned on her car horn and flashed her lights on and off as she was doing this. Meanwhile, yet another Loudoun County marked Sheriff's unit was about to make a left hand turn off of US Route 15 but stopped in the middle of the intersection and let Pam pass. Pam waved at the officer as she passed him, and Tim was convinced that the cop would follow the Land Rover because of Pam's blatant traffic violation.

Instead, the unit continued onto Lovettsville Road. Pam just laughed. "The call to my safe house is a lot more exciting than some traffic infraction," she said as the Land Rover picked up speed.

Sebastian was now in front of Pam and Tim, and he was apparently unaware that they were following. The SUV turned off of US Route 15 and into a gas station on the right-hand side.

"Got you bastards now," Pam said under her breath as she rammed the Mercedes SUV from behind.

The SUV moved up about five feet. The driver's side window came down, and Sebastian stuck his head out.

"He doesn't know it was us who hit him," Tim said as he started to get out.

"Hold on, Tim. He does now." They could both see that Sebastian had produced a gun.

Sebastian took off again and drove back out on US 15, this time turning left and heading north to Maryland. Pam was right on his tail. Sebastian's SUV picked up speed as he approached the Point of Rocks Bridge.

Traffic was still backed up beginning in the middle of the bridge, and Sebastian had no choice but to stop. Pam was now directly behind the Mercedes SUV, and she rammed it once again, this time pushing Sebastian's SUV into the vehicle directly in front of it.

"I'll take care of Sebastian. Tim, you take care of Toby," Pam ordered as she got out of the Land Rover, gun in hand.

The driver in the vehicle in front of Sebastian was apparently getting out of his vehicle to inspect the damage. Tim heard Pam yell, "Sir, please remain in your vehicle! United States Marshals!"

The guy probably saw Pam walking down the middle of the road with the Glock in her hands and decided not to argue. Meanwhile, Tim got out of the Land Rover and racked the shotgun just as Toby emerged from the SUV with the M16 on full automatic. Toby fired a burst of bullets as Tim dove back into the Land Rover. Tim could hear the bullets hit the various parts of the Land Rover and was surprised that none managed to hit him.

Tim knew that he had maybe one chance to stand and fire the shotgun at Toby, but Tim could hear

Toby walking toward him, calling his name. "Come out, Tim!" he heard Toby say in a singsong voice, which was very creepy.

Tim then heard a voice that sounded like Mary Ann's, except he had never heard her sound this way. "Toby, you son of a bitch!" Mary Ann screamed, and Tim stuck his head up to see Mary Ann attack Toby with a tire iron.

Tim watched as Toby tried to hold off Mary Ann with one hand while still gripping his M16 with the other. When he was finally able to wrestle the tire iron away from Mary Ann, he threw it to the side. Toby then grabbed Mary Ann by the hair and banged her head into the side of the SUV. Mary Ann fell to the ground like a rag doll.

Toby looked up and froze. While Toby had been fighting off Mary Ann, Tim had moved closer and had leveled the shotgun directly at Toby's head. The two men stared at each other for a second—and then Tim pulled the trigger.

Nothing happened. The gun must have jammed when Tim was using the butt of the weapon to break into the plumbing van. Tim tried in vain to eject the shotgun shell, but he heard Toby laugh and looked up to see the M16 pointed directly at him.

"It's just not your day, dude," Toby said.

But then his head seemed to explode right before Tim's eyes. Brains and blood came flying out, and Toby's limp body fell to the ground.

Tim took a step back and looked to his left to see Pam holding her Glock 19 9mm. Pam had simply walked over, pointed at Toby's head, and fired. He never saw it coming.

Tim was about to say something to Pam when he noticed that she now had her Glock pointed directly at him. "I've been thinking, Tim, that your presence here at the safe house is going to be difficult for us to explain," Pam said.

"Us?" Tim asked.

"Sebastian and me. You see, when we write this up as an internal security incident, too many people are going to want to know what you were doing here in the first place. After all, you are supposed to be retired and living in Baltimore. You're just going to be hard to explain. Please understand, it's nothing personal."

"Pam, come now. It's time for us to go."

It was Sebastian. He had walked up to Pam, and they were now both standing on the yellow double line of the road.

Pam had turned to say something to Sebastian when Tim saw what looked like all of the blood drain out of her face. Pam must have seen the pickup truck coming straight for them. Sebastian never did.

The truck must have been traveling at 50 miles per hour when it struck Sebastian and then Pam. Sebastian ended up crushed under the truck's wheels, while Pam was found about twenty feet down the road. She had broken her neck, and Tim saw that her eyes were open, staring up to the sky. Tim thought that he saw tears in them. Later on, Tim was told that the driver never saw them because Sebastian's dark overcoat had made them look like part of the black SUV.

Tim looked back to see that there were now several people gathered around Mary Ann, and they appeared to be caring for her. Tim began to hear more sirens, this time coming from both the Maryland and Virginia sides of the bridge. Traffic was jammed in every direction.

Tim turned and walked back to the Virginia side and saw a Loudoun County Sheriff's Deputy standing next to his cruiser. The accident on the bridge would be under the jurisdiction of the State of Maryland, so the Loudoun County officer was just watching. Tim opened his wallet and found the piece of paper that Pam had given him with the name and phone number of the County Liaison Officer. Tim approached the young deputy and handed him the paper.

"Officer, my name is Tim Hall, and I am with the Central Intelligent Agency. I have pertinent information concerning this event on the bridge, and I need to speak with this officer and this officer only."

The young deputy looked at Tim, looked at the piece of paper, and then looked at Tim once again.

"So, you're telling me that you can only speak with Captain Henderson? I'm not sure if Captain Henderson is on duty right now," the deputy said.

"Not a problem, officer. Just call dispatch or your supervisor and tell them that you have a CIA Case Officer who needs to confer with Captain Henderson. They will know what to do." Tim was trying his best to be as nice as possible to the young deputy.

"Okay, sir. You better sit in the car while I make the phone call." The deputy opened the back door to his police cruiser, and Tim got in.

"I guess we will have to see what happens next," Tim said, but he was now alone with no one to hear him.

CHAPTER 31

Tim sat in the back of the Loudoun County Sheriff's car and watched the deputy speak on his cell phone. Tim could tell by the young deputy's body language that he had been placed on hold at least twice. The deputy then began to pace back and forth and appeared to be explaining to someone how a CIA Case Officer happened to be in the back seat of his police car. Tim realized that he was officially retired and was no longer a Case Officer but trying to explain all of that to the young man would just confuse the issue. No, it was always best to keep it simple.

Tim could hear bits and pieces of the conversation, such as, "No, he approached me," and "No, he is not armed." Finally, the phone conversation reached some kind of conclusion, and the deputy got back into his car.

"Mr. Hall? I have been instructed to transport you to Leesburg, where you will be contacted by government officials."

The deputy placed his cruiser in drive and pulled onto Route 15. The road had been closed down in both directions, so there was no traffic for a change.

"I do have one question, Mr. Hall. Do you have anything to do with that house on the hill off of Lovettsville Road?"

"Yes, officer," Tim replied.

"Okay, that's all I need to know." The young officer's attitude toward Tim had changed from one of suspicion to one of deference.

As they drove toward Leesburg, Tim watched a number of marked and unmarked police vehicles heading to the Point of Rocks Bridge. Tim got the feeling that the young deputy wanted to ask Tim if he knew what had happened on the bridge. Tim was trying to figure that out as well.

Although it had appeared that Tim and Pam were working together against Sebastian, this had never really been the case. Sebastian and Pam had always been working together against Tim—and Tim, in his heart, had always known this. Tim had wanted to believe otherwise, but he'd reached the same conclusion the night before. Tim, Pam, and Sebastian were never in a plot together; it had always been Pam and Sebastian.

Tim was now sure that he and Lilly Lin had discovered Pam and Sebastian's plot, but Lilly was murdered by Pam before she could report it. Meanwhile, Tim had foiled Pam and Sebastian's Bitcoin plan by sabotaging their Bitcoin account. Tim had changed the account to require a two-factor PIN number—or, in other words, in order to withdraw and transfer funds, the user would need a second PIN number. A PIN number that neither Pam nor Sebastian even knew about until they'd tried to spend the Bitcoins. Only Tim knew the two-factor PIN number, and Tim now lived in Baltimore with an erased memory. Sebastian had done a very good job of erasing Tim's memory, believing that he and Pam would have no further need of Tim Hall.

Drs. Justice and Lockwood had told Tim and Pam the truth about Tim being drugged in China, but there was no automobile accident, as Sebastian had always claimed. No, Sebastian and Pam, thinking that they'd gotten away with the murder of Lilly Lin, now needed to get rid of Tim, but killing him would have been a major problem. The Agency had sent three agents to China, after all, and it expected three to return. If one of the agents had indeed been killed while on an official mission, there would have been a major investigation.

Sebastian and Pam would never be able to get away with murdering Tim, but what if Tim were to become ill or be involved in an accident? And what if Tim suffered amnesia, or better yet, retrograde amnesia, which was where a person could not recall anything before a traumatic event? Tim had even spoken to Pam and Sebastian about such cases and had unknowingly given them a roadmap for how something like that could happen. He'd even told Sebastian and Pam which drugs could be used to induce such a state. So, it turned out that Sebastian was partially correct. Tim did essentially plan his own amnesia. That was the one aspect of the ordeal that Tim was very embarrassed about. He had trusted both Sebastian and Pam to such an extent that he had given them a way to do him in.

Tim was also feeling badly about Mary Ann and wondering if she was all right. It had been a very long time since Tim had witnessed anyone take the amount of abuse that Mary Ann had been forced to endure. If she really was an undercover cop, then she could have bailed out of the assignment at any point, but she stuck with it. It was also not lost on Tim that Mary Ann's last-ditch effort to fight off Toby with the tire iron had saved his life. Toby had every intention of killing Tim and probably would have, if not for Mary Ann.

Then there was Toby. What had Toby known? Did Toby know what Sebastian and Pam were up to, or was he just doing what he was told? Toby was not supposed to kidnap Pam outside the doctor's office and was definitely not supposed to give her the hypo. That was meant for Tim in a last-ditch effort to discover the second PIN number. Tim also believed that Sebastian sent Toby to kill the two doctors in Leesburg, just as he'd been sent to kill Dr. Gray in Baltimore. If not for Mary Ann's quick thinking, the two doctors in Leesburg would indeed be dead.

And what about the escape from the safe room and the fight in the basement? Did Sebastian know that Pam planned the escape, and was Toby supposed to be waiting for them, or did he just happen to be down there? Was shooting Darrel just an accident? Tim realized that he would probably never know the answers to any of these questions.

On the bridge, Tim was sure that Pam had come around the corner intending to shoot Toby and him, and probably Mary Ann as well. That had been what Sebastian and Pam had been speaking about while Tim and Mary Ann were fighting off Toby. How fucking stupid, it all was, and what a dumb way for his wife to die. Pam had most likely told Sebastian to stay in the SUV, and if he had, then Pam would have finished the job.

No question about it, Pam really did think that killing her husband was the most practical thing to do. Tim tried to recall her last words to him. Something about how he would be hard to explain. Ten seconds later, she was dead, and now it was up to Tim to try to explain everything.

When Tim and the deputy sheriff entered the town of Leesburg, Tim expected to be taken to the Adult Detention Center, which was the new and modern Loudoun County jail. However, the deputy instead drove Tim into the Old Town section of Leesburg and behind the County Courthouse.

The car came to a stop, and the deputy got out and opened Tim's door. "It was good to meet you, Mr. Hall," he told Tim as he returned to his car and drove away.

Tim turned to see two well-dressed men and one very well-dressed woman waiting for him. The woman did the talking. "Mr. Hall? My name is Beverly Andrews. Would you like to tell us what this is all about?"

Tim spent the next seven hours telling the same story to seven different teams of Agency analysts. These interviews took place in a nondescript four-story office building in a nondescript office park outside of the town of Leesburg. Tim told them about Sebastian and Pam, about Mary Ann Layback and the Adults in the Room PowerPoint presentation. They did seem especially interested in the conspiracy to replace the current President with Republicans from past administrations. They were also very interested in how

Tim seemed to know what type of poisons the President had been poisoned with and how he'd managed to determine that. Some of the teams that interviewed Tim played hardball and even suggested that Tim could be convicted of espionage and spend the rest of his life behind bars. Others suggested that Tim should hire a lawyer. A few people called Tim a hero, but one team called him a traitor. And one team even suggested that Tim write a book. However, Tim knew deep down that they did not have anything on him because he'd done nothing wrong except be a houseguest at a home owned by his former employer.

Drs. Justice and Lockwood did not want to press charges. In their opinion, Tim and the woman from the FBI had saved them and their daughter's life, plus the media was calling Joanna a hero for facing down her kidnappers and saving the President's life. Her parents knew the truth, of course, but the entire experience had brought them closer together as a family, so why let the truth get in the way of that?

Tim had also found out that Mary Ann Layback, whose real name was Mary Ann Wilson, was indeed working undercover. Tim only discovered this because some of the interrogation team members kept referring to Mary Ann as Special Agent Wilson. Tim finally put it together, and he was told in no uncertain terms that he was not to have any further contact with Agent Wilson. The FBI was not happy at all about one of their Agents having a relationship while undercover. Lie, cheat, and steal, but for god's sake, do not have a sexual relationship while working undercover. After all, the FBI has standards.

At the eighth hour of the interviews, Tim was ready to call it a day and requested that he either be arrested and charged or set free. That request was ignored. At the ninth hour, Tim was taken to see a man by the name of Robert F. Fredericks, the Director of the Human Resources Resettlement Program. Tim had no clue what Mr. Fredericks wanted to see him about, but he was happy that it appeared to be a one-on-one meeting and not a group interview.

Tim was led to a corner office which overlooked the Dulles Greenway. The Dulles Greenway was the closest thing Loudoun County had to a freeway. Mr. Frederick's administrative assistant seated Tim and asked if he would like a beverage. Tim asked for and received a Coke Zero.

"Mr. Fredericks will be with you in a minute, Mr. Hall," the assistant told Tim, leaving the room. Tim stared out the window and watched the traffic go by. It was dark out, but traffic still appeared heavy. Commuters coming and going, Tim thought. Typical Northern Virginia. Typical DC.

A quick three knocks sounded at the door, and in came a tall man of six foot four, Tim estimated, with thinning salt and pepper hair. He stood at Tim's side and introduced himself. "Mr. Hall? I'm Bob Fredericks."

"Tim Hall, Mr. Fredericks," Tim replied as he began to get to his feet.

"Please call me Bob," Mr. Fredericks told him, walking around to his side of the desk and opening a folder as he sat down. "You've had quite a day, Mr. Hall."

"Please call me Tim," Tim interjected.

"Very well, Tim. I do realize that it has been a traumatic day, with the death of your wife. However, I understand that you were estranged?"

"Yes, three or four years now," Tim replied, though he really no longer remembered how long it had been.

"Yes, quite the day. Tim, my job is to make sure our agents are properly settled once they leave active service, and I will get straight to the point. Would you consider taking over for your wife at the Lovettsville Road secured facility, otherwise known as the safe house?"

The question caught Tim off guard. At best, Tim figured that he would be sent home to Baltimore. At worst, he would be transferred to the jail in Alexandria, VA so he could stand trial for espionage at the Eastern District Federal Court House.

"Yes, I would be happy to do it." Tim's quick response to the question surprised even him.

"Wonderful. Would you consider starting tonight?" Bob asked.

"I don't see why not...but why the hurry, Bob?"

"You may have guests arriving soon, and it's important to us that we have someone there who we can trust," Bob explained. He picked up his phone and dialed a three-digit number. "Gail? Tim Hall is taking the safe house position and will need an ID made before he leaves tonight. Wonderful."

Call finished; Bob placed the phone back in the cradle. "Tim? If you come in next week, we can work out the details, including your new pay package and also the backpay you are owed."

"Backpay, Bob? I admit that you have me there. After all, I'm retired."

Bob Fredericks held up his hand. "Tim, you never retired. You have been paid your salary per month, but you were also eligible for the Danger Pay premium, which we have no record of you receiving since 2012. You were also eligible for a pay increase that you never received."

"So, I never retired?" Tim repeated in surprise.

"No, Tim, you never retired," Bob confirmed. "You are eligible to do so if you would like. Would you like to retire?"

"No, Bob, I would like to continue working for the time being."

"Excellent, Tim. We still need men like you."

Tim took a few seconds to gather his thoughts, then asked, "Is there anything that I need to know about the events this morning?"

Bob nodded. "Yes. They were unfortunate. As you know, the Agency does everything it can to avoid situation such as these, but sometimes they just occur. Nonetheless, you were completely debriefed today, and everyone is satisfied with your explanations."

Tim saw that Bob was smiling at him like they were sharing some kind of inside joke. He decided to press his luck. "Another question," Tim asked. "What is the condition of Special Agent Wilson?"

"To the best of my knowledge, she is okay and is resting at Lansdowne Hospital, but I understand that she had a very traumatic experience."

"Yes, Bob, I'm afraid that she did. And one more question: what happened to the Mercedes? The one at the safe house?"

"That is downstairs and ready for you to drive back to Lovettsville Road tonight. Gail will give you the keys after you have your new ID made. Now, if there are no more questions, I promised my wife that I'd be home before nine tonight."

"No more questions for now, Bob," Tim confirmed. "And thank you."

"No—thank you, Tim. I look forward to working with you."

Tim walked quickly out of Bob Fredericks' office for fear that this had all been a mistake and that he was still about to be arrested.

Bob Fredericks' admin met Tim at the door and escorted him down to a small room where there was a camera. "Now, no smiling," Gail laughed as she took two pictures of Tim. It only took another couple of minutes to produce Tim's new CIA ID card, and Gail gave this to him along with a packet that contained the keys to the house.

"There will be a security detail at your house, Mr. Hall, but they have been alerted that you will be on your way home," she assured him.

"Thank you, Gail," Tim answered. "I just need to make one stop on my way out of town."

Tim was almost running now. He found Pam's Mercedes parked behind the office building, unlocked the door, and jumped into the front seat.

The car smelled like Pam, which stopped Tim cold for a minute. His wife had died tragically on the bridge about eleven hours ago, and here he was running over to his girlfriend's hospital room. The fact that Pam had intended to kill him somehow didn't make much of a difference to Tim. He did still love her. It was also not lost on Tim that he would be returning to her house with all of her things still there, unless they had been moved out already.

But Tim had to see Mary Ann. She might leave the area and return to her home and perhaps her family soon. Maybe she was even married. Wouldn't that be a hoot?

Tim started the Mercedes and made the short drive from the CIA building in Leesburg over to Lansdowne Hospital. He parked and walked into the front entrance, showing the cop at security his newly minted CIA ID. He told the guard that he was with the CIA and that he had to see a Mary Ann Wilson on official business.

The guard gave Tim still another ID and directed him to the 4th floor. Tim got off the elevator and looked for a locked unit, then rang the bell.

The door buzzed open. He showed his new CIA ID once again to the charge nurse, who motioned to a room.

There was a young man sitting in a chair outside the room who immediately got to his feet. Tim showed the young man his new CIA ID, and the man requested that Tim place his hands and arms against the wall. He frisked Tim for weapons, then yelled to someone named Alice that a CIA agent was coming into the room.

Alice met Tim at the door, and Tim noticed that she was holding a Glock 19 9mm at her side. A voice behind her called, “It’s okay, Alice. This one is mine.”

Alice just smiled and holstered her weapon. As she left the room, Tim finally saw Mary Ann.

Except, she didn’t really look or sound like Mary Ann anymore. She actually sounded a lot more like Tim’s late wife Pam. “I thought I gave strict orders that I did not want to see anyone,” Mary Ann said, and Tim could not tell if she was joking or not.

“What have you done with Mary Ann Layback, lady?” Tim said, halfway kidding, halfway not kidding.

“She’s returned to Las Vegas with her very dead boyfriend,” Mary Ann told Tim. “I’m taking messages for her. My name is Mary Ann Wilson, and I am a Special Agent with the Federal Bureau of Investigation.”

"Pleased to meet you, Agent Wilson. My name is Tim Hall, and I am a Case Officer with the Central Intelligent Agency, although I am currently running a safe house in the Lovettsville area of Virginia."

"Really, Mr. Hall? I thought you might be retired."

"Me too, Agent Wilson, but I found out today that that was never the case."

"Well, Mr. Hall, what can I do for you?"

"I just wanted to thank Ms. Layback for saving my life this morning," Tim explained. "I am pretty sure that her crazy boyfriend was going to kill me."

"He's not my boyfriend," Mary Ann said, sounding for the first time like her old self.

"Nonetheless, I wanted to make sure that she knows how much I appreciated that," Tim said.

"I'm sure she does, Mr. Hall, just as I'm sure she appreciates how much everyone has done for her."

Tim smiled at that. "Well, I should be going now, but it was sure nice meeting you, Agent Wilson," he said.

"You too, Mr. Hall."

Tim turned to go, but Mary Ann's voice stopped him. "And Mr. Hall—would you answer a question?"

Tim turned around and faced Mary Ann again.

"Mr. Hall, do you feel it would be possible for you to love a divorced FBI Special Agent who has two children?"

"I think that may be entirely possible," Tim replied with another smile. Then he walked out of the room.

As Tim rode an elevator down to the first floor, he did wonder if he would be able to rekindle his relationship with Mary Ann, but he figured that was something they would need to decide together. After all, they'd fallen in love while believing that they were different people than they'd proven to be. Tim wondered if he could love the real Mary Ann and whether Mary Ann could love the real Tim.

Tim knew that he and Mary Ann would have a lot to consider, so he felt that he should give her a couple of days before he called her again. He was in such deep thought about this as he walked out of the hospital that he did not see that Mary Ann was now standing right in front of him. She must have run down the stairs.

Before Tim could say a word, Mary Ann jumped into Tim's arms and began to kiss him like only Mary Ann could kiss.

"I love you; I love you; I love you," Mary Ann said after each kiss. "And I want to be with you forever. After all, you do need someone to watch your back. I'm the girl to do it."

"As long as you understand that we will be living in my wife's old house with all of her old stuff. That might bother some women," Tim replied.

"But I'm not some woman, Tim," she protested.

"I'm Mary Ann Wilson, and I'm an adult and a professional."

"As a matter of fact, Mary Ann, I'm an adult, too," Tim agreed.

CHAPTER 32

Epilogue

It was now early summer, and temperatures had already surpassed the 90-degree mark. This, of course, emboldened all of the climate change worry warts, but to Tim Hall, it was just another hot day. Much too hot for the sports jacket he was wearing, so he decided to take it off.

Hot summer days did give Baltimore a certain aroma that reminded Tim of his first summer living there. In his mind, Tim felt that he left Baltimore a long time ago, but it had really only been three months. "Time sure flies when you're having fun, or something like it," Tim used to joke, but in reality, the passage of time scared him. Because of this, he'd recently made a commitment to himself to appreciate all of the time that was left in his life.

As Tim walked to the Blue Goose Barbecue, he noticed that nothing much had changed in the neighborhood. Baltimore was like that. No matter how hard anyone tried to improve the city, most of it pretty much stayed the same. Baltimore did not have the success of Brooklyn, NY, for example, which had become a very hip place to live. Maybe this was because Baltimore lived in the shadow of Washington, D.C., except for the notoriety the city received from the numerous TV shows that cited the bad things about Baltimore:

the drugs, the murders, and the racial tension. However, the city was also home to some of the best medical facilities in the world, and the people who lived in Baltimore loved the place and were proud of it. DC, on the other hand, was considered by many to be just an outpost, a place you went to just to get your ticket punched. A place where you spent a couple of years before moving on to wherever you really wanted to live. That was the city's reputation that could never be changed.

As Tim entered the Goose, none of the regulars seemed to recognize him. Tim had cleaned himself up somewhat with a new haircut, and now he was shaving every day. He'd also taken to wearing many of the clothes from his closet at the safe house. His late wife had purchased much of Tim's wardrobe over the years, and she'd of course had immaculate taste.

Referring to Pam as his late wife did leave Tim with a strange feeling of loss. Somehow, when he'd believed that Pam was dead the first time, he'd had a kind of numb feeling about it. Tim's new doctor had explained that this was the result of all the drugs he'd been given; now that he was essentially drug free, all sorts of emotions had returned.

"Secret Agent Tim?" It was Randy, the man who'd said new kidneys could be grown from stem cells. "Professor, where have you been? We all thought you must have died or something."

Tim was not sure what "or something" might mean, but he decided to let it go. "Oh, I just needed to take care of some family business with my uncle. May I buy you a drink, Randy?"

"Well, you know I'm just a fellow who can't say no," Randy replied.

A young man who Tim had not seen before walked behind the bar. "Professor?" Randy said. "Meet Jim. He's Mary Ann's cousin from Ohio."

Randy suddenly looked concerned. He directed his gaze toward a framed picture of Mary Ann that was behind the bar. "You do know that happened, don't you?"

The regulars had made a memorial to Mary Ann. Over the picture, someone had placed a sign that said:

Mary Ann Layback

1976 to 2018

Under that was a story from a newspaper with the headline:

Three Die in Horrific Accident on Point of Rocks Bridge

The news article listed the names of Pam Hall, Sebastian Oak, and Mary Ann Layback, but made no mention of Toby Wheeler. Tim wondered about that and if Mary Ann, or Special Agent Mary Ann Wilson as she was now known, would tell him the reason. The FBI was as anal retentive as usual.

The new bartender and owner of the Goose walked over and introduced himself. "Hi, Jim Jones. And you are?"

"My name is Tim Hall. I'm a regular, but I've been away."

"So, you're Tim Hall?" the new bartender repeated.

"The one and only."

He smiled. "My cousin Mary Ann told me all about you. I hope you won't be a stranger."

"She did?" Tim asked, now knowing that Jim was full of shit.

"Yes. As a matter of fact, my dad, Mary Ann's uncle, would love to hear from you." He handed Tim a business card with a phone number on the back. It had a 703-area code, which was the same as CIA Headquarters in Langley.

"Thanks, Jim," Tim said pleasantly. "I'll be sure to give him a call."

"Thank you, Tim. I'm sure I'll be seeing you around."

Not if I can help it, Tim thought to himself.

Tim bought a round of drinks for everyone at the Goose in honor of the late Mary Ann Layback and started back to his condominium. He did not mention to anyone at the Goose that he would be moving from Baltimore back to Virginia. That would have of resulted in too many questions. It would be better if he were just to disappear, but he did hand Randy one of his new official business cards from his employer, The Central Intelligence Agency. Tim saw Randy showing his card to one of the other regulars as he walked out the door.

"Is that you, my darling?" a voice called as Tim entered his condo.

"The one and only," Tim said again as he followed the sound of the voice.

Mary Ann, now officially known as Special Agent Mary Ann Wilson of the FBI, was on a stepladder in the kitchen going through the cabinets one more time. Mary Ann had taken charge of moving Tim from Baltimore to the safe house in Virginia. She had also taken charge of removing Pam's belongings from the house on Lovettsville Rd, including Pam's wardrobe and personal effects. Mary Ann was able to do all of that within three days. She was incredibly good at searching and organizing, telling Tim that FBI management often requested her when a search warrant was served. "It's one of my specialties," she joked.

Tim had been correct when he surmised that Mary Ann was working undercover when Sebastian entered the picture and that her handlers had told her to maintain her cover to see where it would lead. However, she still would not reveal to Tim why she'd been investigating Toby Wheeler in the first place. "It's an ongoing investigation," was all that she would say about the matter.

Mary Ann also confessed to Tim that she did not believe he was a spy either which was the real reason she started the fist fight with him that day at the Blue Goose.

"When I reported that to Sebastian" Mary Ann

said "He told me that you were a dangerous man but I'm still not sure Tim. Are you?"

"Well I guess you will just have to find that out for yourself" Tim replied not sure why Mary Ann still doubted his abilities to handle himself.

"By the way, you've been replaced at the Goose," Tim said as he opened a Coke Zero.

"Really? By who?"

"Some young good-looking guy named Jim Jones, if you can believe that name."

"Hmm. Well, I don't think he's FBI. Probably one of your guys. After all, Sebastian owned the place."

Tim agreed that Jim Jones was probably CIA. After all, the Agency operated lots of different businesses.

Mary Ann, meanwhile, went back to her searching and cleaning.

She no longer looked like the biker chick he had fallen for over six months ago. Mary Ann had cut her hair, so it was slightly below her shoulders and washed out the red highlights, returning it to her natural color of chestnut brown. Gone also were all of her biker clothes and the heavy mascara. If Tim had taken Mary Ann over to the Goose, most of her regulars probably would not have recognized her.

The real Mary Ann Wilson also no longer sounded like biker chick Mary Ann. She now spoke in more soft and measured tones, which oddly enough made her sound like Tim's late wife Pam. That all said,

Mary Ann's feelings toward Tim had not changed in the slightest. She loved him deeply and was not ashamed to let anyone know it. FBI management was not pleased that Mary Ann had started a sexual relationship while working undercover, but when that was mentioned during her debriefing, Mary Ann simply stated that she would quit rather than give up her relationship with Tim. This effectively called the FBI's bluff, and the subject was never mentioned again. Mary Ann seemed to be a sort of poster child for women in the new and modern FBI, and the last thing anyone needed was for her to quit.

Tim wondered what the real story was between Mary Ann and Toby. After all, they were supposed to be boyfriend and girlfriend. However, Mary Ann had explained that Toby's steroid abuse had essentially rendered him a eunuch. Tim hoped that Mary Ann was telling him the truth, but he had been finding that she would often tell Tim what he wanted to hear as opposed to the truth. Tim was letting that go for the time being, but he knew that Mary Ann's tendency to lie would be a problem down the road. Well, what else was new? Pam lied, and now the new girlfriend did, too.

Meanwhile, the President had fully recovered and resumed his war with the media. As a matter of fact, many in the media never believed there was an attempted assassination at all, preferring to think that the entire matter was a giant hoax. The President's ongoing fight with the media seemed to obscure the fact that a number of CIA and FBI department heads had suddenly decided to retire after the assassination plot was exposed. The press just assumed that these agency heads were leaving because they could no longer work for a President "unqualified to hold office." This phrase was the media's new angle on the President, and they were repeating it ad nauseam.

Often, things happened in the nation's capital for entirely different reasons than the official statements said, and this was certainly not the first time that the media missed a story that happened right under their noses. It actually happened a lot more than anybody in the press corps would like to admit.

Meanwhile, the Agency head who'd been working under the pseudonym Bob Ajacks and who had visited the safe house happened to die in a traffic accident on the GW Parkway. That rated a small article in the Metro section of the *Washington Post*. The man's name was mentioned along with where he lived, but nothing else. He would soon be forgotten. Sebastian Oak and Pam Hall would also be forgotten. Officially, they would be classified as having been killed in the line of service, but Tim doubted that either would receive a star on the Memorial Wall at Langley.

Tim was never able to determine how deeply Sebastian and Pam were involved in the conspiracy, yet just being aware of it and not acting to stop it was bad enough and would get you a number of years in a Super-Max. Tim's guess regarding the kind of poisons used was just pure luck on his part. Pam and Sebastian were probably going to take credit for saving the President, which was another good reason Tim and Mary Ann would need to be killed on the bridge.

Even now, Tim was still having a hard time coming to grips with the fact that his wife had every intention of killing him. He had thought from the beginning that Sebastian and Toby were planning to kill him, but he'd really wanted to believe that Pam was on his side. Tim often confused sex with love—but just because Pam had fucked Tim a couple of times over that weekend did not mean that she still loved him.

In regard to the Bitcoin account, Tim was still considering what he should do about it, if anything. Although he did not have Pam's or Sebastian's PIN numbers, he could probably find them. But Tim had inherited Pam's entire estate and now had more money than he would ever need. The accountants and lawyers couldn't give him an exact total as of yet, but Tim would never need to worry about not having enough money again. This all made the Bitcoin account kind of a moot point...and besides, explaining where you came up with $80 million to the Agency and the IRS would be a problem.

Still, it was something that Tim would need to think over. Perhaps the money could even be used for something good.

Finished with his musings, Tim walked up behind Mary Ann and wrapped his arms around her waist. He could feel the Glock 9mm holstered on her hip. "It's going to take me some time to get used to this extra appendix," he remarked as he kissed Mary Ann on her neck.

"Oh, I can always take it off if you want to play cops and robbers," she replied cheerfully.

"Later on, dear, when we get back to Lovettsville," Tim said as he hugged her tightly.

Like Pam, Tim had found that Mary Ann had a somewhat kinky side. I must just attract the type, Tim thought.

Mary Ann had accepted a training position at the FBI Academy located in Quantico, Virginia. Quantico was almost a two-hour drive from Lovettsville Road, so Mary Ann had arranged to live on campus from Tuesday through Friday. Tim had also arranged clearance for Mary Ann to reside at the safe house on the weekends, as long as she was willing to help entertain some of the guests if the need arose. She was more than happy to do so. Mary Ann, like the late Pam, seemed to enjoy being a cop.

"Do you think my girls can come and visit us at the safe house, Tim?" she asked.

"Sure, I don't know why not. Just as long as nothing is going on," Tim replied.

Until recently, Mary Ann had not seen her children for almost two years, and she was concerned that they were forgetting about her. Mary Ann's ex-husband Dennis was a Battalion Chief with the Cleveland Fire Department, and his wife Sandy was a surgical nurse at the Cleveland Clinic. Mary Ann had a decent relationship with her ex-husband, but she did not trust his wife Sandy whatsoever. "She's stealing my girls," Mary Ann bemoaned to Tim...but she also knew that part of this was her own fault. Mary Ann could have remained a detective with the Cleveland PD, but she wanted a career with the FBI, and that meant moving to different cities. Dennis loved his job as a firefighter and had no intention of moving. Besides it was not easy to transfer from one fire department to another. Their divorce had been amicable enough, although Mary Ann thought that her husband could have been more flexible about following her to her new posts. However, she was still a patrol officer with the Cleveland PD when they were married, and Dennis had no idea that Mary Ann planned to become an FBI agent. In the end, Mary Ann had found that, although she might want it all, she wasn't likely to get it all.

"Are we close to being ready?" Tim asked. "The movers will be here soon."

"Just one last looksee," she responded

"Okay. I just want to be back in Virginia by 6 p.m. Darrel, the security guy, is due back tonight, and I would like to speak with him."

Darrel had survived the gunshot wound to his belly by the skin of his teeth, and the ER doctors credited this to how he'd been prevented from going into shock. That had been all Pam, Tim thought.

"I'm going down to the loading dock to wait for the truck," he told Mary Ann.

As Tim rode down in the elevator, he reached into his top pocket and pulled out the business card that Jim Jones, the new bartender at the Goose, had given him. Tim dialed the number and waited.

The phone rang one time, and a man answered.

"Mr. Hall, we have been expecting your call." He paused, then added, "Mr. Hall, from time to time, we need men like you to help us out in several matters. My question to you, Tim, is simply: do you want back in?"

Recently Tim had been thinking about love and wondering if he had ever really been in love, or even knew what love really was. He'd thought he loved Pam when they were married, but it was obvious now that she'd never loved him in return. Mary Ann did appear to love Tim, and Tim really did care for Mary Ann and felt that she needed to be protected. But was protecting Mary Ann really love, or was that just the fatherly side of Tim coming out? Tim was once told by a girlfriend that, in every relationship, one person loves, while the other person allows themselves to be loved. Tim wondered if there were relationships where both people loved one another equally. Somehow, he doubted it.

Tim thought that running the safe house would be an excellent way to retire from the Agency, and he looked forward to spending many wonderful weekends there with Mary Ann, but how long would that last? Mary Ann was just 38 years old, and soon she would be going back out into the field. Mary Ann was not the "it's just a job" type of cop, meaning that she would throw her heart and soul into each new assignment and case. And, although she would not admit it, Mary Ann had already chosen her career over her children. She may not like her ex-husband's wife Sandy, but she really should be grateful that Sandy was willing to raise her two daughters.

"I want back in," Tim said to the voice on the other end of the line.

The man began to laugh. "Mr. Hall, you still don't get it. You never left."

Tim hung up the phone.

The door opened behind Tim, and out came Mary Ann. She gave Tim a massive hug. "You and I are going to have a great life, honey. Just you wait and see," she said.

Tim took hold of her shoulders and turned Mary Ann around, so she was facing him, then gave her the longest and most passionate kiss he had ever given a woman.

"Mary Ann, we are beginning a journey, and where that will take us is anyone's guess—but there is no one I would rather take it with," he answered.

"Gosh, Tim," Mary Ann whispered. "You took the words right out of my mouth." She laughed. "Now kiss me again like you mean it."

And he did.

A note from the author,

Thank you for reading The Adults in the Room. If you enjoyed my book, please take a minute and provide a rating and a short review (if applicable). Your opinion is very valuable to other readers and to me. Also, you may enjoy my two other novels

The Safe House

and

The Decoys

Which are also available on Amazon and Kindle

Once again thank you for reading Adults in the Room.

Jeffrey D. Mechling

Third Printing

Made in United States
Orlando, FL
17 January 2022

13614700R00219